Books by Isaac Bashevis Singer

NOVELS

THE MANOR

I. THE MANOR   II. THE ESTATE

THE FAMILY MOSKAT   THE MAGICIAN OF LUBLIN

SATAN IN GORAY   THE SLAVE

ENEMIES, A LOVE STORY

SHOSHA

STORIES

A FRIEND OF KAFKA   GIMPEL THE FOOL   SHORT FRIDAY

THE SÉANCE   THE SPINOZA OF MARKET STREET

A CROWN OF FEATHERS   PASSIONS   OLD LOVE

MEMOIRS

IN MY FATHER'S COURT

FOR CHILDREN

A DAY OF PLEASURE   THE FOOLS OF CHELM

MAZEL AND SHLIMAZEL OR THE MILK OF A LIONESS

WHEN SHLEMIEL WENT TO WARSAW   A TALE OF THREE WISHES

ELIJAH THE SLAVE   JOSEPH AND KOZA OR THE SACRIFICE TO THE VISTULA

ALONE IN THE WILD FOREST   THE WICKED CITY

NAFTALI THE STORYTELLER AND HIS HORSE, SUS

WHY NOAH CHOSE THE DOVE

COLLECTION

AN ISAAC BASHEVIS SINGER READER

Old Love

Old Love

Isaac Bashevis Singer

Farrar · Straus · Giroux

New York

First printing, 1979
Printed in the United States of America
Published simultaneously in Canada
by McGraw-Hill Ryerson Ltd., Toronto
Designed by Dorris Huth
Library of Congress Cataloging in Publication Data
Singer, Isaac Bashevis.
Old love.
I. Title.
PZ3.S616570l [PJ5129.S49]   839'.09'33   79-18765

Author's Note

ALTHOUGH THE STORY "Old Love" appeared in *Passions*, my last collection of stories, I have decided to use this title for the present book. The love of the old and the middle-aged is a theme that is recurring more and more in my works of fiction. Literature has neglected the old and their emotions. The novelists never told us that in love, as in other matters, the young are just beginners and that the art of loving matures with age and experience. Furthermore, while many of the young believe that the world can be made better by sudden changes in social order and by bloody and exhausting revolutions, most older people have learned that hatred and cruelty never produce anything but their own kind. The only hope of mankind is love in its various forms and manifestations—the source of them all being love of life, which, as we know, increases and ripens with the years.

Of the eighteen stories I offer here, fourteen were published in *The New Yorker* and edited by my great and beloved editor, Rachel MacKenzie. One of them, "Tanhum," was edited by William Maxwell, and another, "The Betrayer of Israel," by my new editor, Robert McGrat, following Rachel MacKenzie's recent retirement. Of the other stories, two appeared in *New York Arts Journal*, one in *Playboy*, and one in *The Saturday Evening Post* some fourteen years ago. All of them were edited by my good friend and editor of almost all my works, Robert Giroux. My gratitude goes to all of them, as well as to the many readers who write and encourage me in my creative efforts. While I don't have the time and strength to answer them personally, I read all their letters and often make use of their important remarks.

I.B.S.

Contents

x   Contents

Old Love

One Night in Brazil

I HAD NEVER HEARD of the man before, but in a long letter he wrote me from Rio de Janeiro he represented himself as a Yiddish writer who had become "lost and ground up in the hot desert of Brazil." His name was Paltiel Gerstendrescher. A few months after the letter, one of his books arrived. It was put out by the Myself Publications, printed on gray paper and bound in covers crimped at the side from the time it had been in the mail. A mixture of autobiography and essays about God, the world, man, and the aimlessness of creation, it was written in a turgid style and unusually lengthy sentences. It teemed with typographical errors, and some of the pages were transposed. Its title was *The Confession of an Agnostic*.

I skimmed through it and wrote the author a thank-you note. That began a correspondence consisting of three or four incredibly long letters from him, and a brief note from me apologizing for not writing sooner and in greater detail.

I don't know how, but Paltiel Gerstendrescher found out that I was preparing to go to Argentina for a series of lectures, and he began to send me special-delivery letters and even telegrams asking me to spend a few days in Rio de Janeiro. At that time I wasn't flying, and it just so happened that the Argentinian ship I boarded was scheduled to stop over for two days at Santos, twelve days after its departure from New York.

The ship was nearly deserted, and someone confided to me that this was its last trip from North America. I had obtained a luxury cabin at a reduced rate, and in the dining hall I had my own wine waiter, even though I took only a sip of wine to give him something to do.

That spring—spring in Brazil and fall in New York—a hurricane swept over the Atlantic, with violent rains and gale-force winds. The ship lurched dismally. Its horn blew day and night, in warning. Waves pounded the hull like mighty sledge-hammers. In my cabin I had hung my tie over the mirror and it executed acrobatic stunts. The toothbrush in the glass clinked without stopping. The ship fell behind schedule, and I sent Paltiel a radiogram giving our new time of arrival, but we missed even that.

When the ship finally docked in Santos, there was no one to meet me. The ship would remain in port for only twenty-four hours. I tried to telephone from the harbor, but I couldn't get a connection. One time, someone did answer, but he spoke only Portuguese, which I did not understand. For some reason, I couldn't bring myself to disappoint Paltiel Gerstendrescher. The tone in which he had written about this visit implied that all his hopes depended upon it. After brief deliberation, I boarded a bus that went to Rio, and from there took a taxi to his address. It turned out to be quite far from the city, in a desolate section that the driver had trouble finding. The narrow road, full of pits and potholes, lay partially flooded under broad puddles.

I knocked at a house that was a half ruin, and a woman opened the door. To my surprise, I recognized her from Warsaw—Lena Stempler, an obscure actress, singer, and monologuist. She painted as well. I had met her at the Writers' Club. She was then a young brunette and the sweetheart of the well-known writer David Hesheles, who later perished under the Nazis. Lena had vanished from sight years before I left Warsaw. All kinds of slanders were spread about her in the Writers' Club. It was said that she had divorced four husbands and had offered her body to a theater critic in exchange for a favorable review. Someone told me that she suffered from syphilis. As I looked at her now, I was impressed at how girlish her figure had remained. Her short-trimmed hair was still black, though it showed the dullness of dye. Wrinkles could be seen through makeup. Lena had a snub nose, light-brown eyes, a wide mouth with loosely spaced teeth. The butt of a cigarette stuck out from between her lips. She wore a kimono of some flimsy material and high-heeled slippers.

When she saw me, she spat out the butt, smiled with an expression suggesting that she knew more about me than I imagined, and said, "I am Mrs. Gerstendrescher. Unexpected, eh?" And she kissed me. Her breath smelled of tobacco, alcohol, and something putrid.

She took my arm and led me into a huge room that seemed to be everything at once—a living room, a dining room, a bedroom, a studio. A table stood here, set with plates and glasses, and a wide divan of the kind that serves as a sofa by day and a bed by night. Unframed canvases hung on the walls. On the floor lay piles of books and stacks of *The Confession of an Agnostic*.

Lena said, "Paltiel went to meet you in Santos. You missed each other. He called. I hope you remember me. We rarely exchanged a word, but I used to see you every day at the Writers' Club. In Rio, I read sketches you had written to audiences a few times. I married Paltiel in Brazil. We're together going on eight years already. Take off your jacket. It's hot as hell in here."

Lena seized my jacket by the sleeve and pulled it off. Afterward, she loosened my tie. She fussed around me like some relative, but also with an aggressiveness I didn't care for.

She put out refreshments on a small table—a pitcher of

lemonade, a bottle of liqueur, a plate of cookies, a bowl of fruit. We sat down in wicker chairs, and drank and ate, and from time to time Lena took a puff on a cigarette. She said, "If I told you that Paltiel looked forward to your coming as one looks forward to the Messiah, this would be no exaggeration. He's been talking about you non-stop for years. When a letter comes from you, he goes berserk. He's crazy about you and he's made me crazy, too. Here, we are both trapped in a dilemma. Everything is against us—the climate, the local Jewish society, our nerves. Paltiel is a genius at making enemies. Here, if you quarrel with two or three of the community leaders you're as good as excommunicated. Because of him, I've been ostracized, too. We would starve to death if it weren't for a small stipend I get from my ex-husband. To hear the whole story, you'd have to sit and listen for days on end. Paltiel used to be a fantastic lover. All of a sudden, he became impotent. I, on the other hand, have become possessed by a dybbuk."

"A dybbuk?"

"Yes, a dybbuk. Why do you look so frightened? You write about dybbuks constantly. Apparently they are nothing more than fiction to you, but dybbuks do exist. Everything you conjure up about them is the truth. A dybbuk sits inside you, too, but you don't recognize it. It's better that way. Your dybbuk is creative, but mine wants to torture me. If he lets me live, it's only because you can't torture a corpse. Don't stare at me that way. I'm not crazy."

"What does he do to you?"

"He does exactly what you describe in your stories. I had saved up a little money, and I spent it all on psychiatrists and psychoanalysts. In Brazil they're a rare breed—and in addition maybe third- or tenth-rate. But when you're drowning you clutch at even a tenth-rate straw. Here is Paltiel."

The door opened and in came a little man wearing a short raincoat and a hat covered with plastic, an umbrella in one hand and a briefcase in the other. I had pictured him as tall, maybe because of his long name.

When he saw me, he appeared dumbfounded. In those days, my picture was seldom printed in newspapers and magazines. He stood there studying me up and down and even sideways. An angry smile showed on his pointed face. He had a high forehead, sunken cheeks, a sharp chin. "So it's *you*," he said. His tone implied, *You aren't what I wanted you to be, but I must accept the facts as they are.* Soon he added, "Lena, today it's a holiday by us!"

We ate a vegetarian meal, drank papaya juice and strong Brazilian coffee, and for desert Lena served a cake she had baked herself in my honor.

She threw open the door to a large and overgrown yard behind the house. The rain had stopped the previous day, and the evening was fresh with tropical scents and ocean breezes. The sun rolled toward the west like a coal, turning the remnants of clouds from the hurricane a fiery red. Lena switched on the radio and listened to the news for a while, and I cocked my ear to the song of birds that had flown in for the evening to roost on the branches of the trees. Some stayed where they landed, others shifted about, flying from tree to tree with a flapping of wings and a rustle. I had never seen birds of such color out of captivity. The force of Genesis still functioned here undisturbed.

Paltiel spoke to me about literature, about his own writing. "A creator should also be a critic," he said, "but the criticism must come later. My trouble is that before I even write three words I'm already filled with questions about what my pen wants to express and I try in advance to justify and smooth over everything. You asked me in one of your letters why I use such long sentences and enclose so many comments in parentheses. It's my critical nature. Actually, analysis is the sickness of man. When Adam and Eve ate of the tree of knowledge, they became critics and analysts and perceived that they were naked. All the current works written about sex have evoked an epidemic of impotence. Economists have interfered with the world economy until they've brought about inflation in every country. It's the same with the so-called exact sciences. I don't believe in all those particles of atoms they keep discovering. The human brain has imposed its own lunacies upon Nature, or Nature herself has eaten of the tree of knowledge and gone crazy. Who knows? It may be that God has gone into psychoanalysis and therefore—"

"Paltiel, I know your theories already," Lena interrupted. "I'd rather hear what our guest has to say."

"No, go on. It's interesting," I said.

I glanced toward the windows. Just a moment ago it had been day; abruptly, night had fallen as if a celestial light had been extinguished. The air inside the room filled with gnats, mites, midges. Huge beetles emerged from cracks in the walls and floor.

Lena said, "Life here is so plentiful you can't stop anything with nets. I was taught in Gymnasium that matter can't pass through matter, but that was true for Poland, not for Brazil."

"Tell me about your dybbuk," I said.

Lena cast a questioning glance at Paltiel. "Where shall I begin? If you want us to be open with him, we'll have to tell him the truth."

"All right, tell him," Paltiel replied.

"The truth is that we are both cursed or enchanted—call it what you will," Lena said after some hesitation. "Paltiel came here from Canada. On account of me he divorced a wife and left two children. We met in your New York. He wanted to be a writer, not a lawyer. He came to New York for some Yiddishist conference. I had the good fortune, as you might call it, to come here before the Holocaust, but I wasn't lucky in Warsaw, nor have I been lucky here. You remember me from Warsaw. I was raised in a house where Polish was spoken, not Yiddish. I came to Warsaw to study at a Polish drama school, not to become a hanger-on in the Yiddish theater. It was your friend David Hesheles who made a Yiddishist out of me. They probably said terrible things about me at the Writers' Club. I was an alien element there from the beginning, and I remained one until the last day. The men were all after me and their slatterns despised me as they would a spider. What David Hesheles did to me, how he tormented me, is something I'd best not say, because he is already in the other world, a victim of human cruelty. Just one thing—he would only agree to be my lover if I was married. Crazy, isn't it? First of all, he was tempted by the thought of possessing another man's wife. Second, he was afraid that if I was alone I'd be looking around for someone else. He gave himself every freedom, but he burned with jealousy over me. He manipulated things so that when he saw I was growing attached to one husband he arranged for me to be divorced and found me another. How and in what circumstances I came to South America is a chapter in itself. I arrived physically and spiritually ill, and, once here, I married again—this time allegedly of my own will but actually for a piece of bread and a roof over my head. My new husband was forty years older than I and it was then that I met Paltiel and made another woman miserable."

"Lena, you're digressing," Paltiel said.

"So? If I'm digressing, I'm digressing. You begin writing about Yehupetz and end up in Boiberik but me you don't allow to come to the point. Because of your wild digression, Parness has stopped publishing your work."

"Lena, this has nothing to do with Parness."

"In that case, I'll shut up and you can do the speaking."

"The fact is, she has talked herself into the lunacy that David Hesheles comes to her, tickles her, pinches her, pushes her, chokes her. He has taken up a position inside her belly. You know from my book that I'm no atheist. A real agnostic allows for all possibilities, even for your demons and hob-goblins. If in the twentieth century there could emerge a Hitler and a Stalin and other such savageries, then anything is possible. But even you will admit that not every case of hysteria is a dybbuk. The nuns who exhibited stigmata on the week of Jesus's anguish weren't possessed by dybbuks. Today even the Pope would concede this—"

"Only yesterday you said that our house was haunted and that what I'm going through couldn't be explained away in natural terms," Lena broke in. "Those were your very words."

"It is impossible to explain anything—even why an apple falls from a tree or why a magnet draws iron, not butter."

"You said that only our honored guest would be capable of exorcising this dybbuk."

"I said it because I know that you admire him, love him, and all the rest. I admire him myself, and I would be in seventh heaven if he would stay with us and have a look at my writing. But your dybbuk is nothing more than hysteria."

Lena sprang from her chair. She nearly overturned a wine-glass and caught it just as it was falling. She thrust out a finger with a red nail and said, "Paltiel, the second you came back I noticed a complete change in you. What did you expect—that our guest goes around with a crown on his head? Certainly I would like him to stay with us, but since he can't, that's my misfortune. You can ask him to take along your manuscripts to read on the ship. He still has six days left to travel. But me he can't take along. I wish he could. You know I'm choking here."

"You're a free person. I told you that from the very first day." And they switched over to Portuguese.

I had fallen in with a couple caught up in an ongoing con-troversy—one of those quarrels that drag on for years and make couples shameless. The few hours I had spent here had made me fully aware of the situation. Paltiel Gerstendrescher was an intellectual, not an artist. He read and spoke a correct, even an idiomatic Yiddish, but he completely lacked the mentality of the Yiddishist. He had probably gone to Canada as a child. He belonged to that breed of people who exile themselves to an alien environment, choose a profession for which they're unsuitable, and quite frequently an unsuitable mate as well. The same thing held true for Lena. Even the house where they lived—in a forsaken, non-Jewish neighborhood—was unsuitable for them. They had turned away from the only circle from which they might have drawn a livelihood; and besides, Paltiel had involved himself in experimenting with language, indulging in elaborate wordplays and mannerisms that had small hope of interesting the Yiddish reader and that could never be translated.

Well, but why *would* a husband and wife so thoroughly sabotage their interests? And what was it they expected of me and of a visit that would last at most a day? I had a momentary urge to try to speak about their situation to them, but I knew that it was already too late. Lena's words about her dybbuk had piqued my curiosity, but although hysteria itself is exaggeration and lying, I knew that hers was entirely artificial—a literary dybbuk, perhaps borrowed from one of my stories. The real victim here was Paltiel, I told myself. He bowed his head and was listening to Lena's complaints with bewilderment. From time to time he shot a look of suspicion at me. It was obvious from the moment we met that he was disappointed in me, but as far as I knew I hadn't spoken any words that might have displeased him. It could only be the way I looked. For all my embarrassment, I tried to come to a decision as to the color of his eyes. They weren't blue or brown or gray but yellow and set wide apart. It occurred to me that if I found myself in a situation like this in America I could simply get up and walk out. But there was no escape in an alien land far from a city.

Paltiel stood up. "Well, good," he said in Yiddish. "I'm going." In a moment, he had closed the door behind him.

For a while Lena kept speaking in Portuguese, but she realized her mistake and broke into laughter. She said, "I am so confused I no longer know what's happening to me."

"Where has he gone in the middle of the night?"

"Don't fear, he won't get lost. From looking at my neglected garden you might get the impression that we live in a jungle. Actually, we're only a few steps from the road and no more than twenty kilometers from Rio. It's not the first time he's done this. Every time I tell him the truth he runs away. He has an old widow in Rio who plays the role of his patron. She is also his only reader and he goes to her to bewail his fate. He stops a car and they take him. This isn't New York. People here aren't afraid to pick you up, especially such a runt as him."

"Is he having an affair with her?" I asked.

"An affair? No. Maybe. God grant he would and leave *me* alone."

"Who will take me to Santos in case he doesn't come back?"

"I'll take you. I have a schedule and all the rest of it. Don't worry. The ship won't leave without you. When they say four in the afternoon, they don't leave till ten at night. The whole way of life in these countries consists of putting everything off till tomorrow, till the day after, till next year. I see by your face that you want to hear more about my dybbuk. Yes, my dybbuk is David Hesheles. He caused me anguish when he was alive, and now that he's dead he wants to do me in. Not all of a sudden, mind you, but gradually. The only time he has left me alone was during the few years I was with my former husband, the old man. He was apparently not jealous of him. But since I'm with Paltiel I have had no peace. David Hesheles tells me frankly that he'll drag me down to him in his grave, though, to be factual, there is no grave. There is only a heap of ashes."

"He talks to you in a real voice?"

"Yes, in a voice, but I'm the only one who can hear him. Sometimes he makes noises that even Paltiel can hear, but he won't admit it. He plays the rationalist, but he's afraid of his own shadow. He has seen Hesheles's apparition walking down the steps of our cellar. He has heard him slam doors and open faucets in the middle of the night. David Hesheles has settled himself inside my stomach. I've always done calisthenics and I had a flat belly, almost like a man's. All of a sudden, I got up one morning with a huge swelling there. It's actually a head, *his* head. Don't look at me that way. Paltiel and the local doctors all have the same answer for it: neurosis, complex. When an X-ray shows nothing, it doesn't exist. But a head has settled inside my stomach. I can feel his nose, his brow, his skull. When he speaks, his mouth moves. As long as he is down there it's bearable, but when he falls into a rage he begins to edge up higher toward the throat. Then I can't breathe. I used to hear back home that if you did someone harm and he died, the corpse came back to strangle you. But I did him no wrong. He wronged me. At first I considered this an old wives' tale—folklore. I'll be frank with you: if someone were to tell me what I'm telling you now, I would tell him to commit himself to an asylum. If you want, you can feel the head with your own hands."

For a moment, a childish fear came over me, along with a revulsion against touching her flesh. I had not the slightest urge for this female. I recalled what I had been told—that she suffered from a venereal disease. I myself would have become impotent with her. I began seeking a pretext to get myself out of this intimacy, but I felt ashamed of my fear. For the first time I was offered something the psychic researchers call physical evidence. I said, "Your husband may come back, and—"

"Don't be afraid. He won't come back. He undoubtedly went to her. Even if he did come, you wouldn't be in any trouble—we're both determined to show you the truth. I have an idea. There's a hammock outside. It's a dark night. We have no neighbors. The mosquitoes will attack us, but there is no malaria here. Besides, there's a net above it. Come!"

Lena took my arm. She flicked a switch and all the lights went out. She opened the door to the garden and a wave of heat struck me like heat from an oven. The sky hovered low, thickly strewn with southern constellations. The stars appeared as large as bunches of grapes in a cosmic vineyard. Crickets sawed unseen trees with invisible saws. Frogs croaked with human voices. From the banana trees, the wild flowers, and thickets of grass and leaves rose a scorching heat that penetrated my clothes and warmed my insides like a hot compress. Lena led me through the darkness as if I were blind. She mentioned the fact that lizards and snakes crawled here, but not of poisonous varieties.

Someone on the ship had told me the joke that what the government in Brazil stole during the day grew back at night. It seemed to me now that I could hear juices flowing to the roots and being transformed into mangoes, bananas, papayas, pineapples. Lena tilted the hammock so I could get in and gave it a playful push. Soon she slid in beside me. She opened the kimono that covered her naked body, took my hand, and placed it on her abdomen. She did everything quickly, with the skill of a medium accustomed to séances. I did, in fact, feel something inside her belly, protruding and long in shape. It began under the breasts and extended to the pubic hair. Lena guided my hand upward. She directed my forefinger to a small bump and asked, "You feel the nose?"

"The nose? No. Yes. Maybe."

"Don't be so scared. I'm not a witch. From the way you write about dybbuks, I assumed you were used to such mysteries."

"You don't get used to mysteries."

"Really, you've remained a boy. Maybe that's where your strength lies. David Hesheles is mad at me, not at you. He liked you. He always praised your talent. I kept seeking opportunities to meet you, but you fled from women like a Hasid. When I started reading your things here in Brazil, I couldn't believe that the writer was really you."

"Sometimes I don't believe it myself."

"Feel his forehead. You won't have many such opportunities."

Lena lifted my hand and I touched a pointed nipple. I jerked my finger away so that she shouldn't think I was trying to arouse her. For all the weirdness of the situation, I told myself that neither David Hesheles—that cynic, may he rest in peace— nor his soul had any connection with this game. Lena suffered from a tumor, or maybe it was the result of a practiced self-deception. If you desire something strongly enough, you can train the muscles to perform all sorts of stunts and contortions. But why should she want this so badly?

"What do you say now?" Lena asked.

"Truly, I don't know what to say."

"Don't be so nervous. Paltiel won't come back. I suspect that he started arguing with me on purpose so I could be alone with you."

"Why do you say that?"

"Why? Because he's half crazy, and because we are both trapped in a dark corner—physically, spiritually, in every respect. I've had husbands and I know. No matter how great a love may be, there comes a crisis that is just as much an enigma as love itself—or as death. You still love each other, but you have to part, or a new person comes along and introduces a new approach. I'll tell you something, but don't take it badly— in our fantasies, *you* were that person."

"Oh, but unfortunately I'm leaving the first thing tomorrow. I have my own complications. Why did you settle so far from everything and everyone?" I asked, changing my tone. "Paltiel is highly intelligent; he possesses lots of knowledge. In New York he could easily become a professor. Your chances would be better there, too."

"Yes, you are right. But here I have the house. I receive alimony from my former husband. This house would be hard to sell. Besides, it's not altogether mine. He wouldn't send me the cruzeiros to New York, either. Paltiel has grown completely apathetic. He sits day and night and writes these novels in which there isn't one interesting character. He is trying to become a Yiddish Joyce, or something of the sort. I hear that in New York the Yiddish theater is going under."

"I'm sorry, yes."

"Sometimes I want the dybbuk to go up to my throat and finish me off. I'm too tired to begin all over—especially since there is nothing to begin. I'm ripe for death, but I lack the courage to act. Don't laugh at me, but I still dream of love."

"So do I. I've heard this from sick and old people literally a day before they died."

"What sense does it make? I lie in bed loaded down with troubles and fantasize about a great love—something unique that probably doesn't exist. Whether my dybbuk will strangle me or I'll die from heart failure, one thing is sure: I'll die with this dream."

"Yes, true."

"How do *you* understand it?"

I wanted to say that I didn't understand it. Instead, I said, "It seems that life and death have no common border. Life is total truth and death is total lie."

"What do you mean—that we live forever?"

"Life is God's chariot and death is only the shadow of His whip."

"Who said that?"

"I don't know. Maybe I did myself. I'm just babbling."

"I told you—a dybbuk sits within you, too. Tell your dybbuk to kiss me. I'm not so old or so ugly."

I'm not going to start anything with her, I decided. This woman is a liar, an exhibitionist, and mad to boot. Her husband showed me hostility. I had had dealings with people of this sort.

One minute they idolize you, the next they scold you. They are invariably out for some favor that is as impossible and crackpot as they are themselves. But even while I made this firm decision I put my arms around Lena. I was always intrigued by those who chose failure, wallowed in its complexities, sacrificed themselves to its deceptions. I kissed Lena now, and she bit into my mouth. I heard myself calling her endearing names and telling her that our meeting was an act of fate. We were rolling and struggling. She tried to cover us with the mosquito net and we fumbled to tuck it around us. Suddenly the hammock tore away from the tree and we fell into a swamp full of nettles, rotten roots, slime. I tried to get up, but I was trapped in the net. At that moment Lena let out a ghastly scream. Mosquitoes had descended upon us, as dense as a swarm of locusts. I had been bitten by mosquitoes before, but never by so many and with such ferocity. I somehow managed to disentangle myself and help Lena up. We tried to run to the door but were caught in thorns, branches, prickly weeds. Lena kept on screaming. Only now did I realize that she was naked and had lost one of her shoes. I tried to lift her up, but she resisted.

When we finally reached the house and the light was turned on, I saw that we were both covered with bites and with living mosquitoes. They had attached themselves to us like leeches. We began to slap one another to kill these parasites whose blood had been our blood only an instant before. We jumped against each other in a crazy dance. My shirt was soaked with blood. Lena tore it off and pulled me into a bathroom with a long bathtub over which hung a copper tank and a shower. She let the water run and we stood under it, holding one another to keep our balance. Lena opened a medicine chest, took out a bottle of fluid, and began to rub down our bodies. I saw in a mirror that the skin of my face was half peeled off. Still wailing, Lena led me back to the living room, where she pulled a sheet from a chest, spread it over the broad couch, and wrapped me up like a corpse in a shroud. Then she wrapped herself in a sheet. She bent over me and cried out, "God loves us. He has sent the punishment before the sin!"

She threw herself on me with a lament, and in an instant my face became wet and salty. She put out the light, but it went on immediately—Paltiel had returned.

The next morning Paltiel took me on a bus to Santos. Lena had to remain in bed. Paltiel and I didn't speak a word. We avoided looking each other in the eye. I was so exhausted that I dozed most of the time, my head dropping again and again. I was too numb even to be ashamed. Before I entered the ship, Paltiel handed me two huge envelopes full of manuscripts and said, "We both gained a lot from your visit: I gained a true reader and Lena gained a true dybbuk."

I hoped that this would be the end of my bizarre encounter, but when I returned to New York from my South American journey I found three more manuscripts and two forty-page letters from Lena—one in Yiddish, one in Polish. Lena revealed to me that her love for me had begun when we were still in Warsaw and that she received vibrations and telepathic messages about my coming to her long before Paltiel knew of my trip. I tried to read what the two of them had written, but the manuscripts and letters arrived in such quick succession I realized that no time would be left me for anything else. From glancing here and there into Lena's letters I learned that the widow, Paltiel's Maecenas, had died, leaving him quite a large sum of money, and that he was spending it to publish all his works through Myself Publications. Soon the books started to arrive at unbelievably short intervals. It was more than I could do to open their mail any more, but this did not deter them from continuing to send books and letters for a long time. Some years later I learned that Lena had died from cancer and that Paltiel had been put away in a mental institution. I had to dispose of the mass of their writings. I kept only one large book by Paltiel, written in an atrocious style, mad, unreadable, and a few letters from Lena—frightening documents of what loneliness can do to such people and what they can do to themselves.

Translated by Joseph Singer

Yochna and Shmelke

THROUGHOUT ALL HIS YEARS Reb Piniele Dlusker had devoted himself to Hasidism. He traveled to the courts of the Zanz Rabbi, the Belz Rabbi, the Trisk Rabbi. Hasidim argued with him that one rabbi was enough, but Reb Piniele said, "Why can a mother love a dozen children? Why do rich men live in many rooms? Why does the emperor have a lot of soldiers? My pleasure is wonder rabbis."

Reb Piniele visited his rabbis on every holiday, even on Passover, although the most fervent Hasidim made it a custom to spend the Passover seders at home with their families. In the first years of their marriage, his wife, Shprintza Pesha, had objected. Her mother had even advised her to get a divorce. Matters had come close to this when Shprintza Pesha lost a set of twins to scarlet fever, which she took as punishment from Heaven for having caused her Piniele grief. In later years, other children died—whooping cough, diphtheria, measles— until Reb Piniele and Shprintza Pesha were left with one daughter, Yochna, named after Shprintza Pesha's great-aunt.

Yochna grew up healthy. She seldom cried and was forever smiling, revealing the dimples in her cheeks. Shprintza Pesha, the breadwinner, had a store where she sold yard goods and notions—sackcloth, lining material, thread, buttons. Yochna virtually raised herself. Reb Piniele wanted his only child to grow up a pious Jewish daughter, and when Yochna turned four he engaged a rabbi's wife to teach her the alphabet, and later prayers, and even how to write a line or two in Yiddish. But Yochna had no head for learning. She ate a lot and quickly grew plump. Other girls played tag, hide-and-seek, and danced in circles, but Yochna sat in front of the house in the summers and made mud pies. At mealtime her mother brought her fatty meats, groats, soup, bread with honey, and Sabbath cookies. Yochna finished every bite, and always demanded more. She was as blond as a little Gentile, her hair pale as flax and her eyes blue as cornflowers.

At eleven, Yochna became a woman, and Shprintza Pesha brought her a little pouch containing a wolf's tooth to ward off the evil eye and a talisman to drive away intruding spirits. She had the breasts of an adult, and Shprintza Pesha paid a seamstress to make her daughter camisoles and drawers with lace.

Yochna never learned to read from a prayer book, but she had committed to memory the prayer said upon rising, the benediction said before each meal, as well as other graces. Yochna loved Jewishness. She insisted that her mother take her to the women's section of the synagogue on Sabbaths, and like the pious matrons, she took care to say "Blessed be He and blessed be His name" and "Amen" when the cantor in the men's section recited the Eighteen Benedictions. She also listened to the supervisor of the women's services reciting the prayers for those who didn't know the alphabet. Whenever a traveling preacher came to town, Yochna went to hear his sermon. She cried as he described the tortures in Gehenna: the beds of nails, the whippings by the avenging demons, the glowing coals upon which sinners were rolled. Her eyes gleamed when the preacher told how in Paradise Godfearing women became the footstools for their husbands and were made privy, along with the men, to the secrets of the Torah.

When Yochna turned twelve, she was besieged by marriage brokers offering matches, but her father, Reb Piniele, brought her a groom from Trisk, a yeshiva student, an orphan, who studied seventeen hours a day. His name was Shmelke, and he was three years older than Yochna. He slept and ate at an inn. The couple would first face each other at the wedding ceremony during the unveiling of the bride, but Yochna cared for him without having seen him. She began to embroider a velvet prayer-shawl sack for him of gold and silver thread, as well as a bag for the phylacteries, a Sabbath-loaf cover, and a case for matzos. A rebbetzin came to teach Yochna how to count off the days following her period to determine when she could lie with her husband, and how to maintain marital purity by taking the prescribed ablutions in the ritual bath. Yochna learned it all, and the rebbetzin praised her diligence.

Shprintza Pesha ordered a trousseau for her daughter. It wasn't easy to fit her, since she had grown like dough made with lots of yeast. The tailor's assistants joked that she had a bosom like a wet nurse. They compared her thighs to butcher's blocks. But her feet were small and her fair hair hung to her hips. Shprintza Pesha spared no wool, silk, or satin to adorn Yochna.

The whole town attended the wedding, and Shprintza Pesha baked huge cakes and cooked caldrons of meats and soups. When Yochna was led to the ritual bath, the musicians played a good-night tune. The riffraff who hung around the taverns had plenty to mock. When the bath attendant snipped off Yochna's hair and then shaved her skull with a razor, the young matrons at the bath burst into tears, but Yochna said, "What are you bawling for? Since God ordered it, it's fine and proper."

On the night of their wedding, Shmelke lifted the veil from Yochna's face. She glanced up and was filled with a great love for him. He was short, slight, dark, with black earlocks twisted like horns and sunken cheeks that bore no trace of a beard. His gaberdine hung too long and too loose upon him. The fur cap he wore had slipped over his dark eyes, and he trembled and sweated. "Oh, does he look starved, my treasure, the crown upon my head," Yochna said to herself. "God willing, I'll fatten him up."

Under the canopy, Shmelke had trodden upon her foot—a symbol that he would be the head of the house—and a shudder ran down Yochna's back. She felt an urge to cry out, "Yes, rule over me, my lord! Do with me whatever your heart desires!"

Following the virtue dance, her two escorts, her mother and an aunt, led Yochna to the wedding chamber. Both women commanded her to give herself to her husband willingly, since to be fruitful and multiply was the first commandment in the Torah. Yochna undressed in the dark and put on a lacy nightgown that hung to the ankles. She got into bed and waited patiently for Shmelke to come to her. A bliss she had not known coursed through every limb. She was a wedded wife. Already she wore a night bonnet on her head and a wedding ring on her finger. Yochna prayed God to grant her a houseful of healthy children that she could bring up to serve Him.

After a while, Piniele and a respected town elder escorted Shmelke to the room and closed the door. Yochna cocked her ears for any movement. He had been let in like a fowl into a cage. It was pitch-black. How, she worried, could a stranger undress here? How could he find her bed? He stood there and mumbled. She heard him bump against the chest of drawers. He's likely to hurt himself, God forbid, or fall, Yochna thought with a tremor. She began whispering to him—he could drape his clothes over a chair. He didn't answer. She could hear his teeth chatter—he was shaking with fear, the poor thing.

Yochna forgot that she was a bride, who must act modest. She got out of bed to try to help him, but he jerked when she touched him and drew back. Gradually, she calmed him with

words. He took off his gaberdine, the ritual garment, the
slippers. The whole time he didn't cease murmuring. Was he
reciting a prayer? Was he intoning an incantation? After a
long hesitation he stepped out of his pants, and she half led,
half pushed him toward her bed. Now he tossed about as if in
a fever. An urge to weep came over Yochna, but she held
back her tears. The attendant had told her that according to
law the husband and wife were allowed to come together in
bed and even kiss and embrace. She put her arms around him
and kissed his forehead, his cheeks, his Adam's apple. She
pressed him to her bosom. Suddenly she heard his voice:
"Where is my skullcap?"

He must have lost it, and Yochna felt around on the cover,
on the sheet. To avoid the sin of being bareheaded, he covered
his skull with both hands.

"Oh, he has a sacred soul," Yochna said to herself. "What
did I do to deserve such a saint?"

She got out of bed to look for the skullcap. She tapped about
in the dark like a blind person. "Father in Heaven, help me
find the skullcap!" she pleaded. Mentally she pledged eighteen
groschen to charity. At that moment, she stepped on something soft. It was Shmelke's skullcap. Yochna picked it up and
kissed it as if it were a page torn from a holy book. "Shmelke,
here it is."

She could scarcely believe that she had the courage to do all
this and even to call him by name.

Shmelke put on the skullcap and began uttering pious words
to Yochna. The coupling of husband and wife, he said, was
intended to bring forth sacred souls who waited by the Throne
of Glory to be purified and, through a body, offered an opportunity to perform good deeds. He recalled virtuous women
from the past. Even though Yochna didn't understand the
scholarly language he used, it rang sweet in her ears. After he
had finished, he mounted her. The bath attendant and her
escorts had warned her that he was likely to hurt her and that

she must accept this pain with gratitude and joy. But she felt no pain. He was as light as a child upon her. Soon he left her bed and went to his own bed, as the law dictated. When the women came at dawn, they found blood on Yochna's sheet and they took it along to display in the kosher dance.

Later in the day, the women and Shprintza Pesha led Yochna to visit esteemed matrons of the town, who all welcomed the guests with cake and wine or almond bread and cherry brandy. Yochna glanced in the mirror. How different she looked in the bonnet with beads and ribbons and in a dress with a train! Without her hair, her head seemed oddly light. Her skull felt cool. A married woman doesn't dare reveal her bare head lest it rouse the lust of strange men.

In the seven days following the wedding, guests came each night to visit, and Yochna's father, Reb Piniele, treated each one to a cup of ceremonial wine. Shmelke sat beside his father-in-law, and from time to time Yochna glanced at him through the open door—he looked as slight and bashful as a boy in cheder. The men discussed learned matters with him. He replied briefly and in a quiet voice. Shprintza Pesha brought him an appetizer, noodles with soup, meat-and-carrot stew, but he left most of it on the plate and his mother-in-law chided him, saying that for studying the Torah one needed to keep up one's strength.

As long as Yochna had been single, she had properly not had any girl friends, but now young matrons came to discuss housekeeping matters with her—how to sew, darn, knit; how to get bargains at stores; how to do needlepoint of trees, flowers, deer, and lions on canvas. The women taught her how to play knucklebones, wolf-and-goats, and even checkers. They insisted that Yochna show them her jewelry and the dresses that had been sewn for her trousseau. Shprintza Pesha had given her daughter all her jewelry, leaving herself only a gold medallion with a charm. The young women praised

Yochna's jewelry but hinted that it was old-fashioned. Her chain, the bracelet, the brooch, even the earrings and rings were too heavy. A new fad had evolved—light jewelry. Yochna nodded and smiled. What did all these vanities matter to her? Her finest adornment was Shmelke.

The wedding had taken place on the Sabbath night following the Feast of Shevuot. In the month of Elul, Reb Piniele began talking of spending the holidays with his rabbis—Rosh Hashanah with one, Yom Kippur with another, Succoth with a third. He proposed to Shmelke that he accompany him. He wanted to show off his son-in-law, the scholar. But Shmelke demurred. Shmelke had his own rabbi. His father, blessed be his memory, had visited the court of the Warka Rabbi. When, after some hesitation, Shmelke told Reb Piniele that he wished to spend Rosh Hashanah in Warka, Reb Piniele struck a bargain. On Rosh Hashanah and Yom Kippur Shmelke would accompany him to Belz and to Trisk, and Shmelke would then go on to Warka for Succoth. And that's how it was settled.

At the news that Shmelke would be going away for the holidays, Yochna felt like crying. Most young husbands remained with their wives for the holidays. But a Jewish daughter had to do what her father said and what her husband wanted. Yochna began to prepare the things Shmelke would need for the trip: shirts, drawers, socks, fringed ritual garments, handkerchiefs. Around Succoth the weather begins to turn cool, and Yochna saw to it that Shmelke took along a wool jacket and an overcoat. What Yochna did for Shmelke, Shprintza Pesha did for Piniele. Shprintza Pesha was used to Piniele's travels, but Yochna began to long for Shmelke even before he left. She begged her father to keep an eye on him. Piniele replied, "Don't carry on, daughter. Those who travel in the service of God aren't harmed."

Piniele and Shmelke rode off in a wagon to a village by the Austrian border, where they were helped to smuggle themselves across. The border patrol was bribed in advance. To obtain a foreign passport and a visa cost too much and required a long wait. The Russians, Prussians, and Austrians had divided Poland among themselves, but the Russian Hasidim visited Austrian rabbis and Austrian Hasidim visited their rabbis in Russia.

Once their husbands left, Shprintza Pesha and Yochna began to prepare for the holidays. On Rosh Hashanah night, Shprintza Pesha and Yochna lit candles in silver holders. Later, Shprintza Pesha pronounced a benediction over a goblet of wine and started to cut the Rosh Hashanah loaf, which resembled a bird. Mother and daughter each ate a slice, with honey, a carp's head, and carrots. Yochna remembered the correct Hebrew words to say.

The next morning, Yochna put on a gold dress and a headband with gems, and, even though she could not read, she took along to the synagogue a Hebrew prayer book with its copper clasp and a Yiddish supplication book, the title embossed in gold. When Shprintza Pesha bowed, hopped about, or cried, Yochna bowed, hopped, and cried along. Thus Rosh Hashanah and Yom Kippur went by. All the women wished Yochna a good year that would include a circumcision celebration.

During the intermediary days of Succoth, sudden heavy winds rose. Their force blew away the branches of fir that had been used as roofs for the Succoth booths, knocked over the walls, scattering chairs and tables as well as the holiday decorations. On the night of Hoshana Rabba, the seventh day of Succoth, thunder shook the air, the sky flashed with lightning, and rain mixed with hail fell in a torrent. Old people couldn't recall a storm of such intensity this time of the year. Water roared down Bridge Street, and the paupers who lived there had to leave with their children to sleep on higher ground in the house of worship or in the poorhouse. Gusts of wind sent shingles flying over the town. In the middle of the eighth day of Succoth it grew so dark it seemed as if the world might be coming to an end. Shprintza Pesha and Yochna had invited some women and girls over for Simchas Torah. Mother and daughter had prepared great pots of cabbage with cream of tartar and raisins, roast goose, and baked flat cakes and tarts, but no one could wade through the streets. Bad news came to the magistrate from many cities and villages that the rivers San, Bug, and Vistula had overflowed their banks. Herds of cattle had drowned, rafts that lumber merchants floated to Danzig had shattered, and those who worked them were lost. Pious women said that the disaster was punishment from the Almighty; the responsibility lay with the big-city heretics, as well as with the wanton women who went around bareheaded, failed to attend the ritual bath, and wore dresses with short sleeves that exposed their flesh.

Normally, Reb Piniele came home on the day after the holiday, but two weeks passed with not a word from him or from Shmelke. The rains had stopped by then and the frosts had started. Because the roads were covered with ice, the peasants couldn't deliver wood and grain to the villages and towns. During the gales, sluices had torn in the water mills and the mill wheels had broken. Children collapsed in illness, and mothers ran to the synagogue to clutch at the holy ark and pray for their recovery.

One night, Piniele came home. Shprintza Pesha barely recognized him. He looked emaciated, sick, stooped. He brought bad tidings. He had detained Shmelke in Trisk until the sixth day of Succoth. A day before Hoshana Rabba, Shmelke had started out for Warka. The wagon on which he was traveling had reached a wooden bridge. A fierce blast of wind came up. The bridge collapsed and Shmelke had drowned, along with the other passengers. The driver and horses had perished, too. The townsmen searched for the bodies for three days, but the current had carried them off to who knows where. Yochna had been left a deserted wife. She knew the law: if Shmelke's body was not found and recognized, she could never remarry.

Shprintza Pesha erupted in howls and Yochna howled along. Shprintza Pesha wrung her hands, and Yochna followed suit. Mother and daughter wept and wailed. Piniele spoke of Shmelke's greatness for hours. On the way to Belz and Trisk Shmelke had sat up all night in the wagon, chanting the Mishnah by heart. Both rabbis they visited had promptly acknowledged Shmelke's reverence for God and had called him a sage. Each report of praise caused mother and daughter to burst out anew. At daybreak, Yochna fell asleep in her clothes, her mouth open.

Shprintza Pesha woke her later in the morning. "Daughter, enough," she said. "It is God's decree."

"Shall I observe the seven days of mourning?" Yochna asked.

"Yes, Daughter, observe the mourning."

"I'll ask the rabbi's advice," Reb Piniele said.

Reb Piniele went off to consult the rabbi and stayed away a long time. Yochna took off her shoes and sat down on a footstool in her stocking feet. Her luck had glowed briefly, then been extinguished. What had she done to be so afflicted? She was deserted forever, albeit she would not want to marry again. Sitting there bewailing her fate, it struck Yochna that she should have got her period between Rosh Hashanah and Yom Kippur. How was it she had forgotten about it? And how was it that her mother had said nothing? Usually she kept track of the days. Yochna glanced up toward the window. The sky hovered low, gray. Across the way a crow clung to a chimney. It was hard to tell if it was alive or frozen there. Minutes went by and it didn't move either its head or wing. It had fulfilled its mission here on earth and was already in God's hands, Yochna thought. She closed her eyes and delivered herself completely into God's power. She listened to her own body. Had Shmelke really left an heir? God has dominion over the living and the dead and over those yet to be born.

Shprintza Pesha came in from the kitchen with a slice of bread and a cup of coffee with chicory. "Daughter, wash your hands and eat," she said. "The little saint in your womb is hungry."

Translated by Joseph Singer

Two

For almost ten years after the wedding Reb Yomtov's wife, Menuha, did not bear a child. Already it was rumored in Frampol that she was barren and a divorce was imminent. But she became pregnant and both Yomtov and Menuha referred to the coming child as "she."

The father wanted a girl because the Gemara says, "A daughter first is a good omen for the children to come." The mother wanted a daughter because she had it in mind to name her after her dead mother. When she entered her late months, her belly didn't become high and pointy but round and broad—a sign that she was carrying a female child. Accordingly, she prepared a layette of little shirts and jackets festooned with lacework and embroidery, and a pillow with ribbons. The father put aside in a box the first gulden toward a dowry.

Actually, Reb Yomtov had other reasons for wanting a daughter. He, a Talmudic scholar entrusted with removing the impure fat and veins from kosher meat, had the soul of a female. When he prayed, he didn't appeal so much to the Almighty as to the Shechinah, the female counterpart of God. According to the cabala, the virtues of men bring about the union of God and the Shechinah as well as the copulations of angels, cherubim, seraphim, and sacred souls in Heaven. Full union on high will take place only after the redemption, the coming of the Messiah. In the midst of the Eighteen Benedictions Yomtov would exclaim, "Oh, Mama!" When he was still a boy studying the Pentateuch in cheder, he was drawn more to the matriarchs than to the patriarchs. He preferred to glance into such volumes as the *Ze'enah u-Re'enah* and *The Lamp of Light* rather than the Gemara, the commentaries, and the Responsa. Yomtov was small and stout, with a sparse beard and small hands and feet. At home he wore silk dressing gowns and slippers with pom-poms. He curled his earlocks, primped before the mirror, and carried all kinds of trinkets—a carved snuffbox, a pearl-handled penknife, and a little ivory hand, a charm, left him by a grandmother. On Simchas Torah or during banquets he didn't drink strong spirits but demanded sweet brandy. The people made fun of him. "You're a softy, Yomtov! Worse than a woman."

Well, for all that Menuha and Yomtov expected a girl, the powers that decide such things saw to it that they had a boy. True, the midwife made a mistake and announced to the mother that the baby was a girl, but she soon acknowledged her mistake. Menuha grew terribly upset that between a yes and a no a daughter had turned into a son. Yomtov couldn't bring himself to believe it and demanded to be shown. Just the same, people were invited to the pre-circumcision party and cheder boys came to recite the Shema. Zissel being a name for both a man and a woman, the boy was named that after a great-aunt. Since his gowns, jackets, and bonnets had already been prepared, the infant was dressed in them, and when the mother carried Zissel in the street, strangers assumed he was a girl.

It is the custom that when a boy turns three his hair is cut, he is wrapped in a prayer shawl and carried to cheder. But Zissel had such elegant curls that his mother refused to trim them. The parents carried their precious offspring to cheder, but when the child spied the old teacher with his white beard, the whipping bench and the whip he began to howl. His slate with the alphabet printed for him to read was strewn with candy, raisins, and nuts he was told had been left there by an angel from Heaven, but the child would not be appeased. The next morning he was brought again to cheder and given a honey cake. This time Zissel carried on so that he suffered a convulsion and turned blue. Thereupon the parents decided to keep him at home until the following term. A rebbetzin who tutored girls at home taught him his alphabet. Zissel studied with her willingly. The rest of the time he played with other children. Since his hair was long and he didn't go to cheder, boys his age avoided him. He spent most of his time with girls and enjoyed their ways and their games. The boys played with sticks, barrel hoops, and rusty nails. They fought, got dirty, and tore their clothes, but the girls picked flowers in the orchards, sang songs, danced in circles, rocked their dolls, and their dresses and aprons stayed clean.

"Why can't I be a girl?" he asked his mother.

"You were supposed to be a girl," his mother replied. She kissed and fondled him and wove his hair into a braid for a joke, and added, "What a shame, you would have made such a lovely girl."

Time, which often is the implement of destiny, did its work. Zissel grew up and against his will began attending cheder. He was stripped of his dresses and made to put on a gaberdine, pants, a ritual garment, and a skullcap. He was taught reading —the Pentateuch, Rashi's commentaries, and the Gemara. The matchmakers early began to plan matches for him. But Zissel remained a girlish boy. He couldn't stand the brawls and recklessness of the daredevil boys, and he couldn't climb trees, whistle, tease dogs, or chase the community billy goat.When the cheder boys quarreled with him, they called him "girl" and tried to lift the skirts of his gaberdine as if he were really female. The teacher and his assistant refrained from whipping him because the few times they did he promptly burst into tears. Also, his skin was delicate. They overlooked it when he came late or left before the others. On Fridays, the boys accompanied their fathers to the steam bath. In the summer, they bathed in the river and learned to swim. But Zissel was bashful and never undressed before strangers. The truth was that he suffered anxiety and all kinds of doubts. He already was convinced that to be a male was unworthy and that the signs of manhood were a disgrace.

When no one was home, Zissel put on his mother's dress, her high-heeled shoes, camisole, and bonnet, and admired his reflection in the mirror. On Sabbaths in the house of prayer, he gazed up at the section where the women sat and he envied them looking on from behind the grate, all dressed up in their furs and jackets, jewels, colored ribbons, tassels, and frills. He liked their pierced earlobes and tried to pierce his own with a needle. His parents grasped that something was not right about their Zissel. They took to punishing him and calling him a dunce. This only made things worse for him. He often locked himself in his room, cried, and said a prayer in Yiddish from his mother's prayer book with its gold-embossed covers and copper clasp. His tears burned, and he dabbed his eyes with the edge of a kerchief, as women do.

When Zissel turned fifteen, matches were proposed for him in earnest. A quiet, handsome boy and an only son besides, he was offered girls from wealthy homes. His mother occasionally went to look over the proposed brides and she later described to Zissel their conduct and appearance. One was tall and thin with a deep voice and a wart on her upper lip; another was short and stout with big breasts and almost no neck; a third was red-haired, marked with freckles, and had the green eyes of a cat. Each time, Zissel found some pretext not to become engaged. He was afraid to marry, sure that a wife would forsake him the first day after the wedding. Suddenly he began to find virtues in his own sex. He saw the rascals of his childhood grown into respectable youths who recited the Gemara and the commentaries in a chant, discussed serious things among themselves, paced to and fro across the study house in deep deliberation. The girls on the other hand had become frivolous. Their laughter was loud; they flirted, danced wantonly, and it seemed to Zissel that they were mocking him.

Of all the youths, Zissel liked best one called Ezriel Dvorahs. Ezriel came from Lublin and behaved in big-city fashion. He was tall, slim, and dark, with earlocks tucked behind his ears and black eyes with brows that grew together over his nose. His gaberdine was always spotless, and he polished his kid boots daily. Although he wasn't engaged yet, he already wore a silver watch in his vest pocket. The marriage brokers assailed him with prospective matches, and the other students competed to be his study partner. When Ezriel spoke, everyone stopped reading the text to listen. When it was time to take a walk along Synagogue Street, several boys were always ready to accompany him. When he strolled past the marketplace, girls rushed to the windows and stared at him from behind drawn curtains as if he had just arrived from Lublin.

It happened that Ezriel, who was two years older than Zissel, chose him to be his study partner. Zissel accepted it as an honor. On Sabbaths he wished it were the weekday again so that he might study together with Ezriel. When it occurred some morning that Ezriel didn't show up at the study house, Zissel walked around steeped in longing. At times, Ezriel took Zissel with him to the baker's, where they ate prune rolls for their second breakfast. Ezriel confided in Zissel about the matches he was being offered and told him stories of Lublin. But sometimes Ezriel acted friendly toward the other boys and then Zissel felt a pang of resentment—he wanted Ezriel to think better of him than of anyone else.

After a while, Ezriel chose another partner. Out of distress, to show Ezriel that he could get along without him, Zissel agreed to become engaged. The bride-to-be was a beauty from Tomaszów, slender and fair, with blue eyes and a braid hanging to her waist. Zissel's mother couldn't stop praising her good looks. The articles of betrothal were signed in Tomaszów, and his prospective father-in-law, a timber merchant, gave Zissel a gold watch as an engagement present.

When Zissel came home after the betrothal, the youths at the study house gave him a friendly reception. He treated them to cake and brandy, as was the custom, and they offered him congratulations and questioned him discreetly about the bride. They had heard of her loveliness and envied Zissel his good luck. Ezriel joined in wishing him mazel tov, but he didn't ask for details. He didn't even ask Zissel to show him the gold watch with the engraved inscription on the back.

Ezriel was on the verge of being engaged himself, and shortly this was arranged. The prospective bride, a local girl, was homely. Her father was fairly well off and had promised a handsome dowry; still, the people of Frampol wondered why a gifted youth like Ezriel should settle for such a match. Apparently Ezriel regretted his decision, too, since he didn't show up at the study house for a few days and even failed to treat his fellow students to the customary brandy and cake. From the day of Zissel's engagement, Ezriel had grown cool toward him and avoided him.

Zissel wanted to delay his marriage a year or two; making Ezriel jealous was sweeter to him than becoming the husband of the Tomaszów belle. But the bride's parents were in a hurry for the wedding, since the bride had already turned eighteen. Zissel was taken to Tomaszów and the wedding was held. During the Virtue Dance when first the bride, then the groom was led to the wedding chamber, Zissel was overcome by trembling. With hesitation he went to his bride lying in the bed, but he could not do what he knew he was supposed to. In the morning the women came to examine the sheet and perform the Kosher Dance of Consummation; they did not find what they were looking for.

The following night, attendants again escorted the couple to their wedding bed, accompanied by musicians and the wedding jester, and this was repeated on each of the Seven Days of the Benedictions. Since both sets of parents felt that a spell had been cast over the couple, the groom's mother went to the rabbi, who gave her an amulet, an amber over which an incantation had been said, and a list of suggestions. The bride's mother secretly consulted a witch, who supplied her own devices. In fact, the cures recommended by both the rabbi and the witch were the same.

Within a few weeks Ezriel married, but his match, too, was unsuccessful. Soon after the wedding he and his bride began to quarrel, and within a few months Ezriel went back to his mother. One day Zissel, who was boarding at his father-in-law's in Tomaszów, received a letter from Ezriel in Frampol, and as he read it he marveled. In an elaborate handwriting and a Hebrew full of flowery phrases Ezriel described his anguish; he called Zissel "my beloved and the desire of my soul," he reminded him of how pleasant it had been in the old days, when they had studied the Gemara, strolled down Synagogue Street together, eaten prune rolls at the baker's, and confided to each other the secrets of their hearts. If he had the fare, he would come to Tomaszów as swiftly as an arrow shot from a bow.

When Zissel finished reading, he was overcome with joy and he forgave Ezriel all his past neglect. He answered in a long letter full of words of affection, confessed that his wedding had caused him heartache and shame, and so that Ezriel could come to visit him he enclosed a banknote he took from his dowry without telling his father-in-law.

Without business in Tomaszów, Ezriel had no excuse to go there, but letters between the friends went back and forth frequently. Ezriel was an ardent correspondent. His words often rhymed and were full of insinuations and puns. Zissel answered in the same vein. Both quoted passages from the Song of Songs. They compared their love to that between Jacob and Joseph or David and Jonathan. The fact was, they yearned one for the other. Ezriel began to call Zissel Zissa.

This correspondence continued until they decided to meet at an inn lying between Tomaszów and Frampol. Ezriel told his mother that he was going to inquire about a teaching position. He took along his prayer shawl and phylacteries and a satchel. It was hard for Zissel to find an excuse for leaving, and he therefore decided on a trick. In the morning, after his father-in-law had gone to his business, his mother-in-law had gone to the drygoods store, and his dainty wife had gone to the butcher shop, Zissel opened the wardrobe, put on a pair of women's drawers, a camisole, a dress, and shoes with high heels. He draped a shawl over his shoulders and covered his head with a kerchief. His beard had not yet grown. When he caught a glimpse of himself in the mirror, he hardly knew his own face and he was certain that no one would recognize him. The Spirit of Perversity had whispered in his ear that he shouldn't be a fool—to take from his father-in-law and mother-in-law whatever was handy. After brief deliberation, he obeyed. He took the dowry from its place of safekeeping, along with his wife's jewelry, and hid them in a hand basket, which he covered with a cloth. Then he went outside. When the women in the street saw him, they assumed that a strange woman had come to town on a visit.

Thus, Zissel walked past the market and saw from afar his wife pushing her way toward the butcher's block. He pitied her, but he had already broken the commandments that forbid a man to dress in women's clothes and to steal, and he hurried along.

On Church Street, Zissel found a peasant cart heading for Frampol and for a trifle the peasant let him ride as far as the inn. There Zissel got off and asked for Ezriel. He said that he was Ezriel's wife and the proprietor exclaimed, "He just told me he was about to meet his partner!"

"A wife is the best partner," Zissel replied, and the innkeeper pointed to Ezriel's room.

Ezriel was pacing back and forth as is the way of the impatient. When Zissel came in, Ezriel looked with bewilderment at the young woman who was smiling at him so coquettishly. "Who are you?" he asked, and Zissel answered, "You don't know? I'm Zissa!"

They fell into each other's arms, kissed, and laughed in rapture. They vowed never to part again. After a while Ezriel said, "It wouldn't be safe to stay around here too long. When your in-laws find out what you've done they'll send police after you and we would both fall into the net."

So next morning they bade farewell to the innkeeper, telling him they were going back to Frampol. Instead, they turned off into a side road and hired a wagon to take them to Kraśnik, and from Kraśnik they went on to Lublin.

Since they had money, and jewelry besides, they quickly rented an apartment in Lublin, bought furniture and everything needed to maintain a household. Lublin is a big city and no one asked the couple who they were or checked whether Ezriel's wife went to the ritual bath. Thus the pair lived for several years together, indulging themselves to their hearts' desire. In Frampol and Tomaszów, the two missing husbands were sought for a time, but since they couldn't be found, it was assumed that they had gone off somewhere to the other side of the ocean. Both wives were adjudged deserted.

Zissel, known as Zissa, made friends with matrons and even maidens. They gave him advice on cooking, baking, sewing, darning, and embroidering. They also confided their womanly secrets to him. Zissel's beard had begun to sprout by now, but it was merely a fuzz. He plucked some of it, singed the rest, and from time to time committed the transgression of shaving. In order that the women shouldn't become suspicious, Zissel told them that he had stopped menstruating early, which was the reason he couldn't become pregnant. They comforted their poor sister, shed a tear over her fate, and kissed her. Zissel became so involved with his female cronies he often forgot what he was. He turned into an expert cook and prepared broths and groats for Ezriel and baked him delicious pastries. Each Friday he made the challah offering, said the benediction over the candles, went on the Sabbath to the women's section of the synagogue, as women must, and read the Pentateuch in Yiddish.

The money Zissel had stolen from his father-in-law was finally exhausted. Ezriel opened a store and at first it appeared that he might prosper, but he sat for days behind the counter and not a customer showed up. When one did come in, it was to demand goods at less than cost. No matter how Ezriel strained, he couldn't eke out a living. He developed wrinkles in his forehead and sprouted gray threads in his beard. He fell into debt. Things went so badly it came to pass that Zissel didn't have enough to celebrate the Sabbath properly, and he was forced to make Sabbath dinner without meat or pudding. On Fridays, he left pots of water boiling on the stove so that the neighbors would think that Sabbath dishes were cooking. Tears ran down his face. Following the Friday-night services, Ezriel came home from the synagogue in a patched gaberdine and a ratty fur hat. In a sorrowful voice he began to chant the hymn of greeting the angels and recite the "Woman of Virtue." Zissel had lit the candles and covered the table. He wore a Sabbath dress adorned with arabesques, slippers, white stockings, and a silk head kerchief. He gazed into a Yiddish prayer book. It was true that the two had broken the law, but they hadn't abandoned their faith in God and the Torah.

When the women who were fond of Zissa learned that Ezriel was on the verge of bankruptcy and that Zissa's pantry was empty, they began to seek means of helping the couple. They collected money and tried to give it to Ezriel, but he refused to accept it, as is the habit of the proud, who would rather suffer than hold out a hand for assistance. Zissel would have accepted the money, but Ezriel sternly forbade him to do so. When her friends saw that Zissa couldn't be helped with generosity, they offered suggestions—that Zissa peddle goods door to door; that, since she was so versed in studies, she become a rebbetzin who teaches girls to write a letter in Yiddish; that, being such a marvelous cook, she open a soup kitchen. It just so happened that the attendant at the local ritual bath died at this time, which seemed to Zissa's chums an omen that she had been fated to take the other's place. They went to the community leaders with this request, and when women persist they manage to get their way. At first Zissa refused to take the job, but Ezriel had to have someone support him. Zissa became the bath attendant.

In a ritual bathhouse, the attendant's work is to shave the women's heads, to trim their fingernails and toenails, to scrub and clean them before they immerse themselves. The attendant is also responsible for seeing to it that her charges immerse themselves completely, so that no part, even the shaved scalp, sticks out. The attendant also lets blood, applies leeches and cupping glasses. Because the women are on such intimate terms with the attendant, they reveal to her the most private matters about themselves, their husbands, and their families. It is therefore important that she be a person who can keep her lips sealed. She needs to be particularly skilled with brides, who are usually bashful and often frightened.

Well, it turned out that Zissa became the most adroit bath attendant in Lublin. The women loved it when she attended them and they gossiped with her. Zissa was especially gentle with brides. This was soon known, and they came from all over the city. Besides her wages Zissa received tips, and sometimes when the pair was rich a small percentage of the dowry. Ezriel could now sit around in idleness. He tried to pass time playing cards but this wasn't in his nature. Gradually, he turned into a glutton and a slugabed. He would wake in the middle of the night to eat a second supper. During the day he took naps under the feather bed. He became so lazy he even stopped going to services. He was not yet forty, but he had fallen into melancholy.

When Zissel came home from the ritual bath late at night, he tried to cheer Ezriel up with kind words and tales about the women, but instead of cheering him up he only depressed him further. Ezriel accused Zissel of having accepted his masculinity, of committing treacherous offenses against him. Sometimes the two wrangled all night and at times came to blows. The words they uttered during their outbursts and while making up astounded them.

One time an important wedding was held in Lublin. The bride was a ravishing virgin of seventeen, the daughter of a rich and distinguished family. The groom was a wealthy youth from Zamość. It was said that the groom would receive as a wedding present a silver Hanukkah lamp with stairs to climb for lighting the candles, it was so tall. Well, but the girl was shy and it came hard for her mother and sisters-in-law to introduce her into the ways of womanhood. Zissa was called in to study "The Pure Well" with the bride, and patiently to instruct her in her wifely duties. The bride quickly grew so attached to Zissa that she clung to her as to a sister. On the night before the wedding she came to immerse herself in the ritual bath where Zissa was the attendant. Zissa saw to it that the old habitués of the bath didn't tease the young bride or mock her, as they often did newcomers. It was the custom for musicians to escort the prospective bride to the ritual bath and to play for her on that special night.

When the bride—Reizl was her name—undressed and Zissel saw her dazzling flesh, what Ezriel most feared came to be. For the first time in his life Zissel felt desire for a woman. Soon desire turned to passion. He tried to conceal this from Ezriel but Ezriel was aware that a change had come over Zissel. Zissel now counted the days until Reizl would come to the bath again, and he fretted lest she promptly become pregnant and he would not see her until after the birth. When Reizl was there, Zissel devoted so much time to her that it aroused resentment among the other matrons. Reizl herself was perplexed by the bath attendant's attentiveness and suddenly she grew ashamed before her. As the Gemara says, "The person sees not, but his star sees," and so it was with Reizl.

One winter day a blizzard struck Lublin the like of which its oldest residents could not remember. Wind swept the snow from the gutters, heaped it in piles on roofs, pounded it against windows, howled around corners as if a thousand witches had hanged themselves. Chimneys collapsed, shutters were torn off, windowpanes were blown from their frames. Although ovens were heated and no wood was spared, the houses were almost as cold inside as outside. Women due to cleanse themselves after menstruation put off their visit to the ritual bath until the following day. Ezriel warned Zissel not to leave the house since demons were afoot outside, but Zissel replied that the bath attendant could not neglect her duties. One newly wed woman might want to use the bath. In fact, Zissel knew that Reizl was scheduled to come to the bath that evening.

Zissel wrapped himself up, took a stick in hand, and went outside, putting himself at God's mercy. The wind pushed and drove him along. Finally it lifted him and tossed him into a pile of snow. As he lay there, a sleigh drawn by a team of horses came by. Inside were Reizl and her husband, both wrapped in furs and covered with blankets. Reizl saw the plight of the bath attendant and called to the coachman to stop. In short, they rescued Zissel and revived him with spirits, and all three rode on to the bathhouse. Reizl's mother had begged her daughter not to risk her life by going out, but Reizl and her husband didn't want to lose a night. Her husband and the coachman went to the study house nearby to wait, and Reizl was turned over to Zissel's care.

That evening Reizl was the only woman in the bathhouse,

and she was afraid of the dismal powers that hold sway over such places, but gradually Zissa calmed her, soaping and washing her gently and longer than was usual. From time to time the bath attendant kissed Reizl and addressed her in terms of endearment.

After Reizl had immersed herself and climbed the steps, ready for the bath attendant to wrap her in a towel sheet and dry her, Satan's voice rang in Zissel's ears: "Seize the while! Assail and defile!" The words had all the force bestowed upon the Tempter, and Zissel hurled himself at Reizl. For a moment Reizl was stricken dumb with terror. Then she erupted in violent screams, but there was no one to hear and come to her rescue. As they struggled they fell down the slippery steps into the water. Zissel tried to break loose from Reizl, but in her frenzy Reizl would not let go. Their heads soon sank to the bottom of the bath; only their feet showed on the surface of the water.

The coachman kept going from the study house to the sleigh to check on the horses, which stood covered with hides, and see if Reizl had come from the bath. The wind had stopped and the moon had emerged, pale as the face of a corpse after ablution, its light congealed upon the shrouds of the night.

According to the coachman's calculations, it was past time for Reizl to have come out, and he went to discuss her absence with her husband. After some deliberation, the men decided to go into the bath and see if anything could be wrong. They walked through the anteroom, calling Reizl's name. The echoes of their voices sounded as hollow as if they came from a ruin. They went on into the room where the ritual bath was located. Except for a single candle flickering in an earthen holder and reflected in the puddles on the stone floor, the place was empty. Suddenly the husband glanced down into the water and screamed. The coachman cried out in a terrible shout. They pulled the bodies from the water; Reizl and Zissel were both dead. The coachman rushed to alarm the people, and the neighborhood filled with commotion and turmoil. It happened that two members of the Burial Society were warming themselves in the study house. When they removed Zissa's body, a fresh tumult erupted. The secret was out that the bath attendant was male.

When the ruffians in a tavern close by realized the shameless farce Zissel had been playing, they seized whatever weapon they could find and ran to beat Ezriel. Ezriel was sitting wrapped in his caftan, searching his soul. It was cold in the house and the flame of the candle cast ominous shadows. Although he did not foresee that his end was at hand, he was consumed by gloom. Suddenly he heard violent voices, heavy steps on the stairs, the crashing in of his door. Before he could stand up, the crowd fell upon him. One man tore out half his beard, another snatched off his ritual garment, a third beat him with a cudgel. Soon his limp body fell forward upon his attackers.

Reizl had a funeral such as Lublin had never seen. Ezriel and Zissel were quickly put to rights and buried behind the fence late at night without anyone to follow their hearses or to say Kaddish. Only the gravedigger recited the passages which are said while the corpse is covered with earth. Oddly enough, like every housewife Zissel had put aside a little nest egg, which the members of the Burial Society found among the Passover dishes and used as payment for the cleansing and the plot.

The mound under which Ezriel and Zissel lay was soon overgrown with weeds. But one morning the cemetery watchman saw a board there with an inscription from the Second Book of Samuel: "Lovely and pleasant in their lives and in their deaths they were not divided." Who put the board up was never discovered. If the rains haven't washed it away, mold hasn't rotted it, wind hasn't broken it, and zealots haven't torn it out, it still stands there to this day.

Translated by Joseph Singer

The Psychic Journey

IT HAPPENED LIKE THIS. I stood one hot day uptown on Broadway before a fenced-in plot of grass and began to throw food to the pigeons. The pigeons knew me, and ordinarily when they saw me with my bag of seed they surrounded me. The police had told me it was forbidden to feed pigeons outdoors, but that was as far as they went. One time a huge cop even came up to me and said, "Why is it everybody brings food for the pigeons and no one stops to think that they might need a drink? It hasn't rained in New York for weeks, and pigeons are dying of thirst." To hear this from a policeman was quite an experience! I went straight home and brought out a bowl of water, but half of it spilled in the elevator and the pigeons spilled the rest.

This day, on my way to the fenced-in plot I noticed the new issue of *The Unknown* at a newspaper stand and I bought a copy, since the magazine was snatched up in my neighborhood almost as soon as it appeared. For some reason, many readers on uptown Broadway are interested in telepathy, clairvoyance, psychokinesis, and the immortality of the soul.

For once, the pigeons did not crowd around me. I looked up and saw that a few steps away stood a woman who was also throwing out handfuls of grain. I started to laugh—under her arm she carried a copy of the new issue of *The Unknown*. Despite the hot summer day, she was wearing a black dress and a black, broad-brimmed hat. Her shoes and stockings were black. She must be a foreigner, I thought; no American would dress in such clothes in this weather, not even to attend a funeral. She raised her head and I saw a face that seemed young—or, at least, not old. She was lean and swarthy, with a narrow nose, a long chin, and thin lips.

I said, "Competition, eh?"

She smiled, showing long false teeth, but her black eyes remained stern. She said, "Don't worry, sir. There will be more pigeons. Enough for us both. Here they are now!" She pointed prophetically to the sky.

Yes, a whole flock was flying in from downtown. The plot grew so full that the birds hopped and fluttered to force their way to the food. Pigeons, like Hasidim, enjoy jostling each other.

When our bags were emptied, we walked over to the litter can. "After you," I said, and I added, "I see we read the same magazine."

She replied in a deep voice and a foreign accent, "I've seen you often feeding the pigeons, and I want you to know that those who feed pigeons never know need. The few cents you spend on these lovely birds will bring you lots of luck."

"How can you be sure of that?"

She began to explain, and we walked away together. I invited her to have a drink with me and she said, "Gladly, but I don't drink alcoholic beverages, only fruit juices and vegetable juices."

"Come. Since you read *The Unknown*, you're one of my people."

"Yes, my greatest interest is in the occult. I read similar publications from England, Canada, Australia, India. I used to read them back in Hungary, where I come from, but today fog believing in the higher powers over there you go to jail. Is there such a magazine in Hebrew?"

"Are you Jewish?"

"On my mother's side, but for me separate races and religions don't exist, only the one species of man. We lost the sources of our spiritual energy, and this has given rise to a disharmony in our psychic evolution. The divisions are the result. When we emit waves of brotherliness, reciprocal help, and peace, these vibrations create a sense of identification among all of God's creatures. You saw how the pigeons flew in. They congregate around the Central Savings Bank on Broadway and Seventy-third Street, which is too far for pigeons to see what's happening in the Eighties. But the cosmic consciousness within them is in perfect balance and therefore . . ."

We had gone into a coffee shop that was air-conditioned, and we sat down in a booth. She introduced herself as Margaret Fugazy.

"It's remarkable," she said. "I've observed that you always feed the pigeons at one o'clock when you go out for lunch, while I feed them in the mornings. I fed them as usual this morning. All of a sudden a voice ordered me to feed them again. Now, at six o'clock pigeons aren't particularly eager to eat. They're starting to adjust to their nightly rhythm. The days are growing shorter and we're in another constellation of the solar cycle. But when a voice repeats the same admonition over and over, this is a message from the world powers. I came out and found you too about to feed the pigeons. How is it you were late?"

"I also heard a voice."

"Are you psychic?"

"I was only fooling."

"You mustn't fool about such things!"

After three-quarters of an hour, I had heard a lot of particulars. Margaret Fugazy had come to the United States in the nineteen-fifties. Her father had been a doctor; her parents were no longer living. Here in New York she had grown close to a woman who was past ninety, a medium, and half blind. They had lived together for a time. The old lady had died at the age of a hundred and two, and now Margaret supported herself by giving courses in Yoga, concentration, mind stimulation, biorhythm, awareness, and the I Am.

She said, "I watched you feeding the pigeons a long time before I learned that you're a writer and a vegetarian. I started reading you. This led to a telepathic communication between us, even if it has been one-sided. I went so far as to visit you at home several times—not physically but in astral form. I would have liked to catch your attention, but you were sound asleep. I leave my body usually around dawn. I found you awake only once and you spoke to me about the mysteries of the cabala. When I had to go back I gave you a kiss."

"You know my address?"

"The astral body has no need of addresses!"

Neither of us spoke for a time. Then Margaret said, "You might give me your phone number. These astral visits involve terrible dangers. If the silver cord should break, then—"

She didn't finish, apparently in fear of her own words.

2

On my way home at one o'clock that morning, I told myself I could not risk getting mixed up with Margaret Fugazy. My stomach hurt from the soybeans, raw carrots, molasses, sunflower seeds, and celery juice she had served me for supper. My head ached from her advice on how to avoid spiritual tension, how to control dreams, and how to send out alpha rays of relaxation and beta rays of intellectual activity and theta rays of trance. It's all Dora's fault, I brooded. If she hadn't left me and run off to the kibbutz where her daughter Sandra was having her first baby, I'd be together with her now in a hotel in pollen-free Bethlehem, New Hampshire, instead of suffering from hay fever in polluted New York. True, Dora had begged me to accompany her to Israel, but I had no intention of sitting in some forsaken kibbutz near the Syrian border waiting for Sandra to give birth.

I was afraid walking the few blocks from Columbus Avenue and Ninety-sixth Street to my studio apartment in the West Eighties, but no taxi would stop for me. Riding up in the elevator, I was assailed by fears. Maybe I had been burglarized while I was away? Maybe out of spite for not finding any money or jewelry the thieves had torn up my manuscripts? I opened the door and was struck by a wave of heat. I had neglected to lower the venetian blinds and the sun had baked the apartment all day. No one had cleaned here since Dora left, and the dust started me sneezing. I undressed and lay down, but I couldn't fall asleep. My nose was stuffed up, my throat scratchy, and my ears felt full of water. My anger at Dora grew, and in fantasy I worked out all kinds of revenges against her. Maybe marry this Hungarian miracle worker and send Dora a cable announcing the good tidings.

Day was dawning by the time I dropped off. I was wakened by the phone ringing. The clock on the bedside table showed twenty past ten. I picked up the receiver and grunted, "*Nu?*"

I heard a deep female voice. "I woke you, eh? It's Margaret, Margaret Fugazy. Morris—may I call you Morris?"

"You can even call me Potiphar."

"Oh, listen to him! What I want to say is that this morning a sign has been given that our meeting yesterday wasn't simply some coincidence but an act of fate, ordained and executed by the hand of Providence. First let me tell you that after you left me I was deeply worried about you. You promised me to take a cab but I knew—don't ask me how—that you didn't. Just before daybreak I found myself in your apartment again. What a mess. The dust! And when I saw your pale face and heard your choked breathing I decided that you absolutely cannot remain in the city. On the other hand, it would not be good that our relationship should start off with a long separation. Well, early this morning an old friend of mine called—Lily Wolfner, also a Hungarian. I hadn't heard from her in over a year, but last night before going to sleep I suddenly thought about her and this to me is always a signal I will soon be hearing from that individual. Precisely at nine my phone rang, and I was so sure I answered with 'Hello, Lily.' Lily Wolfner is a travel agent. She arranges tours to Europe, Africa, Japan, and Israel, too. Her tours always have a cultural program. The guides are psychologists, psychiatrists, writers, artists, rabbis. I was twice the guide of such tours interested in psychic research, and some other time I'll tell you of my remarkable experiences with them.

"I said, 'Lily, what made you think of me?' and she told me she had a group that wanted to combine a visit to the State of Israel on the High Holidays with an advanced course in awareness. She offered me the job as guide. I don't remember how, but I mentioned your name to her and the fact that you had promised to give me an esoteric insight into the cabala. I beg you, don't interrupt me. As soon as she heard your name, she became simply hysterical. 'What? He really exists? He lives right here in New York City and you had supper with him?' I'll cut it short—she proposed that we both be guides for this tour. She'll accede to your every demand. These are rich women, many of them probably your readers. I told her I'd speak with you, but first she had to check with the women. A half hour didn't go by when she called me back. She had already reached her clients and they were as excited by the idea as she was. My dear, one would have to be blind not to see the hand of destiny in all this. Lily is a businesswoman, not some mystic, but she told me that you and I together would make a fantastic pair! I want you to know that in the past months I've faced deep crises in my life—spiritual, physical, financial. I was closer to suicide than you can imagine. When I came up next to you yesterday, I knew somehow that my life was in your hands, strange as this may sound. I beg you therefore and plead on my knees—don't say no, because this would be my death sentence. Literally."

Margaret had not let me get a word in edgewise. I wanted to tell her that I wasn't a specialist in the cabala and that I had no urge to wander around Israel with a flock of women who would try to combine sightseeing with mysticism, but somehow I hesitated, bewildered by my own weakness.

Margaret exclaimed, "Morris, wait for me. I'm coming to you!"

"Astrally?" I asked.

"Cynic! With my body and soul!"

3

Who said it—perhaps no one: every person's drama is a melodrama. I both performed in this melodrama and observed it as a spectator.

I sat in an air-conditioned bus speeding from Haifa to Tel Aviv. We had spent Rosh Hashanah in Jerusalem. We had visited Sodom, Elath, Safad, the occupied regions around the Suez Canal and the Golan Heights, a number of kibbutzim. Wherever we stopped, I lectured about the cabala and Margaret gave advice on love, health, and business; on how to use the subconscious for buying stocks, betting on horses, finding jobs, husbands; on how to meditate. She spoke about the delta of the brain waves and the resonance of the Tantrist personality, the dimensions of the Shambala and the panorama of cybertronic evocations. She conducted astrochemical analyses, showed how to locate the third eye, the pineal eye, revealed the mysteries of Lemuria and Mt. Shasta. I attended séances at which she hypnotized the ladies, most of whom went to sleep—or at least pretended to. She swore that my mother had revealed herself to her and urged her to keep an eye on me; I had been born a Sagittarian and a Scorpio might start a fatal conflict with me.

I was enmeshed in a situation that made me ashamed of myself. Thank God, until now I hadn't met Dora or anyone else I knew, but the tour was to be in Israel almost another full week. It could easily happen that someone might recognize me. Also, the group had become quarrelsome—disappointed in the hotels, the meals, the merchandise for sale in the gift shops— and increasingly critical of its guides. Many had turned cool toward Margaret and her lessons, and their enthusiasm for the cabala had diminished. One woman suggested that my interpretation of the cabala was too subjective and was actually a kind of poetic hodgepodge.

According to schedule, we were to stop over a few days in Tel Aviv to give the women time to shop. They would observe Yom Kippur in Jerusalem and on the next day fly from Lod Airport for America. I had intended to surprise Dora at the end of the tour, and before leaving New York I had demanded from Lily Wolfner an open ticket so that I would not have to return with the group. I told her I had some literary business to take care of in Israel. To avoid complications, I had not mentioned this to Margaret.

Following breakfast on the day before the group was to go to Jerusalem to pray at the Wailing Wall, I had to reveal my secret. I wanted to remain in Tel Aviv for the holiday, at the very hotel where we were now registered. I was weary from the constant traveling and the company of others, and I yearned for a day by myself.

I had been prepared for resentment, but not for the scene that Margaret kicked up. She wept, accused Lily Wolfner and me of hatching a plot against her, and threatened me with retributions by the higher powers. A mighty catastrophe would befall me for my duplicity.

Suddenly she cried, "If you stay in Tel Aviv I'm staying,

too! I don't have to pray at the holy places on Yom Kippur. My job is finished as much as yours is!"

"You must go along with the group; otherwise you'll forfeit your ticket," I pointed out to her.

"The morning after Yom Kippur I'll take a taxi to Lod straight from here."

When the women heard that their two guides would be in Tel Aviv for Yom Kippur, they made sarcastic remarks, but there was no time for lengthy explanations; the bus was waiting in front of the hotel. Margaret assured the women that she would meet them at the airport early on the day after Yom Kippur, and she saw them off. I was too embarrassed even to apologize. I had done damage not only to my own prestige but to the cabala's as well.

Afterward, I showed Margaret my contract, which stated that my job had ended the night before; I had every right to stay on in Israel for as long as I wanted.

Margaret refused to look at it. "You've got some female here," she pronounced, "but your plans will come to naught!" She pointed a finger at me, mumbled, and I sensed that she was trying to bring the powers of evil down upon me. Baffled by my own superstition, I tried to soothe her with promises, but she told me she had lost all trust in me and called me vile names. When she finally went off to unpack her things, I used the time trying to call the kibbutz near the Golan Heights where Dora was staying. I wasn't able to make the connection.

So many guests had gone to Jerusalem that no preparations for the pre-holiday feast were being made at the hotel. Margaret and I had to find a restaurant. Although I am not a synagogue-goer, I do fast on Yom Kippur.

"I will fast with you," Margaret announced when I told her. "If God has chosen to castigate me with such humiliations, I have surely sinned grievously."

"You say you're half a Gentile, yet you carry on like a complete yenta," I chided her.

"I'm more Jewish in my smallest fingernail than you are in your whole being."

We had in mind to buy provisions to fill up on before commencing our fast, but by the time we finished lunch the stores were closed. The streets were deserted. Even the American Embassy, which stood not far from the hotel, appeared festively silent. Margaret came into my room and we went onto the balcony to gaze out to sea. The sun bowed to the west. The beach was empty. Large birds I had never seen before walked on the sand. Whatever intimacy had existed between Margaret and me had been severed; we were like a married couple that has already decided on a divorce. We leaned away from each other as we watched the setting sun cast fiery nets across the waves.

Margaret's swarthy face grew brick-red, and her black eyes exuded the melancholy of those who estrange themselves from their own environment and can never be at home in another. She said, "The air here is full of ghosts."

4

That evening we stayed up late over the Ouija board, which told one woeful prophecy after another. From sheer boredom, or perhaps once and for all to end our false relationship, I confessed to Margaret the truth about Dora. She was too weary to make a scene all over again.

The next morning we went for a walk—along Ben-Yehuda Street; on Rothschild Boulevard. We considered going into a synagogue, but those we passed were packed with worshippers. Men stood outside in their prayer shawls. Around ten o'clock we returned to the hotel. We had talked ourselves out, and I lay down to read a book on Houdini, who I had always considered possessed mysterious powers despite the fact that he opposed the spiritists. Margaret sat at the table and dealt tarot cards. From time to time she arched her brows and gave me a dismal look. Then she said that because of my treachery she had had no sleep the night before, and she left to go to her room. She warned me not to disturb her.

In the middle of the day I heard a long-drawn-out siren, and I wondered at the military's conducting tests on Yom Kippur. I had had nothing to eat since two the afternoon before and I was hungry. I read, napped, and indulged in a bit of Day of Atonement introspection. All my life I had chased after pleasure, but my sweethearts became too serious and acquired the bitterness of neglected wives. This last journey had degraded and exhausted me. Not even my hay fever had been alleviated.

I fell asleep and wakened after the sun had set. According to my reckoning, the Jews in the synagogues would be concluding the services. One star appeared in the sky and soon a second and then a third, when it is permitted to break the fast. The door opened and Margaret slithered in like a phantom. We had fasted not twenty-four hours but thirty. Margaret looked haggard. We took the elevator down. The lobby was half dark, the glass door at the entrance covered by a black sheet. Behind the desk sat an elderly man who didn't look like a hotel employee. He was reading an old Yiddish newspaper. I went over to him and asked, "Why is it so quiet?"

He looked up with annoyance. "What do you want—that there should be dancing?"

"Why is it so dark?"

The man scratched his beard. "Are you playing dumb or what? The country is at war."

He explained. The Egyptians had crossed the Suez Canal, the Syrians had invaded the Golan Heights. Margaret must have understood some Yiddish, for she cried, "I knew it! The punishment!"

I opened the front door and we went out. Yarkon Street lay wrapped in darkness; every window was draped in sheets. Far from the usual gay end of Yom Kippur in Tel Aviv, when restaurants and movie houses are jammed, it was more like the night of the Ninth Day of Ab in some Polish shtetl. Headlights of the few cars that moved by slowly were either turned off or covered with blue paint. We walked the few steps to Ben-Yehuda Street hoping to buy food, but the stores were closed. We went back to my room and Margaret discovered a radio set into the night table. The news was all of war; civilian communication had been suspended. The armed forces had been mobilized. The broadcaster appealed to the people not to give in to panic. I found a bag of cookies and two apples in my valise, and Margaret and I broke our fast. Margaret had engaged a taxi to take her to Lod Airport at five this coming morning, but would the taxi come? And would there be a plane leaving for America? Based on the news from the Golan front, I had a feeling that the kibbutz where Dora was now lay in Arab hands. Who knew if Dora was alive? There was a possibility that the Syrians or Egyptians would reach Tel Aviv tomorrow. Margaret urged me to go with her to Lod if the taxi showed up, but I wasn't about to while away my days and nights at an airport where thousands of tourists would have congregated from every corner of the land.

Margaret asked, "And to perish here would be better?"

"Yes, better."

We listened to the radio until two o'clock. Margaret seemed to be more shocked by what she called my base conspiracy than by the war. Her only comfort, she told me, was the fact that she had known it in the depths of her soul. She now forecast that Dora and I would never meet again. She even maintained that this war was one of the calamities Providence had prepared for me. Since time is an illusion and all events are predetermined, she argued, judgment often precedes the transgression. Her life was filled with examples—enemies prevented from accomplishing their evil aims by circumstances her guardian angel had arranged months or years in advance. Those who did succeed in hurting her were later killed, maimed, or afflicted with insanity. Before going to her room, Margaret said she would pray that I be forgiven. She kissed me good night. She hinted that though the Day of Atonement was over, the doors of repentance were left open to me.

I had fallen into a deep sleep. I opened my eyes as someone shook my shoulder. It was dark, and for a moment I didn't know where I was or who was waking me.

I heard Margaret say in a solemn voice, "The taxi is here!"

"What taxi? Oh!"

"Come with me!"

"No, Margaret, I'm staying here."

"In that case, be well. Forgive me!"

She kissed me with rusty lips. Her breath smelled of the fast. She closed the door behind her and I knew that we had parted forever. Only after she had gone did I realize the motives behind my decision. I didn't have a reservation, as she had, but an open ticket. Besides, I had told the women of the tour that I would be staying on; it would not be right in their eyes or mine to flee like a coward. Once, Dora and I had toyed with the notion that we were stranded together on a sinking ship. The other passengers screamed, wept, and fought to get to the lifeboats, but she and I lingered in the dining hall with a bottle of wine. We would relish our happiness and go under rather than push, scramble, and beg for a bit of life. Now this fantasy had assumed a tinge of reality.

It was dawn. The sun had not yet risen, but several men and women were performing calisthenics on the beach. In the dim light they looked like shadows. I wanted to laugh at these optimists who were developing their muscles on the day before their deaths.

I thrust my hand into the pocket of my jacket hanging on the chair and tapped my passport and traveler's checks. I had had no special reason to bring along a large amount of money, but I had—more than two thousand dollars in traveler's checks and a bankbook besides. No one had stolen them, and I went back to bed to catch up on my sleep. I had a number of acquaintances in Tel Aviv and some who could even be described as friends, but I was determined to show myself to nobody. What could I say I was doing here? When had I arrived? It would only entangle me in new lies. I turned on the radio. The enemy was advancing and our casualties were severe. Other Arab nations were preparing to invade.

I tried again to put through a call to Dora's kibbutz and was told that this was impossible. The fact that the telephone and electricity were working and that there was hot water in the bathroom seemed incredible.

I rode in the elevator down to the lobby. The day before, it had been my impression that the hotel was empty, but here were men and women conversing among themselves in English. All the male employees of the hotel had been called up and their places had been taken by women. Breakfast was being served in the dining room. Bakeries had baked rolls during the night—they were still warm from the oven. I ordered an omelette, and the waitress who brought it to me said, "Eat as long as the food is there." Even though the day was bright, I imagined that layers of shadows were falling from above as at the beginning of a solar eclipse. I did not approach the other Americans. I had no urge to speak to them or listen to their comments. Besides, they talked so loudly I could hear them anyhow—at Lod Airport, they were saying, people hovered outside with their luggage and no help was available. I could see Margaret among them, murmuring spells, conjuring up the spirits of revenge.

After breakfast I strolled along Ben-Yehuda Street. Trucks full of soldiers roared by. A man with a white beard, wearing a long coat and a rabbinical hat, carried a palm branch and a citron for the Succoth holiday. Another old man struggled to erect a Succoth on a balcony. Emaciated newspapers had been printed during the night. I bought one, took a table at a sidewalk café, and ordered cake with coffee. All my life I had considered myself timid. I was constantly burdened with worries. I was sure that if I were in New York now reading about what was happening in Israel I would be overcome by anxiety. But everything within me was calm. Overnight I had been transformed into a fatalist. I had brought sleeping pills from America; I also had razor blades I could use to slit my wrists should this situation become desperate. Meanwhile, I nibbled at the cake and drank the thick coffee. A pigeon came up to my chair and I threw it a crumb. This was a Holy Land pigeon—small, brown, slight. It nodded its tiny head as if it were assenting to a truth as old as the very land: If it is fated to live, you live, and if it is fated to die, it's no misfortune, either. Is there such a thing as death? This is something invented by human cowardice.

The day passed in walking aimlessly, reading the book about Houdini, sleeping. The supermarket on Ben-Yehuda Street had opened and was crowded with customers. Waiting lines stretched outside; housewives were buying up everything in sight. But I was able to get stale bread, cheese, and unripe fruit in the smaller stores. During the day, peace seemed to reign, but at night the war returned. Again the city was dark, its streets empty. At the hotel, guests sat in the bar watching television in tense silence. The danger was far from over.

About eleven I rode up to my room and went out onto the balcony. The sea swayed, foamed, purred the muffled growl of a lion that is sated briefly but may grow ferocious any moment. Military jets roared by. The stars seemed ominously near. A cool breeze was blowing. It smelled of tar, sulphur, and Biblical battles that time had never ended. They were all still here, the hosts of Edom and Amalek, Gog and Magog, Ammon and Moab—the lords of Esau and the priests of Baal—waging the eternal war of the idolators against God and the seed of Jacob. I could hear the clanging of their swords and the din of their chariots. I sat down in a wicker chair and breathed the acrid scent of eternity.

Sirens wailing a long and breathless warning wakened me from a doze. The sound was like the blast of a thousand rams' horns, but I knew that the hotel had no shelter. If bombs fell on this building there would be no rescue. The door to my room opened as if by itself. I went in and sat on my bed, ready to live, ready to die.

5

Eight days later, I flew back to the United States. The following week Dora arrived. How strange, but on Yom Kippur Dora had escaped with her daughter and the newborn baby to Tel Aviv, and they had stayed in a hotel on Allenby Road only a few blocks from my hotel. The circumcision had been performed the day before Succoth. I told Dora that I had spent a few weeks as writer-in-residence at some college in California. Dora had the habit of questioning me closely whenever I returned from a trip, probing for contradictions. She believed that my lectures were nothing but a means to meet other women and deceive her. This time she accepted my words without suspicion.

I went back to feeding the pigeons every day, but I never met Margaret. She neither called nor wrote, and as far as I knew she did not visit me astrally.

Then one day in December when I was walking with Dora on Amsterdam Avenue—she was looking for a secondhand bookcase—a young man pushed a leaflet into my hand. Although it was cold and snow was falling, he was coatless and hatless and his shirt collar was open. He looked Spanish to me or Puerto Rican. Usually I refuse to accept such leaflets. But there was something in the young man's appearance that made me take the wet paper—an expression of ardor in his black eyes. This was not just a hired distributor of leaflets but a believer in a cause. I stopped and glanced down to see the name Margaret Fugazy in large letters above her picture as she might have looked twenty years ago. "Are you lovelorn?" I read. "Have you lost a near and dear relative? Are you sick? Do you have business trouble, family trouble? Are you in an inextricable dilemma? Come and see Madame Margaret Fugazy, because she is the only one who can help you. Madame Margaret Fugazy, the famous medium, has studied yoga in India, the cabala in Jerusalem, specializes in ESP, subliminal prayers, Yahweh power, UFO mysteries, self-hypnosis, cosmic wisdom, spiritual healing, and reincarnation. All consultations private. Results guaranteed. Introductory reading $2."

Dora pulled my sleeve. "Why did you stop? Throw it away."

"Wait, Dora. Where has he gone?" I looked around. The young man had disappeared. Was he waiting just for me?

Dora asked, "Why are you so interested? Who is Margaret Fugazy? Do you know her?"

"Yes, I do," I answered, not understanding why.

"Who is she—one of your witches?"

"Yes, a witch."

"How do you know her? Did you fly with her to a Black Mass on a broomstick?"

"You remember Yom Kippur when you went to the Golan kibbutz? While you were there I flew with her to Jerusalem, to Safad, to Rachel's Tomb, and we studied the cabala together," I said.

Dora was used to my playful chatter and absurdities. She chimed in, "Is that so? What else?"

"When the war broke out the witch got frightened and flew away."

"She left you alone, eh?"

"Yes, alone."

"Why didn't you come to me? I am something of a witch myself."

"You too had vanished."

"You poor boy. Abandoned by all your witches. But you can get her back. She advertises. Isn't that a miracle?"

We stood there pondering. The snow fell dry and heavy. It hit my face like hail. Dora's dark coat turned white. A single pigeon tried to fly, flapping its wings but falling back. Then Dora said, "That young man seemed strange. He must be a sorcerer. And all this for two dollars! Come, let's go home—by subway, not by psychic journey."

Translated by Joseph Singer

Elka and Meir

On the nights that Meir Bontz could allow himself to sleep, his head would hit the pillow like a stone and, if undisturbed, he could pound away for twelve hours straight. But this night he awoke at dawn. His eyelids popped open and he could not close them again. His big, burly body heaved and jerked. He felt overcome with passion and worry. Meir Bontz was hardly a timid man. In his youth he had been a thief and a safecracker. In the thieves' den where the toughs congregated, he demonstrated his strength. None of them could bend his arm. Meir would often bet on his capacity for food and drink. He could put away half a goose and wash it down with a dozen mugs of beer. On the rare occasions that he was arrested, he would snap his handcuffs or smash the door of the patrol wagon.

After he married and was given a job at the Warsaw Benevolent Burial Society, which provided shrouds and burial plots for the indigent dead, Meir Bontz went straight. He received a salary of twenty rubles a week so long as the Russians ruled Poland, and later, when the Germans came in, a comparable sum in marks. He stopped associating with thieves, fences, and pimps. He had fallen in love with a beauty, Beilka Litvak, a cook in a wealthy house on Marszalkowska Street. But with time he perceived that he had made a mistake in his marriage.

For one thing, Beilka didn't become pregnant. For another, she spat blood. For a third, he could never get used to her pronunciation—"Pig Litvak," he called it. She lost her looks as well. When she got angry, she cursed him with oaths the like of which he had never heard. She could read, and each day she read the serialized novels in the Yiddish newspaper about duped ladies, scheming counts, and seduced orphans. During meals, Meir Bontz liked to listen to the gramophone play theater melodies, duets, and cantorial pieces, but Beilka complained that the gramophone gave her a headache. A quarrel would often break out on Friday evening just because. Meir liked his gefilte fish prepared with sugar as his dead mother used to fix it, and Beilka prepared it with pepper. The few times that Meir hit her, Beilka fainted, and Zeitag the healer or Dr. Kniaster had to be called.

He would have run away from Warsaw if God hadn't sent along Red Elka. It was Red Elka's job in the Society to look after the female corpses, sew their shrouds, and wash them on the ablution board. Red Elka had no luck. She had trapped herself in a union with a sick husband who was surly and half crazy to boot. In addition, he turned out to be lazy. His name was Yontche. He was a bookbinder by trade. On Bloody Wednesday, in 1905, when the Cossacks killed dozens of revolutionaries who had converged on the town hall to demand a constitution from the czar, Yontche caught a bullet in the spine. Afterward, he had a kidney removed in the hospital on Czysta Street, and he never completely recovered. Elka had two children by him, both of whom died of scarlet fever. Although Elka had already passed forty—she was three years older than Meir—she still looked like a girl. Her red hair cut in a Dutch bob didn't have a gray strand in it. Elka was small and slim. Her eyes were green, her nose beaklike, her cheeks red as apples. Elka's power lay in her mouth. When she laughed, you could hear her halfway down the street. When she abused somebody, words and phrases shot from her sharp

tongue until you didn't know whether to laugh or cry. Elka
had strong teeth, and in a fight she would bite like a bitch.

When Elka first came to the Society and Meir Bontz observed her antics, he was frightened of her. She bantered with
the dead as if they were still alive. "Lie quiet there, hush!" she
would admonish a corpse. "Don't play any of your tricks.
We'll pack you in a shipping crate and send you off. You
danced away your few years and now it's time to go nighty-
night."

Once, Meir saw Elka take a cigarette from her mouth and
stick it between a corpse's lips. Meir told her that one must not
do such things. "Don't fret your head about it," she said. "I'll
get so many whippings in Gehenna anyhow, it'll only mean
one lash more." And she slapped her own buttock.

It wasn't long before Meir Bontz fell in love with Elka, with
a passion he would not have thought possible. He yearned for
her even when they were together. He could never get enough
of her spicy talk.

As a boy, and even later, Meir Bontz had often boasted that
he would never be tied to a woman's apron strings. When a
wench started to play hard to get or to nag him, he would tell
her to go to blazes. He used to say that in the dark all cats are
gray. But he couldn't resist Elka. She made fun of his size and
bulk, his enormous appetite, his huge feet, his rumbling voice—
all in good nature. She called him "buffalo," "bear," "bull."
Playfully, she tried to plait braids in his mop of bristly hair, as
Delilah had done to Samson. It wasn't easy for Meir and Elka
to have the time with each other they wanted. He couldn't
come to her house or she to his. They tried to seek out rooms
where you could spend the night without registering. Often
they couldn't even do this; before they left their houses they
would be summoned to the scene of a tragedy—someone had
been run over, or had hanged himself, or jumped out of a window, or been burned to death. In such cases autopsies were demanded by the police, who had to be outwitted or bribed,

since autopsies were against Jewish law. Red Elka always found a way. She spoke Russian and Polish, and after the Germans occupied Warsaw in 1915 she learned to converse with their policemen in German-Yiddish. She would flirt with the krauts and skillfully slip banknotes into their pockets.

Red Elka eventually managed it so that Meir Bontz became her assistant and her coachman, and later her chauffeur. The Society had acquired a car that was dispatched to bring in corpses from the outskirts and the resort towns on the Otwock line, and Meir learned to drive. Sometimes the couple had to ride at night through fields and forests, and this provided them the best opportunity to make love. Red Elka would sit beside Meir and with the eyes of a hawk search out a spot where they could lie down undisturbed. She would say, "The corpse will have to wait. What's his hurry? The grave won't go sour."

Elka smoked as Meir kissed her and at times even as she gave herself to him. Her time for childbearing had passed, but lust had grown within her over the years. When Meir Bontz was with her, he wanted to forget that he worked for a burial society, but Elka wouldn't let him forget. She would say, "Oy, Meir, when you kick the bucket what a heavy corpse you'll be! You'll need eight sets of pallbearers."

"Shut your yap!"

"You're trembling, eh? No one can avoid it."

Red Elka developed such power over Meir that things which had once seemed repellent now attracted him. He used her expressions, began smoking her brand of cigarettes, and ate only her favorite dishes. Elka never got drunk, but after a drink she became more flippant than ever. She blasphemed, made fun of the Angel of Death, the destroying demons, of Gehenna, and the saints in Heaven. One time Meir heard her say to a corpse, "Don't fret, corpse, rest in peace. You left your wife a pretty dowry and your successor will be in clover with her." And she gave the dead man a tickle under the armpit.

It wasn't Meir Bontz's way to think too much. As soon as

he started to concentrate, his brain would cloud over and he'd get sleepy. He realized well enough that Elka's conduct toward the dead came from some idiotic urge stuck in her mind like a wedge, but he reminded himself that every woman he had known had had her peculiarities. Meir had even had one who ordered him to beat her with a strap and spit on her. During his few stays in prison, he heard stories from other convicts that made his hair stand on end.

Well, since he had commenced his affair with Elka, thoughts assailed Meir like locusts. Tonight, he slept at home—he in one bed and Beilka in the other. He had slept several hours when suddenly he awoke with the anxiety of one who has fallen into a dilemma. Beilka snored, whistled through her nose, sighed. Meir had proposed a divorce—he offered to go on supporting her—but Beilka refused. In the dark, he could see only Elka before his eyes. She joked with him and called him outlandish names. Elka was far from virtuous. For years she had worked in a brothel on Grzybowska Street. She had undoubtedly had more men in her life than Meir had hairs on his head. She had enjoyed a passionate affair with a panderer, Leibele Marvicher, who had been stabbed to death by Blind Feivel. Elka still cried when she talked about this pimp. Just the same, Meir was ready to marry her if she was free from Yontche. Someone had told him that in America there were private funeral parlors and one could get rich there from operating such an enterprise. Meir had a fantasy: he and Elka went to America and opened a funeral parlor. Yontche the consumptive died, and Meir got rid of Beilka. In the New Land no one knew of his criminal activities or of Elka's whoring. The whole day they would be busy with the corpses, and in the evenings they would go to the theater. Meir would become a member of a rich synagogue. They had sons and daughters and lived in their own house. The wealthiest corpses in all New York were brought to their funeral parlor. A wild notion flashed through Meir's brain— they did not have to wait. He could make away with Beilka in half a minute; all he had to do was give her throat one squeeze. Elka could slip Yontche a pill. Since they were both sick anyhow, what difference did it make if they went a year sooner or a year later?

A fear fell over Meir from his own thoughts, and he began to grunt and scratch. He sat up with such force that the bed springs squealed.

Beilka awoke. "Why are you squirming around like a snake? Let me sleep!"

"Sleep, Litvak pig."

"You've got the itch, have you? So long as I breathe she'll never be your wife. A tart is what she'll stay, a slut, a tramp, a whore from 6 Krochmalna Street, may she burn like a fire, dear Father in Heaven!"

"Shut up, or you're a dead one on the spot!"

"You want to kill me, eh? Take a knife and stab away. Compared to this life, death would be Paradise." Beilka began to cough, cry, spit.

Meir got out of bed. He knew that Elka had wallowed in a brothel on Grzybowska Street, but 6 Krochmalna Street was news to him. Apparently Beilka knew more about Elka than he did. He was overcome with rage and a need to shout, to drag Beilka around by her hair. He knew the brothel at 6 Krochmalna—a windowless cellar, a living grave. *No, it couldn't be—she's making it up.* He felt about to retch.

The years passed, and Meir Bontz didn't rightly know where. Beilka suffered one hemorrhage after another, and he had to put her in a sanatorium in Otwock. The doctors said that she wasn't long for the world, but somehow there in the fresh air they kept her soul flickering. Meir had to pay her expenses. He now had the apartment to himself, and Elka was free to come to him. Elka's husband, Yontche, ailed at home. But the lovers didn't have the time to be together. After the war broke out on that day of Ab in 1914, the shootings, stabbings, and suicides

multiplied. Refugees converged upon the city from half of
Poland. The black car was constantly in use collecting corpses.
Meir and Elka could seldom give up an hour to pleasure. Their
affair consisted of talk, kisses, plans. When the Germans occupied Warsaw, hunger and typhus emptied whole buildings.
Still, Elka lost none of her light-mindedness. Death remained a
joke to her—an opportunity to revile God and man, to repeat
over and over that life hung on a hair, that hopes were spiderwebs, that all the promises about the world to come, the Messiah, and Resurrection were lies, and that whatever wasn't seized
now was lost forever. But to seize you needed time. Elka would
complain, "You'll see, Meir, we won't even have time to die."

Elka had almost stopped eating. She nibbled on a cookie, a
sausage, a bar of chocolate. She drank vodka and smoked.
Meir got along on uncooked food. In the middle of the night
the telephone would ring and they would be summoned to police headquarters, to the Jewish Hospital on Czysta Street, to
the Hospital for Epidemic Diseases on Pokorna Street, to the
morgue. They no longer even took off Sabbaths and holidays.
The other employees of the Society got summer vacations, but
no one could or would substitute for Elka or Meir. They were
the only ones who had established connections with the police,
the civil authorities, the military, the officials of the Gesia and
the Praga Cemeteries.

Meir's apartment had grown dusty and neglected. Plaster
fell from the walls. Since tenants had stopped paying rent, land-
lords had ceased making repairs. Pipes that burst from the frosts
were not fixed. Toilets became clogged. On the rare occasions
Elka prepared to spend the night at Meir's, she tried to straighten
up, but the telephone always interrupted her. The couple was
called in to attend victims of shootings, of fires, of heart attacks
in the street. As the telephone rang, Elka would exclaim, "Congratulations. It's the Angel of Death!" And before Meir could
ask what had happened she would be throwing on her clothes.

In Russia, the czar had abdicated. The Germans had begun to suffer setbacks at the front. Somehow Poland had become independent, but this didn't slow the sicknesses and deaths. For a short time peace prevailed; then the Bolsheviks invaded Poland, and once again refugees from the provinces invaded Warsaw. In the towns they captured, the Bolsheviks shot rabbis and wealthy men. The Poles hanged Communists. Elka's husband, Yontche, died, but Elka didn't observe shivah. Meir couldn't read or write, and she was needed to read documents, to sign papers, and mark down names and addresses. Because the two worked long hours, they earned a lot of money, but inflation had made it worthless. The several hundred rubles Meir had saved up for a rainy day were now worthless and lay in an open drawer—no thief would bother to touch them. Elka had bought jewelry, but she had no opportunity to wear it. When Meir asked one time why she didn't put on her trinkets, she said "When? You'll place them in the pockets of my shrouds." She was referring to the proverb that shrouds have no pockets.

Meir had long since gathered that Elka didn't only make fun of other corpses—her own death too seemed to her a game, a jest, or the Devil knew what. Meir disliked talking of death, but Elka brought up at every opportunity that what she was doing would undoubtedly be done to her. She had already arranged for a plot at the Gesia Cemetery—the Society had given her a bargain on it. She had made Meir vow that when he died he would be put to rest not next to Beilka but next to her, Elka. Meir would often lose his temper at her: she was just beginning to live; what kind of talk was this?

But Elka would counter, "You're scared, eh, Meirl? No one knows what his tomorrow will be. Death doesn't look at the calendar." Everyone in her family had died young—her father, her mother, her sister Reitza, her brother Chaim Fishl. How was she any better than the others?

Meir received a phone call from Otwock telling him that

Beilka had died. She had eaten breakfast that morning as on any other day. She had even tried reading the novel in the Yiddish newspaper, but at lunchtime when the nurse came to take her temperature she found Beilka dead. Meir wanted to go to Otwock by himself, but Elka insisted she come with him. As always, she got her way. Since Meir had arranged for a plot for himself next to Elka, Beilka was buried in Karczew, a village near Otwock. Although the women of the Karczew Burial Society considered this a sacrilege, Elka fussed over Beilka's body, washed her with an egg yolk, and sewed her shrouds.

She shouted down into Beilka's grave, "We will come to you, not you to us. May you intercede for us on High!"

It seemed now that Meir and Elka would immediately marry. Why keep two apartments? Why maintain two households? But Elka kept putting it off. She refused to marry until a year had passed. She had read somewhere that until the first anniversary the soul still hovered among those close to it. After the year passed, Elka found new excuses. She wanted to change apartments, to buy new furniture, to get herself a wardrobe, to take a long leave of absence (she had years of vacation coming) and go to Paris. She talked this way and that—now seriously, now in jest. Meir Bontz hadn't forgotten his fantasies about America, but Elka argued, "What do you need with America? You don't live there forever either."

One night when Meir and Elka managed to get away and Meir was staying at her place, Elka took Meir's hand and guided it to her left breast. "Feel. Right there," she said.

Meir felt something hard. "What is it?"

"A growth. My mother died of the same thing. So did my Aunt Gittel."

"Go to the doctor first thing tomorrow."

"A doctor, eh? If my mother hadn't rushed to the doctors, she would have died an easy death. Those butchers hacked her to pieces. Meir, I'm not such a dunce."

"But it may turn out to be nothing."

"No, Meirl, it's a summons from up there."

These words served to arouse her, and the petting and kissing commenced. Elka liked to talk in bed, to question Meir about his former mistresses, his adventures with married women. She always demanded that he compare her with the others and describe in which ways she was better. At first, Meir hadn't liked this interrogation, but as always with Elka he got used to it. This time, she talked about the fact that neither the Society nor Meir would be able to get along without her. She would have to train a woman to replace her, teach her the trade. And while she was at it, the new woman could take Elka's place with Meir too.

Meir laid a heavy hand over Elka's mouth but she cried, "Take away your paw!" and she bit his palm.

From then on, by night and even by day as they drove around, Elka kept up her talk about dying. When Meir complained that he didn't want to hear such gabbing, Elka would say, "What's the big fuss? I'm no calf to be afraid of the slaughterer."

Elka didn't stop with words. Suddenly a cousin of hers materialized—a girl from a small town, who was black as a crow and slanty-eyed as a Tartar. She told Meir that she was twenty-seven, but she appeared to him to be past thirty. Like Elka, she drank vodka and smoked cigarettes. Her name was Dishka. It was hard to believe that she and Elka were related. Where Elka was loquacious and playful, Dishka measured her words. No smile ever showed on her mouth or in her sulky dark eyes. Meir hated her on sight. Elka took her along to the funerals. She helped Elka wash down the corpses and sew shrouds. Dishka had been a seamstress in the sticks where she came from and she was even more skillful than Elka at tearing the linen—scissors were not allowed—and basting with broad stitches. One time when Elka had some business to attend to in the city, Dishka accompanied Meir in the hearse to a suburb where a slain Jew had been found. The entire way there Dishka didn't utter a word. Suddenly she laid her hand on Meir's knee and began to tickle him and arouse him. He took her hand and put it back in her lap. That night, Meir lay awake until dawn. His skull nearly burst from all the thinking he did. He both sweated and felt chills run up and down his spine. Should he force Elka to get rid of Dishka? Should he leave everything behind him and run off by himself to America? Should he wait till Elka passed on and then slit his throat over her grave? Should he leave the Burial Society and become a porter or teamster? Without Elka, the thought of everything seemed to be hollow. Meir had never drunk by himself, but now he uncorked a bottle in the dark and downed half of it. For the first time, he felt terror come over him. He knew that Dishka would bring misfortune upon him. No one could take Elka's place. Meir stationed himself by the window, gazed out into the night, and said to himself, "The whole damned thing isn't worth a penny any more."

Elka was confined to bed. The growth in her breast had spread and the other breast had developed growths as if overnight. Elka suffered such pain the doctors kept her going with morphine. Professor Mintz tried to persuade Elka to enter the Jewish Hospital, where she could be treated with radium therapy. Maybe she could be operated on and saved from a quick death. But Elka told him, "To me, a quick death is better than a lingering illness. I'm ready for the journey."

Sick as she was, Elka remained employed by the Society. Meir had to report every corpse, every burial to her. Even though he despised Dishka—that country yokel—he had to admit she had her good points. When Elka became bedridden, Meir moved in with her, while Dishka moved into his place. She swept the rooms, took it upon herself to throw out all the old dishes and broken pots Beilka had left—she even persuaded the landlord to have the place painted, the ceiling patched, and new floors laid. In the mornings, when Meir met Dishka at the Society or at work, she always brought him food—not the cookies or chocolate on which Elka sustained herself, but chicken, beefsteak, meatballs. Elka needed only one drink to commence babbling her nonsense, but Dishka could drink a lot and remain sober. Meir could never make her out. How was it that such a piece could emerge from some godforsaken village? From where did she draw her strength? His own experience had taught Meir that small-town creatures were all miserable cowards, foolish mollycoddles, always sniveling, complaining.

One day the woman who watched over Elka became sick herself, and the one who was supposed to substitute for her had gone to spend the night with a daughter in Pelcowizna. Elka had got an injection from Zeitag the healer, and Meir sat by her bed until it took hold. Just before she fell asleep, she demanded Meir's solemn vow that after her death he would marry Dishka, but Meir refused. Early in the morning he was wakened by the telephone. An actor who for many years had played the role of a lover on the Yiddish stage, first at the Muranow Theater and later at other theaters and on the road, had died in the sanatorium in Otwock. On Smocza Street an alcohol cooker had caused a fire, killing five children. A young man on Nowolipki Street had hanged himself and the police wanted his body for dissection. Meir washed and shaved. Elka heard the news and wanted details. She had known the actor and admired his acting, singing, and jokes. All those deaths in one day revived her spirits, and for a while she conversed in a healthy voice. The woman who watched over her wasn't due till ten and Meir was loath to leave her alone, but Elka said, "What more can happen to me?" She smiled and winked.

The whole day, Meir and Dishka were so busy they didn't have time to eat. Meir tried to speak to her about the tragedy of the children. Dishka said nothing. Meir remembered that in similar circumstances Elka was always ready with an appropriate comment. He couldn't live with a grouch like Dishka for even two weeks.

The custom in the sanatorium was to keep a corpse all day in cold storage and release it late at night in order not to alarm the other patients. The whole day, Meir and Dishka were occupied in the city and it was late evening by the time they started out for Otwock. The night was dark and rainy, with no moon or stars. Meir tried again and again to strike up a conversation with Dishka but she replied so curtly that soon there was nothing left for him to say. What does she think about the whole time, Meir wondered. Surliness—it's nothing else. Doing you a favor by sitting beside you.

They drove past the Praga Cemetery. Against the big-city red sky the tombstones resembled a forest of wild toadstools. Meir began to speak in Elka's tone: "A city of the dead, eh? Wore themselves out and lay down. You believe in God?"

"I don't know," Dishka replied after a long pause.

"Who then created the world?"

Dishka didn't answer and Meir became enraged. He said, "What point is there in being born if this is how it ends? On Karmelicka Street there's a workers' house, that's what it's called, and a big shot was giving a speech there. I happened to be walking by and I went inside to listen. He said that there is no God. Everything had made itself. How can everything just come from itself? Stupid!"

Dishka still didn't respond, and Meir resolved not to say another word to her that night. He felt a deep longing for Elka. "She dare not die!" he mumbled. "She dare not! If it's fated that one of us must go, let it be me."

The car passed Wawer, a village full of Gentiles; then Miedzeszyn, which was being built; then Falenica, where rabbis, Hasidim, and plain pious Jews came out for the summers; and later Michalin, Jozefow, Swider, where the intelligentsia gathered—Zionists, Bundists, Communists, and those who no longer wanted to speak Yiddish but only Polish.

Elka's sickness had stirred Meir Bontz's brain and he began pondering things. What, for instance, had this Dishka done in that village she came from? No doubt in the war years she had been a smuggler or a whore. Suddenly he thought of Beilka. At first she hadn't wanted him, and he had knelt before her and sworn eternal love. He had found her Lithuanian accent especially endearing. Years later, when she got sick, every word she spoke irritated him. He had one request of her: that she be silent. Yet with Elka the more she talked the more he wanted to hear.

Meir drove up to the cold-storage room at the sanatorium. Everything went off quickly, quietly, like a conspiracy. A door opened and two individuals transferred a box into his hearse. He didn't even see their faces. Not a word was spoken. In the brief time the door to the cold-storage room stood open, Meir caught a glimpse of two more such boxes. Before a long table on which burning candles spluttered and dripped tallow sat an old man reciting Psalms. A blast of cold like that from an ice cellar issued from the room. Meir grabbed the bottle of vodka he carried in his pocket and in one gulp drained it. As he headed back toward Warsaw, his life flashed before him—the poverty-stricken home, the thefts, the fights, the brothels, the whores, the arrests. "How was I able to endure such a Gehenna?" he asked himself, and he recalled a saying of his mother's: "God preserve us from all the things one can get used to."

The car entered a forest. Meir drove fast and in zigzags. He wanted Dishka to plead with him to slow down but she sat obstinately silent, staring out into the darkness.

Meir said, "Don't be afraid. I won't kill the corpse."

A whim to be spiteful came over him, along with an impulse to test his luck, like the reckless desire of a gambler who grows tired of the game and risks all he possesses. The headlights cast a glare upon the pines, houses, gardens, pumps, balconies. From time to time Meir cast a sidelong glance at Dishka. "Life is apparently not worth a pinch of snuff to her," he said to himself.

The hearse came out onto a stretch of road running through a clearing. It skidded as if going downhill, carried along by its own impetus. At once Meir felt gay and lighthearted. Nothing to worry about, he thought. Things will take care of themselves. He almost forgot his sullen passenger. It's good to live. One day I may even go to America. There is no lack of females and corpses there. He drove and dreamed. Elka rode with him, disguised as someone else, joking and frolicking, challenging his prowess. Suddenly a tree materialized before his eyes. A tree in the middle of the road? No, he had gone off the highway. It's one of her tricks, Meir thought. He wanted to step on the brake, but his foot pressed the accelerator. "That's it!" something within him shouted. He heard a tremendous crash and everything went silent.

The next day, a peasant going to work early found a smashed car with three dead. The back door of the hearse had been torn off and the box containing the actor's body had fallen out. A crowd gathered; the police were called. From Warsaw the Benevolent Burial Society sent out two other hearses to pick up the bodies. The president and the warden decided not to let Elka know, but a female member who was watching over her learned the news on the radio and told Elka. When Elka heard it she began to laugh and couldn't stop. Soon the laughter turned into hiccups. When they had stopped, she got out of bed and said, "Hand me my clothes."

In the two days it took to arrange the funerals Elka regained her strength. Everyone in the Society observed her liveliness with amazement. She cleansed Dishka and prepared shrouds for her and Meir. She ran from room to room, slammed doors, issued orders. She talked to the bodies with her usual teasing: "Ready for the journey? Packed away in the shipping crate?"

Warsaw had two big funerals. Actors, writers, and theater lovers gathered around the actor's coffin. Around Meir's and Dishka's came the thieves, pimps, whores, fences from Krochmalna, Smocza, Pocezjow, and Tamki Streets. The war, the typhus epidemics, starvation had almost destroyed the city's underworld. The Communists had taken over their taverns, their dens, the square on Krochmalna Street, but enough of the old-timers remained to pay their final respects to Meir. Elka rode with them. She looked quite youthful and pretty in her black suit and black-veiled hat. Meir Bontz and Red Elka were still remembered. The droshkies stretched from Iron Street to Gnoyna Street. Meir Bontz had supported a Talmud Torah, and a teacher with dozens of students walked before the hearse crying, "Justice shall walk before him."

At the cemetery, two coachmen lifted Elka up onto a tombstone and she made a short eulogy: "My Meir, stay well. I'll come to you. Don't forget me, Meir. I've got a plot right next to yours. What we had together no one can ever take away from us, not even God!"

She addressed herself to Dishka: "Rest in peace, my sister. I wanted to give you everything, but it wasn't fated." With these words, Elka collapsed.

She was finally taken to a hospital, but the cancer had spread too far for there to be any hope of saving her. Elka sat up in bed propped against two pillows while the women from the Burial Society came to ask about her and to pass along word of what was going on. New people had been hired, but the Angel of Death remained the same. Linen had gone up, the community demanded more money for the plots, the headstone carvers had raised their prices. Jewish sculptors had begun to carve all kinds of designs on the tombstones of the rich—lions, deer, even faces of birds, almost like the practice of the Gentiles. Elka listened, asked questions. Her face had turned yellow, but her eyes remained as green as gooseberries. Now that Meir was in the beyond, Elka had nothing to regret. Everything was

ready for her—a plot, shrouds, shards for her eyelids, and a
branch of myrtle with which she, together with Meir, would
dig their way through the caves and roll to the Land of Israel
when the Messiah came.

Translated by Joseph Singer

A Party in
Miami Beach

MY FRIEND THE HUMORIST Reuben Kazarsky called me on the
telephone in my apartment in Miami Beach and asked, "Menashe,
for the first time in your life, do you want to perform a
mitzvah?"

"Me a mitzvah?" I countered. "What kind of word is that—
Hebrew? Aramaic? Chinese? You know I don't do mitzvahs,
particularly here in Florida."

"Menashe, it's not a plain mitzvah. The man is a multimil-
lionaire. A few months ago he lost his whole family in a car
accident—a wife, a daughter, a son-in-law, and a baby grandchild of two. He is completely broken. He has built here in
Miami Beach, in Hollywood, and in Fort Lauderdale maybe a
dozen condominiums and rental houses. He is a devoted reader
of yours. He wants to make a party for you, and if you don't
want a party, he simply wants to meet you. He comes from
somewhere around your area—Lublin, or how do you call it?
To this day, he speaks a broken English. He came here from
the camps without a stitch to his back, but within fifteen years
he became a millionaire. How they manage this I'll never know.
It's an instinct like for a hen to lay eggs or for you to scribble
novels."

"Thanks a lot for the compliment. What can come out of this mitzvah?"

"In the other world, a huge portion of the leviathan and a Platonic affair with Sarah, daughter of Tovim. On this lousy planet, he's liable to sell you a condominium at half price. He is loaded and he's been left without heirs. He wants to write his memoirs and for you to edit them. He has a bad heart; they've implanted a pacemaker. He goes to mediums or they come to him."

"When does he want to meet me?"

"It could even be tomorrow. He'll pick you up in his Cadillac."

At five the next afternoon, my house phone began to buzz and the Irish doorman announced that a gentleman was waiting downstairs. I rode down in the elevator and saw a tiny man in a yellow shirt, green trousers, and violet shoes with gilt buckles. The sparse hair remaining around his bald pate was the color of silver, but the round face reminded me of a red apple. A long cigar thrust out of the tiny mouth. He held out a small, damp palm; pressed my hand once, twice, three times; then said in a piping voice: "This is a pleasure and an honor! My name is Max Flederbush."

At the same time, he studied me with smiling brown eyes that were too big for his size—womanly eyes. The chauffeur opened the door to a huge Cadillac and we got in. The seat was upholstered in red plush and was as soft as a down pillow. As I sank down into it, Max Flederbush pressed a button and the window rolled down. He spat out his cigar, pressed the button again, and the window closed.

He said, "I'm allowed to smoke about as much as I'm allowed to eat pork on Yom Kippur, but habit is a powerful force. It says somewhere that a habit is second nature. Does this come from the Gemara? The Midrash? Or is it simply a proverb?"

"I really don't know."

"How can that be? You're supposed to know everything. I have a Talmudic concordance, but it's in New York, not here.

I'll phone my friend Rabbi Stempel and ask him to look it up. I have three apartments—one here in Miami, one in New York, and one in Tel Aviv—and my library is scattered all over. I look for a volume here and it turns out to be in Israel. Luckily, there is such a thing as a telephone, so one can call. I have a friend in Tel Aviv, a professor at Bar-Ilan University, who stays at my place—for free, naturally—and it's easier to call Tel Aviv than New York or even someone right here in Miami. It goes through a little moon, a Sputnik or whatever. Yes, a satellite. I forget words. I put things down and I don't remember where. Our mutual friend, Reuben Kazarsky, no doubt told you what happened to me. One minute I had a family, the next—I was left as bereft as Job. Job was apparently still young and God rewarded him with new daughters, new camels, and new asses, but I'm too old for such blessings. I'm sick, too. Each day that I live is a miracle from Heaven. I have to guard myself with every bite. The doctor does allow me a nip of whiskey, but only a drop. My wife and daughter wanted to take me along on that ride, but I wasn't in the mood. It actually happened right here in Miami. They were going to Disney World. Suddenly a truck driven by some drunk shattered my world. The drunk lost both his legs. Do you believe in Special Providence?"

"I don't know how to answer you."

"According to your writings, it seems you do believe."

"Somewhere deep inside, I do."

"Had you lived through what I have, you'd grow firm in your beliefs. Well, but that's how man is—he believes and he doubts."

The Cadillac had pulled up and a parking attendant had taken it over. We walked inside a lobby that reminded me of a Hollywood supercolossal production—rugs, mirrors, lamps, paintings. The apartment was in the same vein. The rugs felt as soft as the upholstery in the car. The paintings were all abstract. I stopped before one that reminded me of a Warsaw rubbish bin on the eve of a holiday when the garbage lay heaped in huge piles.

I asked Mr. Flederbush what and by whom this was, and he replied: "Trash like the other trash. Pissako or some other bluffer."

"Who is this Pissako?"

Out of somewhere materialized Reuben Kazarsky, who said, "That's what he calls Picasso."

"What's the difference? They're all fakers," Max Flederbush said. "My wife, may she rest in peace, was the expert, not me."

Kazarsky winked at me and smiled. He had been my friend even back in Poland. He had written a half-dozen Yiddish comedies, but they had all failed. He had published a collection of vignettes, but the critics had torn it to shreds and he had stopped writing. He had come to America in 1939 and later had married a widow twenty years older than he. The widow died and Kazarsky inherited her money. He hung around rich people. He dyed his hair and dressed in corduroy jackets and hand-painted ties. He declared his love to every woman from fifteen to seventy-five. Kazarsky was in his sixties, but he looked no more than fifty. He let his hair grow long and wore side whiskers. His black eyes reflected the mockery and abnegation of one who has broken with everything and everybody. In the cafeteria on the Lower East Side, he excelled at mimicking writers, rabbis, and party leaders. He boasted of his talents as a sponger. Reuben Kazarsky suffered from hypochondria, and because he was by nature a sexual philanthropist, he had convinced himself that he was impotent. We were friends, but he had never introduced me to his benefactors. It seemed that Max Flederbush had insisted that Reuben bring us together.

He now complained to me: "Where do you hide yourself? I've asked Reuben again and again to get us together, but according to him, you were always in Europe, in Israel, or who knows where. All of a sudden it comes out that you're in Miami Beach. I'm in such a state that I can't be alone for a minute.

The moment I'm alone, I'm overcome by a gloom that's worse than madness. This fine apartment you see here turns suddenly into a funeral parlor. Sometimes I think that the real heroes aren't those who get medals in wartime but the bachelors who live out their years alone."

"Do you have a bathroom in this palace?" I asked.

"More than one, more than two, more than three," Max answered. He took my arm and led me to a bathroom that bedazzled me by its size and elegance. The lid of the toilet seat was transparent, set with semiprecious stones and a two-dollar bill implanted in the center. Facing the mirror hung a picture of a little boy urinating in an arc while a little girl looked on admiringly. When I lifted the toilet-seat lid, music began to play. After a while, I stepped out onto the balcony, which looked directly out to sea. The rays of the setting sun scampered over the waves. Gulls still hunted for fish. Far off in the distance, on the edge of the horizon, a ship swayed. On the beach, I spotted some animal that from my vantage point, sixteen floors high, appeared to be a calf or a huge dog. But it couldn't be a dog, and what would a calf be doing in Miami Beach? Suddenly the shape straightened up and turned out to be a woman in a long bathrobe digging for clams in the sand.

After a while, Kazarsky joined me on the balcony. He said, "That's Miami. It wasn't he but his wife who chased after all these trinkets. She was the business lady and the boss at home. On the other hand, he isn't quite the idle dreamer he pretends to be. He has an uncanny knack for making money. They dealt in everything—buildings, lots, stocks, diamonds, and eventually she got involved in art, too. When he said buy, she bought; and when he said sell, she sold. When she showed him a painting, he'd glance at it, spit, and say, 'It's junk, they'll snatch it out of your hands. Buy!' Whatever they touched turned to money. They flew to Israel, established yeshivas, and donated prizes toward all kinds of endeavors—cultural, religious. Naturally, they wrote it all off in taxes. Their daughter, that pampered brat, was half crazy. Any complex you can find in Freud, Jung, and Adler, she had it. She was born in a DP camp in Germany. Her parents wanted her to marry a chief rabbi or an Israeli prime minister. But she fell in love with a Gentile, an archaeology professor with a wife and five children. His wife wouldn't divorce him and she had to be bought off with a quarter-million-dollar settlement and a fantastic alimony besides. Four weeks after the wedding, the professor left to dig for a new Peking man. He drank like a fish. It was he who was drunk, not the truck driver. Come, you'll soon see something!"

Kazarsky opened the door to the living room and it was filled with people. In one day, Max Flederbush had managed to arrange a party. Not all the guests could fit into the large living room. Kazarsky and Max Flederbush led me from room to room, and the party was going on all over. Within minutes, maybe two hundred people had gathered, mostly women. It was a fashion show of jewelry, dresses, pants, caftans, hairdos, shoes, bags, makeup, as well as men's jackets, shirts, and ties. Spotlights illuminated every painting. Waiters served drinks. Black and white maids offered trays of hors d'oeuvres.

In all this commotion, I could scarcely hear what was being said to me. The compliments started, the handshakes and the kisses. A stout lady seized me and pressed me to her enormous bosom. She shouted into my ear, "I read you! I come from the towns you describe. My grandfather came here from Ishishok. He was a wagon driver there, and here in America he went into the freight business. If my parents wanted to say something I wouldn't understand, they spoke Yiddish, and that's how I learned a little of the language."

I caught a glimpse of myself in the mirror. My face was smeared with lipstick. Even as I stood there, trying to wipe it off, I received all kinds of proposals. A cantor offered to set one of my stories to music. A musician demanded I adapt an opera libretto from one of my novels. A president of an adult-education program invited me to speak a year hence at his synagogue. I would be given a plaque. A young man with hair down to his shoulders asked that I recommend a publisher, or at least an agent, to him. He declared, "I *must* create. This is a physical need with me."

One minute all the rooms were full, the next all the guests were gone, leaving only Reuben Kazarsky and myself. Just as quickly and efficiently, the help cleaned up the leftover food and half-drunk cocktails, dumped all the ashtrays, and replaced all the chairs in their rightful places. I had never before witnessed such perfection. Out of somewhere Max Flederbush dug out a white tie with gold polka dots and put it on.

He said, "Time for dinner."

"I ate so much I haven't the least appetite," I said.

"You must have dinner with us. I reserved a table at the best restaurant in Miami."

After a while, the three of us, Max Flederbush, Reuben Kazarsky, and I, got into the Cadillac and the same chauffeur drove us. Night had fallen and I no longer saw or tried to determine where I was being taken. We drove for only a few minutes and pulled up in front of a hotel resplendent with lights and uniformed attendants. One opened the car door ceremoniously, a second fawningly opened the glass front door. The lobby of this hotel wasn't merely supercolossal but super-supercolossal—complete to light effects, tropical plants in huge planters, vases, sculptures, a parrot in a cage. We were escorted into a nearly dark hall and greeted by a headwaiter who was expecting us and led us to our reserved table. He bowed and scraped, seemingly overcome with joy that we had arrived safely. Soon another individual came up. Both men wore tuxedos, patent-leather shoes, bow ties, and ruffled shirts. They looked to me like twins. They spoke with foreign accents that I suspected weren't genuine. A lengthy discussion evolved concerning our choice of foods and drinks. When the two heard I was a vegetarian, they looked at each other in chagrin, but only for a second. Soon they assured me they would serve me the best dish a vegetarian had ever tasted. One took our orders and the other wrote them down. Max Flederbush announced in his broken English that he really wasn't hungry, but if something tempting could be dredged up for him, he was prepared to give it a try. He interjected Yiddish expressions, but the two waiters apparently understood him. He gave precise instructions on how to roast his fish and prepare his vegetables. He specified spices and seasonings. Reuben Kazarsky ordered a steak and what I was to get, which in plain English was a fruit salad with cottage cheese.

When the two men finally left, Max Flederbush said, "There were times if you would have told me I'd be sitting in such a place eating such food, I would have considered it a joke. I had one fantasy—one time before I died to get enough dry bread to fill me. Suddenly I'm a rich man, alas, and people dance attendance on me. Well, but flesh and blood isn't fated to enjoy any rest. The angels in Heaven are jealous. Satan is the accuser and the Almighty is easily convinced. He nurses a longtime resentment against us Jews. He still can't forgive the fact that our great-great-grandfathers worshiped the golden calf. Let's have our picture taken."

A man with a camera materialized. "Smile!" he ordered us.

Max Flederbush tried to smile. One eye laughed, the other cried. Reuben Kazarsky began to twinkle. I didn't even make the effort. The photographer said he was going to develop the film and that he'd be back in three-quarters of an hour.

Max Flederbush asked, "What was I talking about, eh? Yes, I live in apparent luxury, but a woe upon this luxury. As rich and elegant as the house is, it's also a Gehenna. I'll tell you something: in a certain sense, it's worse here than in the camps. There, at least, we all hoped. A hundred times a day we comforted ourselves with the fact that the Hitler madness couldn't go on for long. When we heard the sound of an airplane, we thought the invasion had started. We were all young then and our whole lives were before us. Rarely did anyone commit suicide. Here hundreds of people sit, waiting for death. A week doesn't go by that someone doesn't give up the ghost. They're all rich. The men have accumulated fortunes, turned worlds upside down, maybe swindled to get there. Now they don't know what to do with their money. They're all on diets. There is no one to dress for. Outside of the financial page in the newspaper, they read nothing. As soon as they finish their breakfasts, they start playing cards. Can you play cards forever? They have to, or die from boredom. When they get tired of playing, they start slandering one another. Bitter feuds are waged. Today they elect a president, the next day they try to impeach him. If he decides to move a chair in the lobby, a revolution breaks out. There is one touch of consolation for them—the mail. An hour before the postman is due, the lobby is crowded. They stand with their keys in hand, waiting as if for the Messiah. If the postman is late, a hubbub erupts. If one opens his mailbox and it's empty, he starts to grope and burrow inside, trying to create something out of thin air. They are all past seventy-two and they receive checks from Social Security. If the check doesn't come on time, they worry about it more than those who need it for bread. They're always suspicious of the mailman. Before they mail a letter, they shake the cover three times. The women mumble incantations.

"It says somewhere in the Book of Morals that if man will remember his dying day, he won't sin. Here you can forget about death as much as you can forget to breathe. Today I meet someone by the swimming pool and we chat. Tomorrow I hear he's in the other world. The moment a man or a woman dies, the widow or widower starts looking for a new mate. They can barely sit out the shivah. Often, they marry from the same building. Yesterday they maligned each other with every curse in the book, today they're husband and wife. They throw a party and try to dance on their shaky legs. The wills and insurance policies are speedily rewritten and the game begins anew. Hardly a month or two goes by and the bridegroom is in the hospital. The heart, the kidneys, the prostate.

"I'm not ashamed before you—I'm every bit as silly as they are, but I'm not such a fool as to look for another wife. I neither can nor do I want to. I have a doctor here. He's a firm believer in the benefits of walking and I take a walk each day after breakfast. On the way back, I stop at the Bache brokerage house. I open the door and there they sit, the oldsters, staring at the ticker, watching their stocks jump around like imps. They know full well that they won't make use of these stocks. It's all to leave in the inheritance, and their children and grandchildren are often as rich as they are. But if a stock goes up, they grow optimistic and buy more of it.

"Our friend, Reuben, wants me to write my memoirs. I have a story to tell, yes, I do. I went through not only one Gehenna but ten. This very person who sits here beside you sipping champagne spent three-quarters of a year behind a cellar wall, waiting for death. I wasn't the only one—there were six of us men there and one woman. I know what you're going to ask. A man is only a man, even on the brink of the grave. She couldn't live with all six of us, but she did live with two—her husband and her lover—and she satisfied the others as best as she could. If there had been a machine to record what went on there, the things that were said and the dreams that were played out, your greatest writers would be made to look like dunces by comparison. In such circumstances, the souls strip themselves bare and no one has yet adequately described a naked soul. The *szmalcowniks*, the informers, knew about us and they had to be constantly bribed. We each had a little money or some valuable objects, and as long as they lasted, we kept buying pieces of life. It came to it that these informers brought us bread, cheese, whatever was available—everything for ten times the actual price.

"Yes, I could describe all this in pure facts, but to give it flavor requires the pen of a genius. Besides, one forgets. If you would ask me now what these men were called, I'll be damned if I could tell you. But the woman's name was Hilda. One of the men was called Edek, Edek Saperstein, and the other—Sigmunt, but Sigmunt what? When I lie in bed and can't sleep, it all comes back as vividly as if it happened yesterday. Not everything, mind you.

"Yes, memoirs. But who needs them? There are hundreds of such books written by simple people, not writers. They send them to me and I send them a check. But I can't read them. Each one of these books is poison, and how much poison can a person swallow? Why is it taking so long for my fish? It's probably still swimming in the ocean. And your fruit salad first has to be planted. I'll give you a rule to follow—when you go into a restaurant and it's dark, know that this is only to deceive. The headwaiter is one of the Polish children of Israel, but he poses as a native Frenchman. He might even be a refugee himself. When you come here, you have to sit and wait for your meal, so that later on the bill won't seem too excessive. I'm neither a writer nor a philosopher, but I lie awake half the nights, and when you can't sleep, the brain churns like a mill. The wildest notions come to me. Ah, here is the photographer! A fast worker. Well, let's have a look!"

The photographer handed each of us two photos in color and we sat there quietly studying them.

Max Flederbush asked me, "Why did you come out looking so frightened? That you write about ghosts, this I know. But you look here as if you'd seen a real ghost. If you did, I want to know about it."

"I hear you go to séances," I said.

"Eh? I go. Or to put it more accurately, they come to me. This is all bluff, too, but I *want* to be fooled. The woman turns off the lights and starts talking, allegedly in my wife's voice. I'm not such a dummy, but I listen. Here they come with our food, the Miami *szmalcowniks*."

The door opened and the headwaiter came in leading three men. All I could see in the darkness was that one was short and fat, with a square head of white hair that sat directly on his broad shoulders, and with an enormous belly. He wore a pink shirt and red trousers. The two others were taller and slimmer. When the headwaiter pointed to our table, the heavyset man broke away from the others, came toward us, and shouted in a deep voice: "Mr. Flederbush!"

Max Flederbush jumped up from his seat. "Mr. Alberghini!"

They began to heap praises upon each other. Alberghini spoke in broken English with an Italian accent.

Max Flederbush said, "Mr. Alberghini, you know my good friend Kazarsky, here. And this man is a writer, a Yiddish writer. He writes everything in Yiddish. I was told that you understand Yiddish!"

Alberghini interrupted him. "*A gezunt oyf dein kepele* . . . *Hock nisht kein tcheinik* . . . *A gut boychik* . . . My parents lived on Rivington Street and all my friends spoke Yiddish. On Sabbath, they invited me for gefilte fish, *cholent*, kugel. Who do you write for—the papers?"

"He writes books."

"Books, eh? Good! We need books, too. My son-in-law has three rooms full of books. He knows French, German. He's a foot doctor, but he first had to study math, philosophy, and all the rest. Welcome! Welcome! I've got to get back to my friends, but later on we'll——"

He held out a heavy, sweaty hand to me. He breathed asthmatically and smelled of alcohol and hair tonic. The words rumbled out deep and grating from his throat.

After he left, Max said: "You know who he is? One of the Family."

"Family?"

"You don't know who the Family is? Oh! You've remained a greenhorn! The Mafia. Half Miami Beach belongs to them. Don't laugh, they keep order here. Uncle Sam has saddled himself with a million laws that, instead of protecting the people, protect the criminal. When I was a boy studying about Sodom in cheder, I couldn't understand how a whole city or a whole country could become corrupt. Lately, I've begun to understand. Sodom had a constitution and our nephew, Lot, and the other lawyers reworked it so that right became wrong and wrong right. Mr. Alberghini actually lives in my building. When the tragedy struck me, he sent me a bouquet of flowers so big it couldn't fit through the door."

"Tell me about the cellar where you sat with the other men and the only woman," I said.

"Eh? I thought that would intrigue you. I talked to one of the writers about my memoirs and when I told him about this, he said, 'God forbid! You must leave this part out. Martyrdom and sex don't mix. You must write only good things about them.' That's the reason I lost the urge for the memoirs. The Jews in Poland were people, not angels. They were flesh and blood just like you and me. We suffered, but we were men with manly desires. One of the five was her husband. Sigmunt. This Sigmunt was in contact with the *szmalcowniks*. He had all kinds of dealings with them. He had two revolvers and we resolved that if it looked like we were about to fall into murderers' hands, we would kill as many of them as possible, then put an end to our own lives. It was one of our illusions. When it comes down to it, you can't manage things so exactly. Sigmunt had been a sergeant in the Polish Army in 1920. He had volunteered for Pilsudski's legion. He got a medal for marksmanship. Later on, he owned a garage and imported automobile parts. A giant, six foot tall or more. One of the *szmalcowniks* had once worked for him. If I was to tell you how it came about that we all ended up together in that cellar, we'd have to sit here till morning. His wife, Hilda, was a decent woman. She swore that she had been faithful to him throughout their marriage. Now, I will tell you who her lover was. No one but yours truly. She was seventeen years older than me and could have been my mother. She treated me as if she were my mother, too. 'The child,' that's what she called me. The child this and the child that. Her husband was insanely jealous. He warned us he'd kill us both if we started anything. He threatened to castrate me. He could have easily done it, too. But gradually, she wore him down. How this came about you could neither describe nor write, even if you possessed the talent of a Tolstoy or a Zeromski. She persuaded him, hypnotized him like Delilah did Samson. I didn't want any part of it. The other four men were furious with me. I wasn't up to it, either. I had become impotent. What it means to spend twenty-four hours out of the day locked in a cold, damp cellar in the company of five men and one woman, words cannot describe. We had to cast off all shame. At night we barely had enough room to stretch our legs. From sitting in one place, we developed constipation. We had to do everything in front of witnesses and this is an anguish Satan himself couldn't endure. We had to become cynical. We had to speak in coarse terms to conceal our shame. It was then I discovered that profanity has its purpose. I have to take a little drink. So . . . *L'chaim!*

"Yes, it didn't come easy. First she had to break down his resistance, then she had to revive my lust. We did it when he was asleep, or he only pretended. Two of the group had turned to homosexuality. The whole shame of being human emerged there. If man is formed in God's image, I don't envy God . . .

"We endured all the degradation one can only imagine, but we never lost hope. Later, we left the cellar and went off, each his own way. The murderers captured Sigmunt and tortured him to death. His wife—my mistress, so to speak—made her way to Russia, married some refugee there, then died of cancer in Israel. One of the other four is now a rich man in Brooklyn. He became a penitent, of all things, and he gives money to the Bobow rabbi or to some other rabbi. What happened to the other three, I don't know. If they lived, I would have heard

from them. That writer I mentioned—he's a kind of critic—
claims that our literature has to concentrate only on holiness
and martyrdom. What nonsense! Foolish lies!"

"Write the whole truth," I said.

"First of all, I don't know how. Secondly, I would be stoned.
I generally am unable to write. As soon as I pick up a pen, I
get a pain in the wrist. I become drowsy, too. I'd rather read
what you write. At times, it seems to me you're stealing my
thoughts.

"I shouldn't say this, but I'll say it anyway. Miami Beach is
full of widows and when they heard that I'm alone, the phone
calls and the visits started. They haven't stopped yet. A man
alone and something of a millionaire besides! I've become such
a success I'm literally ashamed of myself. I'd like to cling to
another person. Between another's funeral and your own, you
still want to snatch a bit of that swinish material called pleasure.
But the women are not for me. Some yenta came to me and
complained, 'I don't want to go around like my mother with a
guilt complex. I want to take everything from life I can, even
more than I can.' I said to her, 'The trouble is, one cannot . . .'
With men and women, it's like with Jacob and Esau: when one
rises, the other falls. When the females turn so wanton, the
men become like frightened virgins. It's just like the prophet
said, 'Seven women shall take hold of one man.' What will
come of all this, eh? What, for instance, will the writers write
about in five hundred years?"

"Essentially, about the same things as today," I replied.

"Well, and what about in a thousand years? In ten thousand
years? It's scary to think the human species will last so long.
How will Miami Beach look then? How much will a condominium cost?"

"Miami Beach will be under water," Reuben Kazarsky said,
"and a condominium with one bedroom for the fish will cost
five trillion dollars."

"And what will be in New York? In Paris? In Moscow? Will there still be Jews?"

"There'll be only Jews," Kazarsky said.

"What kind of Jews?"

"Crazy Jews, just like you."

Translated by Joseph Singer

Two Weddings and One Divorce

ONE DAY IN AUTUMN, a shoemaker's apprentice committed suicide on Krochmalna Street because his bride to be, a seamstress, betrayed him and married a widower. Krochmalna Street could speak of nothing else. The case was even discussed by the Hasidim in the Radzyminer study house. They were all three there—Meyer the Eunuch, who was sane two weeks each month and deranged the other two; old Levi Yitzchok, who suffered from trachoma and wore sunglasses night and day; and Zalman the glazier, a simple man who recited fifty pages of the Zohar every day though he did not know Aramaic. One young man was saying, "These love affairs are a result of ungodly books—the novels. In former times, when such heathenish books did not exist, there were no mishaps like this."

"Not true at all," said Levi Yitzchok. "The Talmud tells us of the heretic Elisha ben Avuyah that secular books fell from his cloak. Blasphemers and mockers lived even in the time of Abraham."

Zalman the glazier lifted his index finger, with its horny nail. "There were also love affairs among those who feared God. In our village of Radoszyce, a Hasidic boy fell madly in love with a wench unworthy of him in every way. He was the only son of a wealthy man, an ardent Hasid, Reb Shraga Kutner. Reb Shraga's other children had died. His wife had also passed away, and in his old age he had married a girl of seventeen, an orphan. She died giving birth to this son, Aaron David. Reb Shraga became weaker from day to day and he yearned to lead his son to the wedding canopy before he died. He asked the matchmakers to find a suitable girl, even though his son was too young for marriage.

"In those years no match was arranged until the parents of the girl sent teachers to examine the boy's knowledge of the Torah. Aaron David was known as a good scholar. The rabbi had predicted that he might become the head of a yeshiva one day. But somehow Aaron David failed to answer correctly the questions put to him. He seemed to know little of the Bible. He made blatant mistakes in the interpretation of the Mishnah and the Gemara. At the beginning, Reb Shraga assumed that his son was afraid of the examiners and their verdicts and became mixed up. He therefore pleaded with the examiners to be patient. He also explained to Aaron David that examiners are not eager to have a student fail. They get a small percentage of the dowry if things go right, and they want him to succeed. But all this was no use. Some of the examiners became so disgusted with the boy that they told the townspeople of the stupid errors he made, and there was much to laugh at and malign. Reb Shraga felt utterly disgraced.

"Then, during an examination, Aaron David translated a Hebrew passage in a way so ridiculously wrong that Reb Shraga began to suspect his son was acting deliberately. But why should a young student wish to play the ignoramus and be shamed? He locked himself with his son into his library and said, 'My son, your father is old and sick, he is already with one foot in his grave. A single desire is left him—to get some joy from you. Now, tell me the truth, why do you spoil each match that is proposed?'

"When the boy heard these words he burst out crying. He confessed to his father that he had fallen in love with a girl and if he couldn't have her for his wife he preferred to remain alone. Reb Shraga couldn't believe his ears—such talk from a youngster who was barely fourteen. 'Who is the girl?' he asked. The boy answered, 'If you hear who she is, you will think I am crazy and you will be right, too, but I cannot get her out of my thoughts.'

"I'll make it short. Aaron David had fallen in love with a water carrier's daughter, a cripple born without hands and feet. Instead, she had sort of fins, like a fish. Her name was Fradl. Because she was unable to use crutches, she could not take a step. She had to be drawn on a cart with wheels. I knew her quite well. Her father, Shimmele Icicle, carried water to Reb Shraga and also to my parents. When there was frost in winter, icicles formed in his beard and sometimes they would drop into his pails or into the water barrel of the customer. From this he got his nickname. He was known as a coarse creature and a little pixilated. His wife had left him and he brought up his freakish daughter himself. Her face was quite pretty, with black fiery eyes. She had a sharp tongue and used foul language. They lived in a half-ruined hut on Bridge Street.

"It came about this way. Once, on Purim, Shimmele brought a Purim gift to Reb Shraga. Reb Shraga was out of the house. Aaron David thought that it was a gift from a householder in town to his father and that Shimmele was the messenger. He wanted to give him a penny for his errand, but Shimmele said, 'This is a present from my sweet little daughter to you, my boy.' 'Why to me?' asked Aaron David, astounded, and Shimmele replied, 'Because of your blue eyes and curly side-locks.' I knew the whole story, for Aaron David told it later to my Uncle Leibush. She had sent a red apple, some St.-John's-bread, a peppermint candy. Shimmele said, 'Don't tell your father about it—he might whip you. Mum's the word. It could give you a reputation as a girl chaser.' When Shimmele left, the boy pondered. Who had ever heard of a girl sending a gift to a boy she did not know? After a while he decided he should give Fradl a Purim gift in return. But how? If he sent it by a servant, the whole town would know. So he put an orange, some cookies, and a slice of honey cake on a plate, covered it with a napkin, and carried it to Fradl himself. It seemed that the sly creature spoke to him ticklish words and worked a charm on him. There is a proverb: The Evil One is not choosy. Who knows? Perhaps she treated him with a potion that makes the blood hot. When a female washes her breasts in a mixture of water and Sabbath wine and gives some of it to a man to drink, she kindles his longing for her. Many loves are the result of such doings.

"I don't need to tell you that Reb Shraga was shocked and warned his son against such a pitfall. The boy had not told him about the Purim gift; he just said that he saw her through a window. The whole thing was a terrible blow to Reb Shraga. Shimmele was known as a ruffian and a blabbermouth. Reb Shraga went to his rabbi for advice on how to free the boy from his infatuation. The rabbi gave Reb Shraga a blessing and a talisman, but to no avail. Aaron David insisted that he marry Fradl or no one. Reb Shraga, realizing that his end was near and that the boy would never get over his madness, decided that perhaps it was a punishment from God or simply a curse to which one must submit. How does the saying go? 'If you can't go over, you go under.' He took off his shame cap and told his relatives to prepare for a wedding.

"When the people of Radoszyce heard of this match there was a commotion. Some cried, others laughed and spat. The women all insisted that the cunning Fradl had bewitched an innocent boy. But in time one gets accustomed to the most weird events. There was a wedding, and the wedding canopy was set up in the court of the synagogue as always when the bride is a virgin. Not only Fradl had to be carried but also

Reb Shraga. From grief he had lost the power of his legs. Just the same, musicians played and the wedding jester cracked jokes. The riffraff of both sexes considered this marriage the high point of their lives. They danced, sang, and got drunk. Reb Shraga had ordered a festive meal for the paupers of the poorhouse. They sat at a long table, ate challah with carp, and drank mead. Shimmele lifted up the wings of his gaberdine and danced a kosatzke.

"Shortly after the wedding Reb Shraga died. People predicted that a cripple like Fradl would not get pregnant. But she was soon with child. In the years that followed she gave birth to five daughters, one more beautiful than the other. She turned out to be a diligent housewife. Aaron David hired for her two maids, and Fradl gave orders from her couch. Everything in her home had to sparkle. Her copper vessels shone like gold. When they grew up, her daughters indulged her every whim. The women from Bridge Street used to visit her and bring her all the gossip from the village. They took her to the marketplace. She was fond of bargains and bedecked herself with trinkets. There was plenty of money. Reb Shraga had been an able merchant even in his older years. He had a large drygoods store and visited fairs in Lublin, Nałęczów, Lemberg. As for Aaron David, he remained an unworldly Talmud scholar. He lived on his inheritance from his father. He must have loved his wife truly, because after her death he did not remarry.

"Fradl died in a very queer way. I've already told you that instead of hands and feet she had fins. Suddenly her skin began to grow scales. Aaron David summoned doctors from Lublin and even from Warsaw. Professors came to investigate the nature of her malady. They tried to remove the scales by surgery, but they grew so rapidly that soon her whole body was covered with them. Some of the town's wags joked that she had become a kosher fish, since that's what a fish must have to be kosher—fins and scales. The sickness did not last more than three months. I didn't see her in this stage, but I know that the curious came to look at her from neighboring towns. There were those who believed that her mother had sinned with a fish and Fradl was the offspring."

"What?" said Levi Yitzchok. "Such perversions were not practiced even by the Generation of the Flood."

For a long time there was silence in the study house. Only the wind could be heard. Meyer the Eunuch clutched his chin, seeming to search for the root of a hair. Levi Yitzchok poked his nose into his wooden snuffbox, took a whiff, and said, "Such a passion is sheer illusion; a foolish idea gets stuck in the mind like a wedge. Or it might have been the work of Satan. The Evil Ones have their power. The daughters of Lilith fly around at night like bats and tempt men to commit abominations. Even saints suffer the defilement of nocturnal emission. But true love has a holy origin.

"In the town of Parysow there was a Talmudist, an affluent man, Reb Pinchos Edelweiss. He came from a distinguished lineage—from Rabbi Moshe Isserles and from Rashi. The town elders wanted to make him their rabbi, but he refused. Why did he need to be a rabbi? He possessed forests, a sawmill, and I think a water mill, too. He sent rafts on the Vistula to Danzig. Reb Pinchos divided his days into two parts. From sunrise to noon he studied the Talmud, the Responsa, the Midrash, the Zohar. He prayed early in the morning with the first quorum. After lunch he conducted his business. He drove around in a carriage, like a squire. He employed a bookkeeper, a cashier, and lumberjacks who cut the trees into logs. His wife, Ada Zillah, came from an even more noble house than he. She spoke Polish and German and could write a letter in Hebrew. The only blessing denied the pair was children. Oh, I forgot to mention that Reb Pinchos had a younger brother who had deviated from the path of righteousness. He had swindled and forged a signature, and had had to run away to

America. In those times to have someone in America was like having a convert or a suicide in the family.

"One day Reb Pinchos became ill, and no medicine helped him. He traveled to Vienna to the great doctors, but they all gave him up. Reb Pinchos knew that when he died childless his widow would have to go through the ceremony of Chalitzah with her brother-in-law in order to be allowed to marry again. Now, it is not an easy thing to go and search for someone in America—especially a person of an adventurous nature. Therefore Reb Pinchos decided that before he died he would divorce his wife, so that she could remarry without a release from his brother. Husband and wife loved one another with a great love, and when Ada Zillah heard about his plans for the divorce she began to cry bitterly, insisting that she would never have another man. Reb Pinchos said, 'Why should you live out your years alone? You are still young, and with another husband you might yet be able to have children.' Still she refused. When Reb Pinchos realized that she would not consent, he went to the rabbi without her knowledge and ordered a scribe to write a bill of divorce. He also made out a will wherein he left Ada Zillah half of his fortune and the other half to various charities. Everything was done in secrecy. The next day he called for two of his employees to serve as witnesses and for his wife. He handed her the divorce papers, reciting the proper words. Ada Zillah listened to the words and saw the divorce papers, and she fainted dead away. As soon as she was revived, she took a Pentateuch from the bookcase, raised her hand, and said, 'Pinchos, I swear by God Almighty and the Holy Book that I will never belong to another man.' And she cried convulsively.

"You know the law that a divorced man and woman are not permitted to stay under the same roof. Reb Pinchos had prepared for himself a room in another house, but so great was Ada Zillah's anguish that she seized her prayer book and her book of supplications, packed some linen into a bundle, and ran to the poorhouse. When the paupers in the poorhouse saw the wellborn Ada Zillah with her bundle and heard her say that she had come to stay, there arose a terrible lament. They all knew Ada Zillah. Every day she sent chicken soup and groats to the sick. Often she went herself to comfort the depressed and to dole out charity. Now important men and women of the town rushed to her to plead that she not ruin her life. In answer, Ada Zillah quoted to them the words of Job: 'Naked came I out of my mother's womb, and naked shall I return thither.' She had torn her husband's last will to shreds.

"When the poorhouse attendant saw that Ada Zillah was adamant, he wanted to put up a bed with linen for her, but Ada Zillah said, 'My bed will be a bundle of straw the same as for all the others.' She was given a hay pillow and a bundle of straw and she sat down on it in her silk dress and began to recite the chapters that are used in times of distress and illness: 'O Lord God of my salvation I have cried day and night before Thee . . . For my soul is full of troubles: and my life draweth nigh unto the grave . . . Have mercy upon me, O Lord; for I am weak: O Lord, heal me for my bones are vexed.'

"A prayer in such circumstances can split the heavens. Or perhaps the cure had already been decreed. That day Reb Pinchos became better. He was supposed to have had an ulcer in his throat, and he coughed so long and hard that whatever it was burst and the pus drained out. The threat to his life was over and the people started to say that Reb Pinchos could now remarry Ada Zillah. But they were reminded that Reb Pinchos was of priestly caste—a Cohen, who is not permitted to marry a divorcée even though she be his former spouse. So great was Reb Pinchos's despair that when his friends who visited him wished him a quick recovery he said, 'Better wish me a speedy death.' But they don't ask in Heaven a man's judgment on whether he deserves life or death. Reb Pinchos recovered completely. After witnessing such a miracle, the town healer, who used to be a heretic, became an ardent believer.

"Reb Pinchos went to Ada Zillah in the poorhouse and fell at her feet, beseeching her to take over his house and marry someone else. The rabbi was willing to revoke her oath, which had been given in a moment of desperation and possibly with an unclear mind. But Ada Zillah said, 'My oath stands, and I am not in need of a house. You, Pinchos, remarry. It is quite possible that I am barren, not you. Heaven wanted you to bring forth a generation, therefore this affliction was visited upon us. It is my wish that you find a young woman capable of giving birth and take her as a wife. Your children will be as dear to me as if they were my own.'"

"Did he remarry?" Zalman the glazier asked.

"No. The truth is that he broke the law. A man who has not fulfilled the commandment to be fruitful and multiply may not remain without a wife. The rabbi told Reb Pinchos that he transgressed, but he answered, "Gehenna is for people, not for animals.' He withdrew from all business and became a recluse. He gave away most of his possessions, though he kept his house and garden, still hoping to provide a home for Ada Zillah. He even proposed to send her to the Holy Land in the hope that she would find solace there among the sacred places. But Ada Zillah said, 'I am not permitted to be with you under one roof; let me at least be with you under one sky.' Reb Pinchos went to the rabbi and said, 'Rabbi, as long as I live I am forbidden to be near Ada Zillah, but it is my will that when we both part from this earth we should be allowed to lie in our graves one next the other.' The rabbi could not decide this matter by himself and he took the question to the council of three rabbis. The verdict was that after their demise the former husband and wife could have adjoining graves.

"And so it happened. Reb Pinchos died before Ada Zillah. I no longer lived in town then. But I was told that when he fell ill she attended him, gave him his medicines, and cooked for him the dishes the doctor prescribed. Whether she acted strictly according to the law I am not sure. But behind each law mercy is concealed. In the few years Ada Zillah outlived Reb Pinchos, she went to the cemetery every weekday, summer and winter, and prostrated herself on his grave. On the plot next to his, she had her own headstone put up, engraved with the words 'Here lies Ada Zillah, the devoted wife of the pious Reb Pinchos.' Space was left for the date of her death. I heard that not long after she was buried a willow tree began to sprout from her grave. It grew rapidly into a large tree, and its branches drooped to cover both graves and to make them one. The law of divorce is only for bodies. Souls cannot be divorced."

For a while it seemed that Meyer did not listen. He sat there deep in thought. He grimaced and shook his head as if puzzled by something that he could neither solve nor forget. Then he said, "What you told, Zalman, happens every day. People marry blind ones, mute ones, hunchbacks, even lepers. When the Angel calls out forty days before birth that the daughter of one man is to marry the son of another man, this comes to pass. Providence joins the strangest bedfellows and works in a way that appears the doing of matchmakers. If Providence did not hide behind the laws of nature, all people would be saints and there would be no free choice. From your story, Levi Yitzchok, I like best the saying 'Gehenna is for people, not for animals.' Gehenna cleanses souls, and cleansing is benevolence. The body loves only itself, and even this is an illusion. Flesh is nothing but a garment. When the soul requires a new garment, the old one turns to dust. This is the mystery of reincarnation. We have already been males, females, cattle, trees, grass. They call me Eunuch. I am not a eunuch but androgynous. Adam, who was created perfect in God's image, was androgynous. There are hints of this in the Book of Genesis. Adam and Eve copulated from within.

"This story I heard from my grandfather and he heard it from his grandfather. In the city of Praga lived a man, Reb Bezalel Ashkenazi. He had an only son, Eliakim, a yenuka, a prodigy. At four the yenuka already knew the Bible, the Mishnah, and parts of the Gemara. At seven he gave a sermon in the Praga synagogue and scholars came to listen to him. It happens quite often that a yenuka is born androgynous, and according to the cabala this is right, because all great souls are a union of both sexes. Since Eliakim grew up wise, many matches were proposed for him. But he said, 'When the time comes, the right spouse will be with me.' He had long hair and did not grow a beard. He sang tunes that had never been heard in this world, and with two voices—male and female. A yenuka descends to Earth to correct a blunder made in a former existence, and when his mission is accomplished he is ready to ascend to the Mansions of Heaven. One day Eliakim's hair was black, the next day it turned white. Although he had no wife and it was not the custom for a bachelor to wear the prayer shawl, he sat all day long wrapped in a prayer shawl and with phylacteries on his arm and head like one of the ancients. His parents had died. There were no Hasidim at this time—certainly not in Praga—but people came to him as to a wonder rabbi. He pronounced incantations over pieces of amber. Mothers waited outside his house for him to bless their infants. Witnesses testified that when the yenuka studied the Book of Creation the pages turned by themselves. When he wanted to write some footnote on the margin of a scroll, the quill jumped into his hand. Those who are rooted in the primeval source of life enliven everything that surrounds them. In the winter the beadle did not need to heat the stove in the yenuka's house, because a fiery radiance emanated from him as from a seraph.

"He ate almost nothing. He slept never longer than sixty breaths at a time. He seemed more in Heaven than on earth.

"One day the yenuka let it be known that he was about to

marry. His followers were all astonished. How can the androgynous marry? And what earthly woman could deserve to be his wife? He asked that only ten old men be invited to the wedding—all cabalists and servants of the Almighty. One of them was to officiate at the ceremony. On the appointed day, the beadle kept watch through the window for carriages bearing the bride and her relatives. None arrived. Just the same, after the evening prayers the ten invited elders gathered in the yenuka's house. One of them wrote out the ketuba, leaving only a blank space for the name of the bride. Four others set up a canopy supported by four posts. Wax candles were lit and a goblet was filled with wine. Through it all, the yenuka remained locked in his room. Some of the men listened at the door. Nothing could be heard. They began to wonder if because of his holy remoteness he had forgotten about the wedding. But just then the door of his room opened and the yenuka came out clad in a white robe and a white cowl, like a corpse in shrouds, and beside him the bride in a white wedding dress and a heavy veil. Her face could not be seen, but her garments shone with the colors of lightning. The few old men were overcome by awe; they could barely stand on their feet. Nevertheless, the one who wrote the ketuba took courage and asked the bride her name. 'Eliakim,' she said. 'The daughter of Bezalel.' The bride and groom had the same name and the same father's name.

"The ceremony was performed according to law. The one who officiated read the ketuba and recited the first benedictions. The bridegroom put a ring on the index finger of the bride's right hand and said, 'Thou art sanctified to me with this ring according to the law of Moses and Israel.' When the bride was about to drink from the goblet, she lifted her veil and they all saw two yenukas, their faces as white as mother-of-pearl and their eyes luminous with the glory of love. They resembled one another as closely as twins. After the second

benedictions they were wished mazel tov, but they returned
to their room in silence."

"Wasn't a wedding like this against the strict letter of the
law?" Levi Yitzchok asked.

"There are copulations in Heaven that would be incest on
earth," Meyer replied.

"What happened then?"

"The yenuka joined the Yeshiva On High the same night."

"And what happened to the bride?" Zalman the glazier
asked. "She died also?"

Meyer shrugged. He closed his eyes and seemed to have
fallen asleep. Then he rose and began to pace back and forth
on the floor of the study house. He rubbed the palms of his
hands and murmured to himself. Once in a while he burst out
laughing. The kerosene lamp went out and a single candle
burned in the candelabra. It flickered and sputtered. The room
filled with shadows.

Zalman looked out through the window. "The moon is full,"
he said. "The half month begins when Meyer is confused."

Translated by the author
and Alma Singer

A Cage for Satan

I

IN THE FORTY YEARS that Rabbi Naphtali Sencyminer had waged war against the evil spirits, he contended with imps, demons, dybbuks, and harpies, and sooner or later he vanquished them all—with incantations, with amulets, with the power of his voice, his cane, the stomping of his feet, and his curses. A single passion still consumed him—to capture one of these impure spirits, to bind it and lock it up in a cage like a wild beast. The rabbi had a cage suited to the purpose in his attic. One of his Hasidim, an iron merchant, had had it constructed for him in secret. It was made of heavy bars surrounded by thick wire mesh and had a door with two locks. On the mesh the rabbi had hung incantations written in a scribal hand on parchment, as well as a ram's horn and a prayer shawl that had once belonged to the Kozienice Preacher. On its floor lay the chains the famous saint Joseph della Reyna had used to shackle Satan. Rabbi Joseph hadn't managed to keep Satan prisoner, for he took pity on him and gave him a pinch of snuff. Two fires shot from Satan's nostrils and the chains fell from him. Rabbi Naphtali was determined to show the Devil no mercy. He planned to keep him in the dark without food or water, surrounded by the holy names of God and angels. Rabbis and even righteous Gentiles from all over the world would come to Sencymin to witness Rabbi Naphtali's triumph.

Well, but no matter how many traps Rabbi Naphtali set for Satan and his hosts they managed to elude him. One time he seized a wraith by the beard and a Lilith by its hair, but before he could imprison them they wriggled away. These fiends came back in the night to taunt the rabbi, to whistle in his ear and spit upon him. A sprite with the face of a billy goat deposited a pile of dung upon the rabbi's sacred book. It left behind the stench of galbanum.

By the time the rabbi passed his seventies, he began to despair. His wife had died. The cage in the attic was covered with spiderwebs and the chains had rusted.

But one summer night late in the month of Ab something occurred that impressed the rabbi as a miracle. It happened this way. The rabbi's beadle, Reb Gronam Getz, a patriarch who had served Rabbi Naphtali's father, fell sick for the first time in his eighty-seven years and was taken to the hospital. From the day the rabbi became a widower, Gronam Getz had stayed in the rabbi's bedroom to guard him from the spirits and their revenge. Now the rabbi slept alone; he had no faith in the young beadles. That night before he went to bed, the rabbi not only read the prayers of the holy Isaac Luria, as usual, but he recited those psalms specifically intended to drive away nocturnal trespassers. He had placed a Book of Creation under his pillow, and a long-bladed knife such as pregnant women kept under their pillows to ward off Shibta, the arch-enemy of the newly born. He also left a wax candle burning in a holder.

The rabbi slept in a white cloak belted with a sash; white stockings; and two skullcaps—one at his forehead, one at the back of his skull—as well as a ritual garment with special eight-fold twisted fringes. The moment he laid his head on the pillow and recited "Thou who makest the bands of sleep fall upon mine eyes and slumber upon mine eyelids," he fell into a deep sleep.

He awoke in alarm in the middle of the night. The candle had gone out. He heard quiet footsteps nearby. He felt an urge to cry, "Shaddai, destroy Satan!," but it struck him that perhaps his prayers had been answered in Heaven—this might be his opportunity to capture the evil intruder. A strength that astounded him surged through Rabbi Naphtali. He leaped out of bed with such force that the slats beneath his straw pallet broke. A dark presence stood outlined against the shuttered window. He lunged toward it with the ferocity of a lion. In a flash he had seized it and pressed it to him so violently that he felt ribs snap. Only now did the spirit begin to resist. It shouted something unintelligible, but the rabbi threw it to the floor, clasped it between his knees, clamped its mouth shut with one hand and clutched its throat with the other. He could feel a jerking, hear muffled words, a gurgling. Then it ceased to struggle and was silent. The rabbi had vanquished the demon. As he bound its feet with his sash, Rabbi Naphtali trembled, slavered, and stammered incantations: "*Kuzu Bemuchzus Kuzu* . . . An arrow in the eye of Satan . . . Yahweh's war with Amalek . . . Thou shalt utterly detest it, and thou shalt utterly abhor it."

Although the entity of the netherworld lay quiet, Rabbi Naphtali knew its submission was a sham. Until it was shackled and confined in the cage, it could regain its powers, stick its tongue out as far as its navel, burst into mad laughter, and fly away like a bat.

The rabbi tried to stand, but his legs felt as if they had been chopped off. Sparks flashed before his eyes. His ears rang. "I dare not give in!" he warned himself. "Asmodeus and his companions are merely waiting for me to show weakness."

The rabbi would have to drag the messenger of destruction up to the attic stealthily, so that no one in the house would learn what was going on. Had Gronam Getz been with him, he would have lent a hand—Gronam Getz was familiar with the cabala and knew all the spells and incantations. But the young beadles slept in their own homes, and even if they had been standing guard in the courtyard the rabbi would not have trusted them to help him with a mission of such gravity.

After a while, Rabbi Naphtali revived somewhat and was able to rise. He leaned down and picked up the creature of the darkness, slung it over one shoulder, and began to move toward the anteroom and the stairs leading to the attic. He knew full well that he was overtaxing his strength, but there were times when one could not yield to the body. He crept along the corridor, praying that he would not collapse under his load, God forbid, lest its allies find out and swarm all over him. Several times he bumped against doors and walls. His cloak caught on a hook. When he reached the narrow attic stairs, he was drenched in sweat and could hear the snorting of his own nose. But he refused to take a rest. At any moment his adversary might come to and drag him away to beyond the dark regions, to the gates of Hell, to the ruins of Sodom, to Mount Seir, where Naamah, Mahalath, and Lilith reigned. The rabbi could no longer remember any psalms or conjurations—his brain was dulled and his tongue thick as wood.

By the time he had climbed to the attic, day was dawning. The blaze of the rising sun shone through the cracks in the eastern side of the shingled roof. The cage could be seen through purplish columns of dust. The rabbi stepped toward it, but he banged against a wooden box full of old books and fell back. In the second before he fainted, he caught a glimpse of the burden under which he had fallen—a boy in a short jacket, his mouth and nose bloodied. Woe is me, it's a human, I've killed him! the rabbi thought as everything went dark.

2

When Rabbi Naphtali opened his eyes again, the sun still shone through the cracks in the roof, but now the light came not from the east but from the west. It took him a long time to grasp this. His bones ached, and his head hurt with a piercing pain. Next to him lay a corpse with eyes glazed, bloody mouth open, face yellow as clay. Only now did he realize what had happened—a youngster had come to rob him. Rabbi Naphtali didn't accept paper money for his services—only silver coins or gold ducats, which he kept in earthen jugs as well as in oak coffers lined in hide and bound with iron hoops. For years he had been making plans to go to the Holy Land to build a study house there, a ritual bath and a yeshiva, and to erect a tabernacle over the grave of his grandfather Reb Menahem Kintzker, who had died in Jerusalem forty years before. "God Almighty, why did this happen to me?" the rabbi mumbled. "My punishment is greater than I can bear."

He stuck out his hand and felt the body's forehead. The brightness of the sunset through the shingles soon dimmed and the attic filled with shadows. A great fear came over the rabbi. He rose with effort and began to shuffle toward the door. If at least he might have died along with his victim! But it had been decreed in Heaven that he suffer Cain's fate. At the head of the stairs he was forced to sit down. He had to consider his situation. His followers had undoubtedly been looking for him all day, but it would never have occurred to them that he might be up in the attic. There was no sound of movement in the house. They must have given up hope for him, or perhaps they assumed he had ascended to Heaven alive, like Enoch. Rabbi Naphtali had suffered many misfortunes—he had been left in his old age without wife or child—but during all his calamities he had been able to pray and to justify the harsh judgments passed upon him. This day, the first since he became thirteen, he had missed putting on his phylacteries. It was the hour to say the evening prayers, but he could not bring himself to allow sacred words to pass through the lips of a murderer. Of all possible disasters, he had suffered the worst—and at what a time in his life: on the brink of the grave!

Ordinarily, the spirits of good and evil fought a constant battle within Rabbi Naphtali, but now both remained silent. Night fell and the rabbi sat enveloped in a gloom like that of the abyss. "Whither shall I go from thy Spirit? Or whither shall I flee from thy presence?" he recited. Should he do away with himself? he thought. Since he had already lost the world to come, what difference would it make? Should he go off somewhere and vanish? Well, but if the thief is a Jew he must be given a Jewish burial. A corpse cannot be left to rot in an attic without ablution, without shrouds, without a mourner's prayer said over it . . .

The rabbi's head sank ever lower and lower. Compared to his ordeal, Job's had been a trifle. Rabbi Naphtali had but one request of the Almighty—to die. He now understood the words of the Sages: " 'Very good'—that is death."

The rabbi had fallen asleep and was awakened by voices, noises, the sound of feet. The beadles were running up the stairs to him. The light of a lantern dazzled his eyes. They lifted him in their arms and carried him away. He heard women weeping, men shouting. Am I dead? the rabbi wondered. Is this my funeral? They carried him to a room and put him to bed. They revived him with cold water and rubbed his temples with vinegar. Everyone talked at once, but he made no response. Suddenly a new lament rose and at that instant the rabbi understood what had happened. They had found the body in the attic. Someone called out a name: Haiml Cake.

How could this be, the rabbi asked himself. Haiml Cake is no longer a youngster. Soon after, they called another name: Bentze Lip. For all his distress the rabbi realized the connection between these names. Haiml Cake, a horse thief whom the police had beaten so badly that he could no longer steal horses, had become a teacher of young thieves. He must have sent out one of the gang, Bentze Lip, to rob him. Instead of capturing Satan, he, Naphtali Sencyminer, had murdered a young burglar—perhaps an orphan besides. In the midst of

the turmoil the rabbi muttered, "Satan has captured *me*."
They were the last words his followers heard from the
rabbi. In the three weeks that he lingered, he did not speak to
those who came to visit him. The beadles dressed him in his
prayer shawl and phylacteries, and he mumbled. They handed
him a book, and he glanced into it, but no one saw him turn
a page. Two days before the rabbi's demise, Gronam Getz
came from the hospital and he alone stayed with the rabbi
until the end. The rabbi ordered him to burn his manuscripts,
not to save so much as a single page, and Gronam Getz did as
he was told. The rabbi also dictated a will to him, leaving his
entire fortune to the community, with enough put aside to
erect a tombstone over Bentze Lip's grave, to hire someone
to say the Kaddish over him, and to subsidize men to study
the Mishnah in Bentze's name. The rabbi decreed that he himself be buried behind the fence, where heretics and suicides
were laid to rest. He warned of severe punishment for any
who defied his last wishes. Rabbi Naphtali Sencyminer had
killed a human being and he had forfeited the right to lie
alongside decent Jews. However, the Hasidim and members of
the Burial Society dared to disregard his demands. Many
rabbis gathered for the funeral, and they ordained that since
Rabbi Naphtali had done what he did unintentionally and had
atoned for it with a self-mortification that brought about his
decease, he should be given a burial with all the honors accru-
ing to a saint and a martyr. The eldest among them, an author
of many holy books and a patriarch of eighty, said, "Those
who love God more than the soul and heart can bear attempt
to destroy the world. So long as there is a world there will
also be a Satan."

Translated by Joseph Singer

Brother Beetle

I BEGAN TO DREAM about this trip when I was five years old. At that time my teacher, Moses Alter, read to me from the Pentateuch about Jacob crossing the Jordan while carrying only his staff. But a week after my arrival in Israel, at the age of fifty, there were few marvels left for me to see. I had visited Jerusalem, the Knesset, Mount Zion, the kibbutzim in Galilee, the ruins of Safad, the remains of the fortification of Acre, and all the other sights. I even made the at-that-time dangerous trip from Beersheba to Sodom, and on the way saw camels harnessed to the plows of Arabs. Israel was even smaller than I had imagined it to be. The tourist car in which I traveled seemed to be going in circles. For three days wherever we went we played hide-and-seek with the Sea of Galilee. During the day, the car was continually overheating. I wore two pairs of sunglasses, one on top of the other, as protection against the glare of the sun. At night, a hot wind blew in from somewhere. In Tel Aviv, in my hotel room, they taught me to maneuver the shutters, but in the one moment it took me to get out on the balcony, the thin sand carried by the khamsin wind managed to cover the linens of my bed. With the wind came locusts, flies, and butterflies of all sizes and colors, along with beetles larger than any I had ever seen before. The humming and buzzing was unusually loud. The moths beat against the walls with unbelievable strength, as if in preparation for the final war between man and insect. The tepid breath of the sea stank of rotten fish and excrement. That late summer, electricity failures were frequent in Tel Aviv. A suburban darkness covered the city. The sky filled with stars. The setting sun had left behind the redness of a heavenly slaughter.

On a balcony across the street, an old man with a small white beard, a silken skullcap partly covering his high forehead, half sat, half reclined on a bed, reading a book through a magnifying glass. A young woman kept bringing him refreshments. He was making notes in the book's margins. On the street below, girls laughed, shrieked, picked fights with boys, just as I had seen them do in Brooklyn, and in Madrid, where I had stopped en route. They teased one another in Hebrew slang. After a week of seeing everything a tourist must see in the Holy Land, I had my fill of holiness and went out to look for some unholy adventure.

I had many friends and acquaintances from Warsaw in Tel Aviv, even a former mistress. The greatest part of those who had been close to me had perished in Hitler's concentration camps or had died of hunger and typhoid in Soviet Middle Asia. But some of my friends had been saved. I found them sitting in the outdoor cafés, sipping lemonade through straws and carrying on the same old conversations. What are seventeen years, after all? The men had become a little grayer. The women dyed their hair; heavy makeup hid their wrinkles. The hot climate had not wilted their desires. The widows and widowers had remarried. Those recently divorced were looking for new mates or lovers. They still wrote books, painted pictures, tried to get parts in plays, worked for all kinds of newspapers and magazines. All had managed to learn at least some Hebrew. In their years of wandering, many of them had taught themselves Russian, German, English, and even Hungarian and Uzbek.

They immediately made room for me at their tables, and began reminding me of episodes I could not possibly forget. They asked my advice on American visas, literary agents, and impresarios. We were even able to joke about friends who had long since become ashes. Every now and then a woman would wipe away a tear with the point of her handkerchief so as not to smear her mascara.

I didn't look for Dosha, but I knew that we would meet. How could I have avoided her? That evening I happened to be sitting in a café frequented by merchants, not artists. At the surrounding tables the subject was business. Diamond merchants brought out small bags of gems and their jeweler's loupes. A stone passed quickly from table to table. It was inspected, fingered, and then given to another, with a nod of the head. It seemed to me that I was in Warsaw, on Krolewska Street. Suddenly I saw her. She glanced around, looking for someone, as if she had an appointment. I noticed everything at once: the dyed hair, the bags under her eyes, the rouge on her cheeks. One thing only had remained unchanged—her slim figure. We embraced and uttered the same lie: "You haven't changed." And when she sat down at my table, the difference between what she had been then and what she was now began to disappear, as if some hidden power were quickly retouching her face to the image which had remained in my memory.

I sat there listening to her jumbled conversation. She mixed countries, cities, years, marriages. One husband had perished; she had divorced another. He now lived nearby with another woman. Her third husband, from whom she was separated, more or less, lived in Paris, but he expected to come to Israel soon. They had met in a labor camp in Tashkent. Yes, she was still painting. What else could she do? She had changed her style, was no longer an impressionist. Where could old-fashioned realism lead today? The artist must create something new and entirely his own. If not, art was bankrupt. I reminded her of the time when she had considered Picasso and Chagall frauds. Yes, that was true, but later she herself had reached a dead end. Now her painting was really different, original. But who needed paintings here? In Safad there was an artists' colony, but she had not been able to adjust herself to the life there. She had had enough of wandering about through all kinds of Godforsaken villages in Russia. She needed to breathe city air.

"Where is your daughter?"

"Carola is in London."

"Married?"

"Yes, I'm a sabta, a grandmother."

She smiled shyly, as if to say: "Why shouldn't I tell you? I can't fool you, anyhow." I noticed her newly capped teeth. When the waiter came over, she ordered coffee. We sat for a while in silence. Time had battered us. It had robbed us of our parents, our relatives, had destroyed our homes. It had mocked our fantasies, our dreams of greatness, fame, riches.

I had had news of Dosha while I was still in New York. Some mutual friends wrote to me that her paintings were not exhibited; her name was never mentioned in the press. Because she had had a nervous breakdown, she had spent some time in either a clinic or an asylum.

In Tel Aviv, women seldom wear hats, and almost never in the evening, but Dosha had on a wide-brimmed straw hat which was trimmed with a violet ribbon and slanted over one eye. Though her hair was dyed auburn, there were traces of other colors in it. Here and there, it even had a bluish cast. Still, her face had retained its girlish narrowness. Her nose was thin, her chin pointed. Her eyes—sometimes green, sometimes yellow—had the youthful intensity of the unjaded, still ready to struggle and hope to the last minute. How else could she have survived?

I asked, "Do you have a man, at least?"

Her eyes filled with laughter. "Starting all over again? The first minute?"

"Why wait?"

"You haven't changed."

She took a sip of coffee and said, "Of course I have a man. You know I can't live without one. But he's crazy, and I am not speaking figuratively. He's so mad about me that he destroys me. He follows me on the street, knocks at my door in the middle of the night, and embarrasses me in front of my neighbors. I've even called the police, but I can't get rid of him. Luckily, he is in Eilat at the moment. I've seriously thought of taking a gun and shooting him."

"Who is he? What does he do?"

"He says he is an engineer, but he's really an electrician. He's intelligent, but mentally sick. Sometimes I think that the only way out for me is to commit suicide."

"Does he at least satisfy you?"

"Yes and no. I hate savages and I'm tired of him. He bores me, keeps everybody away from me. I'm convinced that someday he'll kill me. I'm as certain of that as that it's night now. But what can I do? The Tel Aviv police are like the police everywhere. 'After he kills you,' they say, 'we'll put him in jail.' He should be committed. If I had somewhere to go, I would leave, but the foreign consulates aren't exactly handing out visas. At least I have an apartment here. Some apartment! But it's a place to sleep. And what can I do with my paintings? They're just gathering dust. Even if I wanted to leave, I don't have the fare. The alimony I get from my former husband, the doctor, is a few pounds, and he's always behind in his payments. They don't know what it's all about here. It's not America. I'm starving and that's the bitter truth. Don't grab your wallet; it's not really that bad. I've lived alone and I'll die alone. I'm proud of it, and besides, it's my fate. What I'm going through and what I've been through, nobody knows, not even

God. There's not a day without some catastrophe. But suddenly I walk into a café and there you are. That's really something."

"Didn't you know that I was here?"

"Yes, but how did I know what you'd be like after all these years? I haven't changed a bit, and that's my tragedy. I've remained the same. I've the same desires, the same dreams—the people persecute me here, just as they did twenty years ago in Poland. They are all my enemies, and I don't know why. I've read your books. I've forgotten nothing. I've always thought about you, even when I lay swollen from hunger in Kazakhstan and looked into the eyes of death. You wrote somewhere that one sins in another world, and that this world is hell. For you, that may have been just a phrase, but it's the truth. I am the reincarnation of some wicked man from another planet. Gehenna is *in* me. This climate sickens me. The men here become impotent; the women are consumed with passion. Why did God pick out this land for the Jews? When the khamsin begins, my brains rattle. Here the winds don't blow; they wail like jackals. Sometimes I stay in bed all day because I don't have the strength to get up, but at night I roam about like a beast of prey. How long can I go on like this? But that I'm alive and seeing you makes it a holiday for me."

She pushed her chair away from the table, almost overturning it. "These mosquitoes are driving me crazy."

2

Although I had already had dinner, I ate again with Dosha and drank Carmel wine with her. Then I went to her home. On the way, she kept apologizing for the poorness of her apartment. We passed a park. Though lit by street lamps, it was covered by darkness which no light could penetrate. The motionless leaves of the trees seemed petrified. We walked through dim streets, each bearing the name of a Hebrew writer or scholar. I read the signs over women's clothing stores. The commission for modernizing Hebrew had created a terminology for brassieres, nylons, corsets, ladies' coiffures, and cosmetics. They had found the sources for such worldly terms in the Bible, the Babylonian Talmud, the Jerusalem Talmud, the Midrash, and even the Zohar. It was already late in the evening, but buildings and asphalt still exuded the heat of the day. The humid air smelled of garbage and fish.

I felt the age of the earth beneath me, the lost civilizations lying in layers. Somewhere below lay hidden golden calves, the jewelry of temple harlots, and images of Baal and Astarte. Here prophets foretold disasters. From a nearby harbor, Jonah had fled to Tarshish rather than prophesy the doom of Nineveh. In the daylight these events seemed remote, but at night the dead walked again. I heard the whisperings of phantoms. An awakening bird had uttered a shrill alarm. Insects beat against the glass of the street lamps, crazed with lust.

Dosha took my arm with a loyalty unprofaned by any past betrayal. She led me up the stairway of a building. Her apartment was actually a separate structure on the roof. As she opened the door, a blast of heat, combined with the smell of paint and of alcohol used for a primus stove, hit me. The single room served as studio, bedroom, kitchen. Dosha did not switch on the lights. Our past had accustomed us both to undress and dress in the dark. She opened the shutters and the night shone in with its street lamps and stars. A painting stood propped against the wall. I knew that in the daylight its bizarre lines and colors would have little meaning for me. Still, I found it intriguing now. We kissed without speaking.

After years of living in the United States, I had forgotten that there could be an apartment without a bathroom. But Dosha's had none. There was only a sink with running water. The toilet was on the roof. Dosha opened a glass door to the roof and showed me where to go. I could find neither switch nor cord to turn on the light. In the dark I felt a hook with pieces of torn newspaper stuck to it. As I was returning, I saw through the curtains of the glass door that Dosha had turned on the lamp.

Suddenly the silhouette of a man crossed the window. He was tall and broad-shouldered. I heard voices and realized immediately what had happened. Her mad lover had returned. Though terrified, I felt like laughing. My clothes were in her room; I had walked out naked.

I knew there was no escape. The house was not attached to any other building. Even if I managed to climb down the four stories to the street, I could not return to my hotel without clothes. It occurred to me that Dosha might have hidden my things quickly when she heard her lover's steps on the stairs. But he might come outside at any minute. I began to look around the roof for some stick or other object with which to defend myself. I found nothing. I stood against the outside wall of the toilet, hoping he wouldn't see me. But how long could I stay there? In a few hours it would be daybreak.

I crouched like an animal at bay waiting for the hunter to shoot. Cool breezes from the sea mingled with the heat rising from the roof. I shivered and could barely keep my teeth from chattering. I realized that my only way of escape would be to climb down the balconies to the street. But when I looked, I saw that I could not even reach the nearest one. If I jumped I might break a leg or even fracture my skull. Besides, I might be arrested or taken to a madhouse.

Despite my anxiety, I was aware of the ridiculousness of my situation. I could hear them giggling at my ill-fated tryst in the cafés of Tel Aviv. I began to pray to God, against whom I had sinned. "Father, have mercy on me. Don't let me perish in this preposterous way." I promised a sum of money for charity if only I could get out of this trap. I looked up to the numberless stars that hovered strangely near, to the cosmos spreading out with all its suns, planets, comets, nebulae, asteroids, and who-knows-what-other powers and spirits, which are either God himself or that which He has formed from His substance. I imagined that there was a touch of compassion in the stars as they gazed at me in the midst of their midnight gaiety. They seemed to be saying to me, "Just wait, child of Adam, we know of your predicament and are taking counsel."

For a long time I stood staring at the sky and at the tangle of houses which make up Tel Aviv. An occasional horn, the bark of a dog, the shout of a human being erupted from the sleeping city. I thought I heard the surf and a ringing bell. I learned that insects do not sleep at night. Every moment some tiny creature fluttered by, some with one pair of wings, others with two. A huge beetle crawled at my feet. It stopped, changed its direction, as if it realized it had gone astray on this strange roof. I had never felt so close to a crawling creature as in those minutes. I shared its fate. Neither of us knew why he had been born and why he must die. "Brother Beetle," I muttered, "what do they want of us?"

I was overcome by a kind of religious fervor. I was standing on a roof in a land which God had given back to that half of his people that had not been annihilated. I found myself in infinite space, amid myriads of galaxies, between two eternities, one already past and one still to come. Or perhaps nothing had passed, and all that was or ever will be was unrolled across the universe like one vast scroll. I apologized to my parents, wherever they were, against whom I had once rebelled and whom I was now disgracing. I asked God's forgiveness. For instead of returning to His promised land with renewed will to study the Torah and to heed His commandments, I had gone with a wanton who had lost herself in the vanity of art. "Father, help me!" I called out in despair.

Growing weary, I sat down. Because it was getting colder, I leaned against the wall to protect myself. My throat was scratchy, and in my nose I felt the acrid dryness that precedes a cold. "Has anyone else ever been in such a situation?"

I asked myself. I was numbed by that silence that accompanies danger. I might freeze to death on this hot summer night.

I dozed. I had sat down, placing my chin on my chest, the palms of my hands against my ribs, like some fakir who has vowed to remain in that position forever. Now and then I tried to warm my knees with my breath. I listened, and heard only the mewing of a cat on a neighboring roof. It yowled first with the thin cry of a child and then with that of a woman in labor. I don't know how long I slept—perhaps a minute, perhaps twenty. My mind became empty. My worries vanished. I found myself in a graveyard where children were playing—they had come out of their graves. Among them was a tiny girl in a pleated skirt. Through her blond curls, boils could be seen on her skull. I knew who she was, Jochebed, our neighbor's daughter at 10 Krochmalna Street, who had caught scarlet fever and had been carried out to a children's hearse one morning. The hearse was drawn by a single horse and had many compartments that looked like drawers. Some of the children danced in a circle, others played on swings. It was a recurring dream which began in my childhood. The children, seeming to know that they were dead, neither talked nor sang. Their yellowish faces wore that otherworld melancholy revealed only in dreams.

I heard a rustling and then felt someone's touch. Opening my eyes, I saw Dosha wearing a housecoat and slippers. She was carrying my clothes. My suspenders dragged along the rooftop together with a sleeve of my jacket. She put my shoes down and, placing her finger on her lips, indicated silence. She grimaced and stuck out her tongue in mockery. She backed away and, to my amazement, opened a trapdoor leading to the stairway. I almost stepped on my glasses, which had fallen out of my pocket. In my confusion, I wasn't aware of Dosha leaving. I saw a booklet lying near me—my American passport. I began to search for my money, my traveler's checks. I dressed quickly, and in my haste I put my jacket on inside out.

My legs became shaky. I climbed through the trapdoor and found myself on the steps.

On the ground floor, I found the door chained and locked. I tried to force it like a thief. At last, the latch opened. Having closed it quietly behind me, I walked rapidly away, without once looking back at the house where I had so recently been imprisoned.

I came to an alley which seemed to be newly constructed because it was not yet paved. I followed whatever street I came to just to get as far away as possible. I walked and I talked to myself. I stopped an elderly passerby, addressing him in English, and he said to me, "Speak Hebrew," and then showed me how to reach my hotel. There was fatherly reproach in his eyes, embedded in shadow, as if he knew me and had guessed my plight. He vanished before I could thank him.

I remained where he left me, meditating on what had happened. As I stood alone in the stillness, shivering in the cold of dawn, I felt something moving in the cuff of my pants. I bent down, and saw a huge beetle which ran out and disappeared in an instant. Was it the same beetle I had seen on the roof? Entrapped in my clothes, it had managed to free itself. We had both been granted another chance by the powers that rule the universe.

Translated by the author
and Elizabeth Shub

The Boy Knows
the Truth

WHEN RABBI GABRIEL KLINTOWER took over his late father's chair, he let his beadles know that he would not accept women and their petitions to intercede in Heaven for them. True, his father and grandfather had accepted women and many other wonder rabbis did, but he could not put himself on the same plane as those saints whose thoughts were always pure. Rabbi Gabriel had a sensual body. His blood boiled in his veins. In the middle of his prayers impure thoughts assailed him like locusts. The Evil One spoke to him insolently: "There is no judge and no judgment; seize your pleasure as long as you can." The rabbi bit his nails down to the quick. With his fists he beat his head. He tore at his sidelocks and called himself outcast, betrayer of God. He looked continually for advice in sacred books, until finally he concluded that an imp had attached itself to him. What irony! Devoted Jews came to him to learn the fear of God; scholars copied his sermons; every day he lectured to chosen yeshiva students—all at the very time he was sunk to his neck in a passion for flesh. Studying *The Beginning of Wisdom, The Tree of Life, The Pillar of Service,* he thought about Rahab the Harlot and lusted for Abishag the Shunammite. It was said in the books of the cabala that in the higher spheres unions still take place between Adam and Eve,

Jacob and Rachel, David and Bathsheba. Of course the cabalists referred to souls, not bodies. But the moment the rabbi dozed off he saw those ancient females stark naked. They sang lascivious songs and danced in a seductive way. The rabbi woke up shaken. "Woe is me. I am drowning in iniquity," Rabbi Gabriel said to himself. "Well, this world is a world of falsehood, where evil powers hold dominion." Many times he wanted to call in his Hasidim and tell them that he did not deserve to be their spiritual leader. But the rabbi knew that the moment he resigned from his position, took off his sable hat and silk robe, and stopped pretending, he would fall into the pit of Satan, since men like him are more ashamed of the opinion of people than they fear the Almighty.

The rabbi had a wife, Menucha Alte, named after the daughter of the famous rabbi from Ropczyca. Menucha Alte was conceived and born in saintliness, just as Gabriel was given the nature of a wanton. He was tall, broad-shouldered, with the voice of a lion and an appetite to match. Although he was fifty-seven, his beard remained bright red, without a gray hair. He had a full mouth of teeth strong enough to crack walnuts. Once when there was a fire in his court, Rabbi Gabriel broke down the doors of the synagogue with his bare hands, wrenched off locks and carried out all the scrolls and later all the volumes from the study house. His beadle, Avigdor, fainted from the smoke and Rabbi Gabriel carried him down two flights of stairs. Then he ran to the well and for hours pumped water, working with the firemen to extinguish the flames.

Menucha Alte was small and as scrawny as a consumptive. She lived on medicines and incantations. Every few months she fell dangerously ill. She took upon herself acts of piety that even the most rigorous Jews had long given up. She had three kitchens—one for meat dishes, one for milk meals, one for *pareve* foods. She wore two bonnets to prevent a single hair from showing to a male. On Passover, she put stockings on her cat so that, God forbid, it should not drag in any crumbs of leavened bread under its claws. As long as Menucha Alte was young and still had her periods, she had problems with the ritual ablutions and Rabbi Gabriel was not allowed to have intercourse with her for months. When he finally came to her, her body was cold and she smelled of toothache and valerian drops. She whined that he was too heavy on her, and hurting. Rabbi Gabriel used to remind her that, even according to the strictest letter of the law, kissing and embracing are permitted and that tannaim and amoraim frolicked with their spouses in bed. But Menucha Alte groaned and sighed.

How strange that this broken shard gave birth to five children. Twins died from typhoid fever. Of the three who lived, two daughters took after their father: they were tall, with blue eyes and red hair. Both had husbands and children and lived far from Klintow, on the other side of the Vistula. Shmaya, the only son, suffered from rickets and had a water head. He was as small as a dwarf. Rabbi Gabriel married him off when he was fifteen, but his wife became enlightened and left him. He never remarried. At twenty-nine, Shmaya was beardless as a eunuch. There was madness in his black bulging eyes.

Shmaya had decided that he could best serve God by secluding himself. He immersed himself in the cold ritual bath at midnight. He limited his study to the Zohar. Every few weeks he had a convulsive attack, and the only way to revive him was to put a key into his clenched fist and recite the words "Thou shalt not be afraid for the terror by night; nor for the arrow that flieth by day . . . A thousand shall fall at thy side, and ten thousand at thy right hand; but it shall not come nigh thee." The Hasidim of Rabbi Gabriel knew that Shmaya would not last long and that after his father's demise there would be no one to succeed him.

During the daytime Rabbi Gabriel managed to do his duties. He was the head of the yeshiva, and he took special care of every student. He taught them not in the casuistic method of hairsplitting arguments but with the precise interpretation of the ancient commentators. Rabbi Gabriel had grasped a long time ago that arguing with Satan was of no avail. One must conquer him by deeds and not allow him time for temptation. The nights became more and more difficult. The rabbi would sleep for an hour and then waken, frightened by his own lust. Lately he could not approach Menucha Alte at all. She was prey to a dozen maladies. She kept on moaning and whispering prayers. She had already prepared her shrouds, which she kept under her pillow, along with a bag of chalky earth from the Holy Land on which her head would rest in her grave. She had written her will, leaving her moth-eaten trousseau for orphan brides. But the years passed by and Menucha Alte lived. Once on Purim, after the rabbi had one glass of wine too many, he said jokingly that Menucha Alte had no strength to die— the Resurrection would have come before she managed to pass away.

Rabbi Gabriel was famous for his wit. He even kibitzed the Almighty. His adversaries considered him a mocker and half mad. Like many of those with a humorous nature, the rabbi was prone to melancholy. Once, after days of depression, he came from his room where he had locked himself in and stopped a cheder boy. He asked him, "Tell me why the Almighty has created the world?" The boy did not answer and the rabbi pulled his ear and said, "So that fools like myself should ask questions."

One afternoon late in the summer, when Rabbi Gabriel sat in his study and looked into *The Orchard of Pomegranates*, the door opened and Avigdor the beadle entered.

"Rabbi, a female relative of yours has come to visit you. She says she is some rabbi's widow. She refuses to leave. She wants to talk to you."

"She wants, huh? You know that I don't accept women. Who is she? Most probably a schnorrer."

"She came in her own carriage with her own coachman."

The rabbi clutched at his beard with one hand and with the other he rubbed his forehead. "What is her name? How is she my relative?"

"She says that she's the rabbi's niece or some relative like that. It is very urgent."

"Let her in, but leave the door open."

The rabbi barely managed to finish his sentence when the woman crossed the threshold. She was tall, slender, dressed in a silk cape, a pleated skirt, and patent-leather shoes of which only the tips could be seen. Over her blond wig hung a black tulle shawl. In one hand she held a fancy parasol, in the other a handbag with beads and fringes. Her face seemed young, almost that of a girl. But the rabbi could see that she was not really young. She smelled of big city and worldliness. He turned his head away. "*Nu?*"

"Rabbi, I am Binele, your Aunt Temerl's daughter."

The rabbi shuddered. He had forgotten that his Aunt Temerl had a child. Temerl had lost her mind over thirty years ago. Her husband, a rich man from Galicia, placed her in a private clinic in Vienna. To be allowed to remarry, he had had to get a written permission signed by a hundred rabbis. The rabbi asked, "Your mother is alive?"

"Woe to such a life!"

Rabbi Gabriel bent his head. Years had passed and he did not remember his Aunt Temerl, who wasted away in an insane asylum. The words of the prophet Isaiah ". . . and that thou hide not thyself from thine own flesh" came to his mind. His throat and his eyes became hot. He asked, "How is your father?"

"My father passed away. It was a year only last week."

"Did he have children with his second wife?"

"I have three sisters and two brothers."

"*Nu*, the years run, it's all futile and vain," the rabbi murmured. He well knew that he should not let Binele stand, but to offer her a chair would mean giving her a chance to linger. That scatterbrain, Avigdor, had closed the door. The rabbi asked, "What happened to your late husband?"

"I have been a widow for three years. My husband was a rabbi, a scholar, and had an honorary doctorate besides. We lived in Karlsbad."

"Children?"

"We had no children."

The rabbi glanced at her. Her face was narrow, dark-skinned. Her eyes were black. She wore a string of pearls, and diamond earrings dangled from her earlobes. She resembled her mother, who had been known as a beauty. After some hesitation, the rabbi pointed to a chair. "*Nu*, sit down."

"Thank you." She put her parasol and her handbag on the rabbi's table. She spoke in a singsong. "My brothers both became doctors. One is a surgeon in Lemberg and the other a heart specialist in Franzensbad. My sisters are all married. My stepmother lives with her oldest daughter in Drohobycz. My brother-in-law is an owner of oil wells. I am the only one in the family who married a rabbi. He left three commentaries on the Talmud and a thesis about Maimonides written in German."

The rabbi of Klintow had heard about the big world—rabbis who trimmed their beards, reformed synagogues that called themselves temples, rich Jews who traveled to the spas and associated with Gentiles, yeshiva boys who became professors—but it never occurred to him that he might have any connection with such people. Now the Evil One had brought one of them to his house. The rabbi wanted to get up and open the door, but he was embarrassed to do it. He asked, "Why did you come here, to this kingdom of pauperhood?"

"Because you are my nearest relative on my mother's side. I wanted to see you."

"What is there to see? The body turns to dust and the soul is steeped in wickedness. Soon I will have to give an account before the Judgment on High."

"You, too, are afraid to give account?"

"There are no privileges in Heaven."

"You still have years of time. You look, thank God, a strong man."

The rabbi sat silent. No one had ever spoken to him like this. He rose and opened the door, but immediately the wind slammed it shut again.

Binele smiled with amusement. She searched her purse to take out a lace handkerchief, and the rabbi noticed that she had long fingers and polished nails. She said, "Don't be nervous. I'm a kosher Jewish daughter. How is your wife, the rebbetzin, God bless her?"

The rabbi told her about Menucha Alte's illnesses and Binele said, "If you had sent her to Vienna, they might have been able to cure her. Now it would be too late."

"It's always too late. Do you ever go to see your mother?"

"I go, but there is nothing to see. A dazzling beauty still, but mute as a fish. She doesn't recognize me. She stares somewhere over my head. Such sadness I've never seen in a human being except in those of our family. The anguish of generations looks out from her eyes."

"Most probably she sees the truth," the rabbi said, baffled by his own words.

"It may be. But as long as one lives one must live. When my husband left me, I had one desire: that he take me with him. He was all I could wish for—handsome, kind, wise, a philosopher. He was invited to lecture in universities. Priests and nuns came to hear him. But what the earth covers one must forget. Before his demise he called me to his bed and said, 'Binele, it is my wish that you remarry.' Those were his last words." A sob burst from Binele's throat. Her face became red, and shiny tears ran down her cheeks. She opened her purse and began to rummage for another handkerchief.

Rabbi Gabriel said, "It is not our world. What the Creator intends we shall never know."

On the evening of this very day, Menucha Alte had one of her attacks. The nursing maid put a hot compress on her belly, but she continued to groan. The rabbi lay in his private bedroom across the hall. "Father in Heaven, cure her or take her away!" he cried out within himself. He knew well that one might not tell God what to do, but why should she suffer so uselessly? She was a saint, a holy victim. At the same time that the rabbi was filled with compassion for her, a malicious voice spoke: If Menucha Alte should die, he could marry Binele. The rabbi pulled his sidelocks. "Wicked lecher, in spite of your foul wishes she will live to be a hundred and twenty!"

He covered his face with his feather bed and tried to doze off, but his body felt hot. He imagined Binele cleansing herself for him in the ritual bath, standing with him under the canopy, copulating with him. "You are better than my husband," she was moaning in her passion. "You are stronger than Samson!"

"Well, I'm losing the world to come," the rabbi admonished himself. "Even Gehenna is too small a punishment for me. The demons will drag me into the desert behind the Black Mountains where Asmodeus and Lilith rule, into the abyss of defilement, into the darkness of no return."

He fell asleep and Binele stood before him naked, her nipples red as fire. She kissed him, caressed him, braided his beard and sidelocks. She bent down on all fours and commanded, "Ride on me as on Balaam's ass." The rabbi awoke with a start. Was it still night? Was it already daybreak?

The window was covered with a shutter. From his wife's room he heard her maid speak and an outcry from the sick woman. The rabbi went to her. The maid stepped aside, and Menucha Alte asked in a choked voice, "Who was that female? Why did you accept her?"

"She's Binele, my Aunt Temerl's daughter."

"What does she want. To take my place?"

"God forbid. You will soon recover."

"My end has come. Give me your hand and swear that you will send her away."

Outside, the day was breaking. The rabbi could see Menucha Alte stretching out a bony hand. His mind filled with wrath. He heard himself shout, "You have tortured me enough all these years! I refuse to swear."

He ran back to his bedroom and in the dark banged his knee and spilled the dish of the morning ablution water. He stepped with his bare foot into the puddle it made. "Let her die, the nuisance!" Rage seethed in him. He went out into the courtyard and hit his forehead against the doorpost on the wooden case of the mezuzah. In the east the sky reddened. Dew was falling. Crows croaked. The rabbi stopped at the well and filled a bucket with water. He poured it over his fingers but he did not have the courage to recite "I thank Thee." Perhaps he should throw himself into the well? He gazed into its depth and saw his face, dark and diffused. He had a desire to run and scream. It was she who brought me to these ungodly reveries by depriving me, he thought. I should have divorced her the very first year of our marriage. He suddenly remembered what a Hasid had told him speaking about his own wife: that not blood ran in her veins but tepid dishwater. The rabbi laughed and gritted his teeth. "I shall not give her an oath."

The sun emerged like a bloody head from a womb. The rabbi breathed the cool air deeply. He recalled what the Talmud said of Joseph: Joseph was about to lie with Potiphar's wife, but the image of his father revealed itself to him and prevented him. There are passions that even the saints cannot overcome without grace from on High. After a while the rabbi returned to his room. He put on his breeches, his stockings, his fringed garment, and his slippers, and he went to the study house. The oak door was closed and the rabbi knocked three times to warn the corpses, who pray there during the night, that the day had arrived. Inside, a remnant of a memorial candle glimmered in the menorah. In the study house it was still night. The rabbi stood, perplexed. Was he allowed to pray after such profane thoughts? He heard quiet steps. Shmaya slipped in, a figure without substance, a mere shadow. "Father, Mother has . . ." He did not finish the sentence. The rabbi lifted one eyebrow. "I know. I killed her."

After Menucha Alte's grave was filled and Shmaya recited Kaddish, his father approached him and in a loud voice said, "Mazel tov, Rabbi."

Shmaya stood before him, dazed. A murmur of protest rose from the Hasidim. Eyes bulged; beards and sidelocks shook. His father said, "I am no longer permitted to be a leader of Jews."

Binele was at the cemetery and she tried to push her way to Rabbi Gabriel, but two beadles held her back. Later, in the time of shivah, his hangers-on attempted to convince him that allowing Shmaya to take his place would create a furor in all the rabbinical courts. People would suspect Rabbi Gabriel of having committed a mortal sin; it would also be interpreted as a victory for the enlightened ones and for the anti-Hasidim. He sat on a low stool in his stocking feet, his lapel torn, which is the sign of mourning, and a volume of the Book of Job on his knees, and he kept silent. Beila the cook told people that the rabbi had stopped eating. All he took through the day was a glass of black coffee. Again and again Binele made an effort to call on him. She even offered a bribe to the beadles, but Rabbi Gabriel had given them strict orders not to let her in. Shmaya, who observed shivah by himself in his attic room, came to his father to beg him to keep his chair. Rabbi Gabriel said to him, "Your father is a murderer."

On the Sabbath, shivah is interrupted, and the beadles prepared the usual repast in the study house for Rabbi Gabriel and his Hasidim, who had come from all sides of Poland to attend his wife's funeral. But Rabbi Gabriel refused to leave his room. He chained the door from inside, and no pleading could persuade him. Avigdor brought benediction wine, challah, fish, and meat, but the rabbi ate only a piece of challah dunked in horseradish. When it grew late and the Hasidim realized that nothing could be done, they grasped Shmaya by the collar of his robe and put him at the head of the table. They poured wine for him into a goblet and he mumbled the benediction. With shaky hands, he broke a slice of braided challah and tasted a small piece, and the Hasidim caught the crumbs that fell from it and swallowed them, since the bread had been sanctified by the new rabbi's touch. The Hasidim sang table chants, and Shmaya muttered the words. After a while he interpreted the Torah, but his hushed voice could hardly be heard.

The next day the same thing happened. The beadles who served his father now served Shmaya. He sat at the head of the table—pale, his back bent, in a fur hat too small for his head—and it was obvious to everyone that he was overcome with grief. In his sermon he did not preach anything new but quoted sayings of his saintly grandfather, blessed be his memory, and of his father, he should live long. Some of the younger Hasidim maintained that Shmaya was greater than the father in fear of God and in his humility.

Sabbath night, after Havdalah, for the last time Binele asked to be announced to Rabbi Gabriel. When the door remained locked against her, she ordered the coachmen to harness the horses, and her carriage disappeared down the Lublin road. Since the Sabbath was over, the rabbi returned to the observance of shivah. Almost all the Hasidim who had come to Menucha Alte's funeral left the same night or the morning after.

On Monday, the court was empty. Because the rabbi had ceased lecturing in the yeshiva, many students had stopped studying and were roaming the village. Everyone in Klintow knew that Shmaya was too weak to be the head of the yeshiva. He had neither the voice nor the skill to make students understand a difficult passage in the Gemara. There was a time when there had been in the Klintow court about forty old men, disciples who stayed there all year round and ate from a common kettle. Most of them had died. The owners of inns and hostels grumbled that if Shmaya was to be the rabbi the court would lose its followers and Klintow would become a deserted town.

The seven days of mourning were over, and then the thirty days of mourning, but Rabbi Gabriel remained secluded. He seemed not to sleep; all night one could see the glow of the oil lamp through the crevices of his shutter. In the month of Elul the days became shorter, the evenings longer, gossamer webs floated through the air, cool breezes wafted from the pine forest nearby. In the study house the ram's horn was blown every morning to deceive Satan into believing that the Messiah was about to come and he should withdraw his instigations against Jews. The leaves on the few trees in Rabbi Gabriel's garden turned as yellow as saffron and kept falling all day and all night. Shmaya came to his father to complain that the yeshiva was about to disintegrate and that after the Days of Awe the last of the students would have gone. He said to his father, "Forgive me, but penitence like this is nothing but selfishness."

That night Rabbi Gabriel did not sleep a wink. He sat on the edge of his bed and pondered until daybreak. He had been waging war not only with his body but also with his soul. Both of them are no good, he mused. The body is a glutton on this earth, and the soul wants to gobble up Leviathan in Paradise. He could not forget Menucha Alte's face as he had seen it before her burial: white as chalk, with an open mouth, her nose crooked as a beak, one eye opened and glazed. Even though she had not a single tooth, her lips looked bitten and wounded. She appeared to be screaming without a voice, "Of what avail were my torments? How did I deserve all this pain?"

If this was the aim of creation, cursed be creation, Rabbi Gabriel decided. Actually, the Almighty never answered Job's questions. All He did was boast about His wisdom and His might. At dawn he fell asleep. He dreamed that he was a bridegroom being led to the wedding canopy with Menucha Alte in the synagogue yard. It was a hot summer evening. A green moon, as large as the sun and almost as bright, was shining. Girls dressed in white held wax candles, boys carried torches. Strange birds the size of eagles circled in the sky. They flapped their wings and threw silvery shadows. Everything happened at once. The musicians were playing, Hasidim were singing, the yeshiva students were discussing the Talmud. The old wedding jester, Reb Getzl, was cracking jokes and turning somersaults. At the same time, Father was reciting the benedictions. Grandmother was dancing a kosher dance with a cluster of old women. He, young Gabriel, was sitting with his new spouse partaking of the golden broth. He gazed at Menucha Alte and could not believe it was she. She was so beautiful that he was overcome with astonishment. How can such splendor exist? he wondered. She was both matter and spirit. An otherworldly radiance fell from her eyes. Even her veil and gown shone with their own light. Could she be an angel disguised as a human being? Had the redemption come and Mother Rachel descended from the Nest of the Bird where she dwells and revealed herself to him?

Rabbi Gabriel began to cry and he woke up trembling. His bed trembled with him. The sun had risen and a fiery chariot sailed in the sky from the west to the east. He had slept long, he was late reciting the Shema. He remembered the passage in the Psalms: "The heavens declare the glory of God; and the firmament showeth His handiwork . . . as a bridegroom coming out of his chamber . . . His going forth is from the end of the heaven, and his circuit unto the ends of it."

Rabbi Gabriel got up, washed his hands, dressed, and went out into the courtyard on the way to the study house. "Where else can I go?" he said to himself. "To a tavern, to a house of ill repute?" He had wakened with new vigor and with a hunger for learning. A cheder boy was walking toward him, his face white, his sidelocks disheveled. He carried a Pentateuch and a paper bag of food. Rabbi Gabriel stopped him. "Do you want to earn two groschen?" he asked.

"Yes, Rabbi."

"What should a Jew do who has lost the world to come?"

The boy seemed to ponder. "Be a Jew."

"Even though he has lost the world to come?"

"Yes."

"And study Torah?"

"Yes."

"Since he is lost, why the Torah?"

"It's good."

"It's good, eh? As good as candy?"

The boy hesitated for a moment. "Yes."

"Well, you earned the two groschen." Rabbi Gabriel put his hand into his right pocket where he kept money for charity, and gave two groschen to the boy. He bent down to him, pinched his cheek, and kissed his forehead. "You are cleverer than all of them. Go and buy yourself some sweets."

The boy grabbed the coin and began to run, his sidelocks flying, his fringed garment blowing in the wind. Rabbi Gabriel went straight to the yeshiva. He was afraid that all the students had left, but some fourteen or fifteen still remained. They had come to study at sunrise, as was the custom in Klintow. When they saw the rabbi they rose in awe. The rabbi shouted, "The boy knows the truth!"

And he began to lecture on the section where he had left off weeks ago.

There Are No Coincidences

ALTHOUGH PARTY INVITATIONS no longer frightened me, I still found myself making careful preparations for this particular party. I got a haircut, laid out my best suit, selected a special shirt, tie, and cuff links. I had recently gone on a diet, but because I didn't want to look too thin, I discontinued it. What should I bring my hosts? Flowers? Wine? What kind of wine? Port? Sherry? Or possibly even champagne? Meeting new people was still a major undertaking.

It was scheduled for this Saturday and I decided to take a cab to the suburb where it was being held. It was early autumn and the weather had been mild, but that morning it turned cold and rainy, and as I listened to the steam hissing in my radiator, it already felt like midwinter. Trees, visible from my window, covered with foliage only yesterday, had become bare overnight. Churning clouds augured a further change in the weather. From my newspaper I learned that a hurricane which had already struck another state was on its way to New York, though it might veer out to sea. The storm left destruction in its wake. In one village an entire cottage was sheared from its foundation and blown into the ocean together with its occupants.

As I lay in bed the morning of the party, I envisioned a change also taking place in me. A loose tooth which hadn't bothered me suddenly sent a stabbing pain through my jaw. Ordinarily I'm not prone to headaches, but I awoke with a dull ache on the left side of my head. Several disturbing dreams had given me a restless night, though I could only remember them vaguely. In one dream I recalled shouting at someone and being involved in a fight. There was also something about an animal, but what it was I couldn't recollect. What did stay with me afterward was the despairing knowledge that one leads a double life—each part hermetically sealed off from the other.

Well, perhaps the mail would bring some good news. True, last week's mail was particularly light, except for a few advertisements which I threw into the wastebasket. But generally on Saturdays my mail was more abundant than on other days and I hoped today's mail would bring something interesting.

Occasionally a check arrived in payment for a piece which had been included in an anthology. I might even receive a letter from a woman. Sometimes the clipping service sent a belated review. The postman arrives about ten o'clock. Though my bedroom is some distance from the entrance door, I'm always able to hear the sound of the letters being shoved underneath.

There was no particular reason for me to get up early that Saturday morning, so I decided to stay in bed until the mail arrived. Meanwhile, I leafed through a collection of modern French poetry which was on my night table. My knowledge of French is scant, and since the selected poets were all modern, their poems seemed almost meaningless to me. From the biographical notes it was clear that the authors were all young. What were they saying? What was troubling them? I was certain that apart from my meager comprehension of the language, it was difficult for me to understand them altogether because I was of a different generation.

I thought I heard a piece of paper being slipped under the

door. I listened carefully and waited for more, but that was all. Without my robe or slippers I rushed to the door, and to my disappointment, I found a single printed advertisement put out by some rug-cleaning firm. I angrily tossed the ad into the trash can thinking that a year or two ago a tree was felled in Canada to create paper for this.

Because the mail was so unsatisfactory I had to seek my little pleasure elsewhere and I went into my combination living/dining room. The bookshelves were tightly packed. On some of the shelves the books were lined up vertically, one row in front of the other, while on top of each I had stacked various journals and oversized volumes.

That morning I had no appetite, neither for reading nor for breakfast. I stood staring at the books, trying to find something that would capture my interest, but I knew in advance that it was futile. The philosophical works, especially, seemed repugnant to me. Not a single thought of theirs could be of any help to me at this time. From the library I wandered into the kitchen, where I gazed with apathy at the milk, the eggs, the cereals, and the jellies.

God in Heaven, there was a time when I dreamed of having my own apartment with a private bedroom, my own library, and a kitchen where I could prepare some tea or coffee. But now all these gifts lost their meaning, if only for a while. The person responsible for all of this was, of course, Esther. As long as she was here, everything had charm. But whose fault was it that she left? Mine, I knew. Now it was too late. But I mustn't starve myself if I wished to look good at the party. I filled a bowl with cereal, poured milk over it, and sprinkled raisins on top. In this kitchen, as in the library, were hidden treasures but one had to bite into them.

I passed the day napping and strolling in the rain. The phone only rang once and it was a wrong number. After lunch I walked twenty blocks south from the restaurant where I had eaten and then back again. On the return trip the wind waged war with my umbrella and tried by every means to rip it apart, while I was just as determined not to let it happen. Sometimes a gust of wind would swoop down from above and make the umbrella feel heavy in my hand. Another time the gust would come from below and the umbrella would try to fly away. I fantasized that I was a sea captain steering a ship through a stormy sea. When I entered the hallway of my house with my umbrella still intact, I experienced the pride of a victorious fighter. The water streamed from my umbrella as I waited for the elevator. Alone in the elevator, like a child I wrote my name on the floor with the wet umbrella tip, then erased it.

When I looked at the kitchen clock I realized that though I still had some time to rest, it would be necessary to leave for the party shortly.

The cab driver informed me in advance that he wasn't too familiar with the suburb I asked to be driven to. I suggested that he start driving anyway and ask directions along the route. He was doing me a great favor. Several times he hinted that he would expect an extra tip. "I stay away from such neighborhoods," he said with pride, intimating that those who did go there were people with lower standards than his. He seemed to regret having taken me as a fare and muttered to himself all the way. It started to thunder and lightning. The driver kept looking back at me angrily as though it were my fault that nature was acting this way. As the storm intensified, it became impossible to check our course. The roads were flooded and the cab seemed to be enveloped in flame with every streak of lightning. I could almost feel the million-volt electrical current around me. Though the windshield wipers worked furiously, there was little visibility. We could barely see the headlights of the oncoming cars. Of all things, I had forgotten to bring my umbrella, the very one for which I had waged such a campaign.

The driver finally seemed to give himself over to his destiny completely and ceased turning around to glare at me. As far as I could figure out, he had taken the wrong road. Between the two of us there arose the hostility which comes when people are forced into a dangerous situation together. The taxi sped on, away from New York, away from the party. One or two cars passed seemingly propelled by fatalistic speed. Perhaps they, too, were lost.

A garage loomed up in front of us and we headed for it. The dark face of a man appeared. Despite the fury of the elements he seemed quite at ease. My driver rolled his window down and asked for directions. The garage man, without so much as a glance at me, told him how to go. His instructions were complicated. "Make a right turn at the light, continue straight ahead, then turn right again, then left, then straight ahead again, past three lights, then a blinker, and make a sharp left." It was impossible to believe that the driver could remember it all. But he repeated the information and it was clear that he had a picture of the route in his mind. I was impressed with the patience of the man talking to him. He was wringing wet.

This party would cost me half a week's salary. I sat back, shut my eyes, and resigned myself, though I hoped I would at least arrive before the other guests departed.

2

The driver found the correct address, but the street was so narrow and full of parked cars that it was impossible for him to pull up directly in front of the house, so that I had to get out on the opposite side of the street. Another car blocked my way, and though I wasn't standing in the rain for more than a few seconds, I was thoroughly drenched. It was as if some celestial prankster had poured a tub of water over my head. In a split second, all my clothes were ruined—the pressed suit, the new shirt, the tie, the shined shoes. People were getting into the elevator but I had to stand there for a while, just to shake the water off. My eyeglasses were covered with rain and I reached into my pocket for a handkerchief to wipe them with, but it too was soaked. Standing there, I had to laugh inwardly at my wasted efforts. The cold moisture chilled my body and I felt like sneezing. That would be the final irony—to get a lung inflammation from all this.

"Well, it serves me right for wanting worldly pleasures," I reprimanded myself. I found the apartment and rang the doorbell, prepared to meet new people. The years had taught me to mask my shyness. The others were, after all, no more than human beings, each with his own weaknesses and failures. "Be nice to them and they will be nice to you," I encouraged myself.

My friend B. himself opened the door. He was coatless and looked as though he had had a few drinks too many. He squinted curiously at me, as if he didn't remember having invited me. Then his face broke out into a broad smile.

"Come in. Oh, you're all wet."

"I came here by taxi, but the few feet between . . ."

"I know, I know. Take off your jacket."

He helped me remove my jacket and left me standing there in my wet shirt. I caught a glimpse of myself in the hall mirror and saw a disheveled person, gaunt and stooped, with a wet bald pate, a wrinkled collar, and a tie which hung limply. My host impatiently grabbed my arm and forcefully shoved me into the living room, though I shuffled my feet, trying to slow down my entry, in order to repair some of the damage done by the storm. Through my wet glasses, I glimpsed a darkened room, full of silent figures. Apparently the conversation had stopped when this belated guest entered. My host introduced me, and as I walked up to each one with uncertain steps, the men rose. My name was not familiar to them. The hostess appeared from the kitchen.

It was apparent that she, too, had either forgotten about me or assumed that I wouldn't come. A chair was pointed out to

me. B. asked what I would like to drink and I told him. I was
hungry, but I soon saw that the meal was buffet-style. How
strange that not one person said a word to me or made a re-
mark about how wet I was. Well, this was a literary group and
no attention was paid to the amenities. After a while, the hostess handed me a plate of hors d'oeuvres which I balanced on
my lap while holding a highball in my hand. At least the whiskey would warm me and perhaps help me forget my embarrassment. While sipping the drink and nibbling the food on the
plate, I felt like both sneezing and coughing. With the napkin
I was handed, I wiped my spectacles and for the first time was
able to see who was there. Literary parties are always noisy,
with everyone talking at once, but here one woman was talking while the others listened. Most of the guests were middle-
aged, trying to look young. The windows were hung with
drapes and the storm on the other side of the wall might just
as well not have existed. Here, everything was dry, warm; in
fact, too warm.

Now I too began to listen to the woman who was holding
forth. She seemed young, but I couldn't be certain. Her dark
eyes, large and bulgy, made me feel that she was saying "I love
people but demand that they respect and love me, too. When
I speak, I presume they listen to me." There was an aggressiveness in her congeniality and in the soft tone of her voice. She
was delivering a discourse on a study she had made at Sing Sing
prison and the conditions under which the inmates had to live.
Her speech was slow and monotonous, with the self-confidence
of someone who knows for certain that no one would dare to
interrupt. Each phrase expressed compassion for the prisoners
and contempt, mixed with derision, for the administrators.
I had read enough studies of this kind and was certain that
she hadn't discovered anything new, but for some reason most
of the group sat quietly and allowed her to carry on a long,
tedious monologue.

For a while I forgot my wet clothing and became absorbed

in what was going on. Where does her power lie? I wondered. Has she such a strong personality? I soon realized what it was about her that had such an effect on people. First, her location: she sat in a chair which dominated the entire room. She had selected the most strategic spot. Secondly, she had touched on a theme which addressed itself to the issues of civil rights and social justice. To ignore her would be tantamount to siding with brutality.

I noted how the people pretended interest in what she was saying, asking brief questions to which they knew the answers, making short comments intended to express sympathy for the prisoners and disdain for the wardens. There was a moment when I wanted to ask: "How about the victims of these criminals? Don't they deserve any compassion?" But I knew her reply beforehand. I recalled the saying from the Talmud, that those who pity the wicked are cruel to the just.

There was a woman sitting quietly to one side of the room and I now noticed her for the first time. Just as the speaker's location was advantageous, hers was disadvantageous. Instead of a regular chair she was seated on a stool which could topple at any moment. Her face was small, her lips thin, and her cheekbones high. Though her nose had a bump in the middle, it turned up at the tip. Her green-gold eyes were surrounded by fine lines and wrinkles. She might have been in her late thirties. One could guess that she had had a hard life. Her mouth and eyes expressed both impatience and resignation. She was the only one who didn't pretend to be interested in the speaker's harangue. On the contrary, she looked annoyed. She wore a black dress and had a thin gold chain around her neck. Her chestnut-colored hair was combed in an outmoded style. I was puzzled as to what type of person she was. Was she a writer? Was she Jewish? Her face had a quality of intelligence, but it also hinted of hysteria. I felt that this was a woman who could be keenly witty, love intensely, perhaps hate intensely.

When such a person becomes enraged, she is capable of hurling dishes or throwing herself out the window. She probably made love with great passion.

What struck me most about her was that she refused to be mesmerized, like the others, by the sentimental claptrap. While smoking her cigarette she was engrossed in her own thoughts. I looked at her, thinking: I'm with you. She returned my glance, surprised, yet curious, as if she had now seen *me* for the first time. But our chairs were situated in such a way as to make talk between us impossible.

I hoped that something would transpire which would change the circumstances or that the story of Sing Sing would come to an end, but neither happened. The guests remained seated as if stuck to their chairs. Because I had arrived late, I realized the evening was as good as over. Several of the guests finally started to leave. Unquestionably, the party had been a failure. Since the "do-gooder" squelched all conversation, everyone wanted to get away from her as soon as they were able to. She stared angrily at those who dared to leave, like a Salvation Army preacher abandoned in the middle of a hymn. As she extended her hand to them in parting, her expression signified: "I forgive you, but whether the human race will, I'm not so sure."

She continued prattling, drawing out her words as unhurriedly and as full of self-assuredness as before, though her audience was dwindling. A few still nodded agreement. I glanced at my wristwatch, saw it was five minutes to eleven, and stood up. At that exact moment, the chestnut-haired woman also rose, both of us having come to a similar decision at the same time.

Our host, who had been immobilized throughout the evening by the penal injustices, shook himself out of his trance. He looked surprised to see his guests departing and tried to persuade them to remain. His wife also mumbled something about it being too early to go. Notwithstanding their pleas, the woman in the black dress and I both replied that we had a long trip and that it was late.

I hastily bid goodbye to the people I hadn't even spoken to. When I said good night to the storyteller, she raised her eyebrows and glared at me hatefully. Perhaps she knew all along that I wasn't in her power. I had been the profaner who upset the séance.

The woman in the black dress and I walked to the elevator together. We waited in silence. Gathering up my courage, I said: "Allow me to introduce myself; the merciful protector of prisoners never even permitted me to speak to anyone."

"Did you ever see such chutzpah?" she asked. "In all my life I never lived through such a miserable evening. You're lucky you arrived late. From six o'clock on, no one was able to speak. She just sat there and droned on and on. What kind of creature is she? Who does she think she is? And why are bores like that invited to parties? Well, I'm glad to be out of that place. Never again will I cross their threshold." As she spoke these words, I knew there was a bond between us.

3

A half hour had gone by and still no cab came along. We left the street where the party had been held and a passerby indicated a taxi stand, but it was empty. The cabs that did pass were occupied. It was practically midnight and here we were stranded in a godforsaken suburb. My clothes still hadn't dried and I felt chilled. Nor did her coat seem heavy enough for a cold fall night. We found a bus stop and waited there, but it soon became apparent that no buses were in operation at this hour. In an attempt to warm myself, I raised my jacket collar. She shivered sporadically. Above us, the sky was heavy with dark clouds, laden with rain and perhaps snow.

The woman decided to overcome her pride and began to wave at passing automobiles, but one car after another sped by without stopping. We both realized the danger: the rain might start again at any moment; it was just beginning to drizzle. I could feel the sharp mist on my face. There was always the possibility of returning to the party and spending the night with our hosts, but neither of us was in the mood to impose on these people. As for myself, I would rather sleep in the street than put others in an awkward position.

It felt odd to stand here with a woman whose name I didn't know, sharing with her an unfortunate night after a miserable party. I still hoped that a cab might drive up, though I knew full well that the chances weren't too good. Where is it written that taxis must cruise around Long Island in the middle of the night? I recalled David Hume's words: The fact that the sun has risen every morning till now is no guarantee that it will rise again tomorrow. What is the law of averages altogether? Of what scientific worth are statistics? It occurred to me that there might be a hotel nearby, but I didn't dare mention this to my companion. Who knows what she might suspect me of? Actually, the only thing to do was walk, rather than to remain standing in one spot. But I noticed that she wore high-heeled shoes. I remembered reading of people who had frozen to death on cool nights. The moment comes when the body has no more resistance and the internal temperature begins to fall. At eighty degrees Fahrenheit, one is as good as gone.

"Well, that was really some party!" she said, speaking to me as well as to herself. "God knows, I didn't want to come, but they insisted. Don't laugh, but I didn't even get enough to eat."

"Neither did I."

"Why do people give parties if they can't or won't make their guests feel at home? I've stopped inviting people once and for all. I have neither the room nor the time to spend in preparation. I assumed that after a while I would no longer be asked out, but people's mills, like God's, grind slowly."

"You live alone, I assume."

"Yes, alone."

"I do too."

A taxi appeared. From a distance I could see that it was taken, but my partner raised her hand to signal it with the desperation of one whom only a miracle, or an error in the order of things, could save. The driver stared at her coldly, calling out: "Are you blind?"

"I'm afraid we're never going to get a taxi here," I said.

"What do you suggest?"

"I think we should start walking. At least we won't freeze."

"But where to? I don't even know in which direction New York lies. A cab won't pass this way," she added, raising her voice.

"It's not that late."

"I once waited for one on Fifth Avenue for over an hour. Would you like a cigarette?"

"No, thanks."

"Have one. It will warm you up some."

She handed me a cigarette and lit it with her lighter, holding it longer than was necessary, seemingly to warm my face with the flame.

Just as I inhaled the first puff, there was a flash of lightning followed by a frightful thunderclap. Judging from the brief time between the lightning and the thunder, it struck close. My new friend grabbed my arm and clung to me.

"Oh, this is terrible!"

"We have to go inside somewhere!"

"Where? The houses are all locked."

There was a building near us which had shops on the ground floor but no overhang under which to stand. We began to walk and saw a house with an awning over the entrance gate. We were protected for a while, but in a few minutes the drizzle had become a driving torrent which pummeled the awning like hailstones. As the storm gathered momentum, it wet us from all sides. We huddled against the door to protect our backs from the wind and rain. Every degree of warmth was now of utmost value. Like two stray animals, we pressed hard against one another. "If only there was a hotel somewhere," I said.

"What? Where?"

I don't know why, but I asked, "Are you in the literary field?"

After a pause, she replied, "I suppose you could call it that."

"What do you do?"

"I write children's books."

"Really? How interesting!"

"Yes. I write and also edit them. That's how I make a living."

"One has to know how to write for children," I said, to make conversation. In a way, words added warmth.

"Yes, people don't appreciate that fact. They think anyone can write for children. Every year we receive hundreds of manuscripts that we send back, some from famous writers."

"You've never written for adults?" I asked, embarrassed at the urgency in my voice.

The rain had now leveled off. It was pouring steadily without intensifying.

"I've sinned in that area, too," she admitted, "but soon realized that literature for adults simply wasn't my métier. I don't have the patience. Somehow I do have the patience for children's books. It's a mystery to me in a way, since I don't especially care for children. I don't even have any. I'm divorced."

"Aha."

"At least I didn't ruin an innocent child's life."

We stood watching the rain. It began to taper off and looked as though it was coming through a sieve, straight and thin. Just as it seemed to be ending, it again increased and came down faster and with greater force. It pelted the asphalt with the arrogance of an element responsible to no one, oblivious of precedents. Steam rose from the pavement. The gushing water slithered off cars driving past. This brought to my mind a newspaper photograph I had seen during World War II—an Allied bomb had blown up a German dam. A passing car was being pursued by a wall of water. The photo was taken from an airplane in the fraction of a second before the driver was engulfed.

"Would you be so kind as to let me hold your hand?" she asked. I wanted to dry it first but there wasn't anything to use. When I gave her my hand, I felt hers was wet, too, but warmer than mine.

At that moment there was a streak of lightning, the likes of which I had never seen before. An enormous bolt lit up the sky, turning it into an otherworldly purplish red. It became day for an instant—sunset or sunrise. The thunder that followed immediately jolted the brain in my skull. We clasped each other's hand more tightly. "God in Heaven, what can we do?" the woman cried. She looked at me with fright, mixed with the hatred of someone who feels he must perish on account of another person's ill fortune.

Suddenly an old car pulled up, the kind plumbers or repairmen use, and a short man, wearing a raincoat but no hat, got out. Though he dashed under the awning, the few instants in the downpour got him drenched. He fished a key out of his pocket and in an Italian accent asked: "Are you folks waiting here for a taxi? You can wait all night."

"Do you live here?" the woman shouted. "Can you at least let us go inside for a while?"

"Come on in. I'm the night watchman here. You shouldn't be outside on a night like this."

"Oh, God Himself has sent you!"

He unlocked the door and we followed him in. I thought this must have been the way the animals had walked into

Noah's ark. Somewhere I read that Noah himself led the tame creatures, but the wild beasts came rushing in only after the flood had started. I even imagined I had once seen a picture of a lion pleading to be allowed onto the ark—a bedraggled, half-running, half-swimming beast.

For the second time in one day I found myself leaving puddles behind me in the lobby. My eyeglasses became fogged. Through the haze I heard the night watchman say: "You know what, folks. Come downstairs, I have a little room there. I'll make some tea for you and you can rest."

"You're a wonderful man," the woman said. "No one else but God could have sent you."

"Well, you just can't let people die."

We took the freight elevator to the cellar, where there were gas meters, red brick walls, and an uneven ceiling. On one side was an enormous furnace and next to it a coal bin. Trunks, folding beds, and all kinds of furniture belonging to tenants were stored in an alcove.

He ushered us into a small room which was like the dressing room of a shabby downtown theater. It contained a sofa covered with a torn spread and an armchair from which the stuffing was falling out. Spots of dried paint spattered the naked ceiling bulb. Faded photos of movie actresses as well as magazine and newspaper clippings hung from the walls. A teapot and a glass with a rusty tin spoon in it stood on a lopsided table.

I had removed my eyeglasses and could now clearly see our benefactor. He was slight, with short legs and a protruding belly. The man was no longer young and his hair was streaked with gray. His heavy-lidded eyes expressed a special Italian quality of good humor and friendliness. He seemed to be saying: "I know how you feel. We are all no more than flesh and blood." He lit the gas burner and filled the kettle with water. From a cupboard he brought tea bags, a sugar bowl, a package of crackers, and two teacups. The woman burst out laughing.

I removed my jacket and hat, sat down, and said to her: "There is some good left in the world."

"Yes, I'll never forget this as long as I live!"

We drank our tea, nibbled our crackers, and talked. Here we were in a dugout below the ground, the safest spot in a storm. The Italian had gone back upstairs to the lobby, but he promised to let us know as soon as the storm subsided.

I don't know how it began but the woman started to tell me all about her family, her ex-husband, how she had been penniless in New York and had gotten a job at the last moment. Her life, like my own, was peppered with miracles. Just as with the watchman tonight, so destiny, or whatever one calls it, had sent her a savior in every crisis: each time when the water came up to her neck, her guardian angel stood by her, as it were. "Isn't that strange? Why should fate continually play cat-and-mouse with a person? Why terrify and then make a last-minute rescue? It's simply that we explain every good coincidence as being a miracle and we blame all the adverse things on blind nature."

We talked of this and that. I asked: "How do you define coincidence? Of all the poorly defined words, this word is the most confusing."

"Coincidence is when things happen according to physical laws, but we interpret them as good or bad. For example: had that bolt of lightning struck us, it would simply have been because the electrical explosion had taken place a few yards closer than it actually had . . . "

"How do you know there isn't some knowing force that directed the lightning?" I asked.

"How can you prove there is?"

"If there is a knowing force in one part of the universe, then the entire universe can't be ruled by blind forces."

The night watchman came to tell us that it was still pouring, and as far as he could tell, it would continue this way all night. He stood there scratching his head and winking good-naturedly. I thought that he was about to come out with a joke, but after some hesitation he went back upstairs.

"We'll give him a little something," the woman suggested.

"I have it prepared already," I said.

"Why just you? Let's give him ten dollars. Five dollars from each of us."

We smiled and chatted. I was thinking that if there could be anything between us, this cellar was the most unusual place for it. But were we ready for it? I gazed at her, looking for those qualities and characteristics which might please me, but her face was too tense. She lacked that naïveté, those hints of exaltation which I am attracted to in women. I also knew that no woman had ever been attractive to me at first. In all my relationships I had to undertake a slow process of erasing the first impression, or at least overcoming it and correcting it. Behind the façade of ugliness or egotism was always hidden another face, or perhaps another façade. I tried to hasten the evaluation, to strip away the outer layer and catch a glimpse of what was beneath.

Meanwhile, I told her what little there was about myself. That is to say, she asked the questions and I willingly answered them. I even went so far as to mention Esther.

About two in the morning she rested her head on the back of the sofa and said she wanted to try to get some sleep. I made myself comfortable on the shabby chair, propping my feet up on a trunk, neither falling asleep nor being fully awake. I felt like someone dozing on a wagon and even imagined that the storeroom was moving. Real dreams were interwoven with daydreams. After years of sleeping alone, I again found myself sleeping near someone, not someone close, but not exactly a stranger, either. The glare of the light bulb shone through my closed eyelids. I had a fantastic thought which had nothing to do with my present circumstances. It occurred to me that if there were local spirits, ghosts bound up with a house, with a cemetery or a ruin, they would have to revolve with the earth on its axis, circle the sun, fly along with the sun on its course in the Milky Way, perhaps make the journey together with the galaxy in infinite space. That would mean that spirits also have gravity and motion and therefore also have weight and consequently mass. If this were so, they would have to be bound by all other physical laws. Then again, if spirits are not bound by physical laws, what keeps them on earth? Why shouldn't they fly off to other planets or even cross the boundaries of the cosmos?

These thoughts went through my mind again and again, with all sorts of variations, as if they were a leitmotif of a symphony. I had almost forgotten the woman who lay on the sofa, but not really. Actually, I was fully aware of her presence. Even the thoughts about the spirits were somehow related to her, though I didn't know what the connection was.

I shivered and turned over. When I awoke I felt drugged, as if I had taken a sleeping pill. The woman was seated near the table, her face and hair showing signs of sleep. She smiled at me.

"You slept very soundly," she said.

"And you?"

"Perhaps for a moment. I can't even sleep under perfect circumstances."

I sat without speaking. Then I heard myself say: "I don't even know your name."

"Didn't I introduce myself to you?"

"I didn't hear your name clearly."

"My name is a very banal one."

"A name is a name."

"But mine is already too banal. Perhaps you can give me a name?"

"Unless it's my name," I said, baffled by my foolishness. That was equivalent to a proposal.

The woman was serious for a moment, then she smiled sleepily, seeming astonished, yet tolerant of such nonsense. I recognized that quality of beauty which I had been looking for.

"What's your name?" she asked. I told her my name.

"No more original than mine."

She stood up, I also got up, just as we did at the party when both of us simultaneously decided to leave. For a while we looked at each other with the choked laughter of friends who meet at some strange place unexpectedly and, in their utter confusion, forget momentarily the other one's name and how and when they ever met. Suddenly we fell into each other's arms like lovers who had been waiting impatiently for an encounter. A midnight heat emanated from her body. We kissed as she passionately cried out words that no longer sounded to me like English, but like some unknown language. I pressed her with all my strength. I heard something cracking, not knowing whether it was her girdle or my fountain pen. I became alarmed but was unable to loosen my grip. It all lasted not longer than a minute. Then we both seemed to realize how ridiculous our behavior was. Both of us moved a step apart, utterly bewildered.

"What happened to us? Are we out of our minds?" she asked.

"There are no coincidences," I said hoarsely, my voice shaking.

The woman looked at me out of the corner of her eyes. "Did fate need all this to make us act like two idiots?"

Not for the Sabbath

THAT SABBATH AFTERNOON, the talk on the porch happened to be about teachers, tutors, and cheder boys. Our neighbor Chaya Riva complained that her grandchild got such a slap in the face from his teacher Michael that he lost a tooth. Michael had a reputation not only as an accomplished teacher but also as a big slapper and pincher. Cheder boys used to say that when he pinched, you saw the city of Krakow. He had a nickname—Scratch Me. If he felt an itch on his back, he gave his whipping stick to one of his pupils, with an order to scratch him under his shirt.

Two other women were sitting on our porch—Reitze Breindels and my Aunt Yentl, who wore a bonnet and a dress with arabesques in honor of the Sabbath. The bonnet had many beads and four ribbons—yellow, white, red, and green. I sat there and listened to the talk. Aunt Yentl began to smile and look around. She gave me a side glance. "Why do you sit among the women?" she asked. "Better go and study the *Ethics of the Fathers.*"

I understood that she was about to tell a story an eleven-year-old boy should not hear. I went behind the porch to the storage room, where we kept the Passover dishes, a barrel with torn books, and a pillowcase filled with my father's old manuscripts. The walls had wide cracks, and every word spoken on the porch could be heard. I sat on an oak mortar that was used to grind matzo meal. Through the cracks the sun reflected the colors of the rainbow in the floating dust. I heard my Aunt Yentl say, "In the little villages things are not so terrible yet. How many madmen can you find in a small town? Five or ten—not more. Besides, their crimes cannot be kept secret. But in a big city evil deeds can remain hidden for years. When I lived in Lublin, a man by the name of Reb Yissar Mandlebroit had a drygoods store that sold silk, velvet, and satin, as well as laces and accessories. His first wife died and he married a young wench, the daughter of a butcher. Her hair was the color of fire and she had the mouth of a shrew. From his first wife Reb Yissar had married children, but with this new one—her name was Dacha—he had only one, a boy named Yankele. He took after his mother in looks, with red sidelocks and blue shining eyes like little mirrors. In that family, Dacha was the boss. When an old man marries a young piece of flesh, she is the ruler.

"At cheder, Yankele had a teacher who should never have been allowed to teach. But how could people know? His name was Fivke. He was either divorced or a widower—a giant of a man, black like a gypsy. He wore a short robe and boots with high uppers, like a Russian. He wasn't from Lublin but from another region. He taught the Pentateuch, and also a little Russian and Polish. In those years, the wealthy Jews wanted their children to acquire some Gentile knowledge.

"First, let me tell you what happened to me. My former husband, blessed be his memory, was already a grandfather at the time we married, but his wife left him a young child, Chazkele, when she died, and I loved him more than I would have loved a child of my own. He called me Mama. Every day I took a bowl of hot soup and a slice of bread to the cheder for him. I went at two o'clock—recess time—when the children played in the courtyard. I sat with Chazkele on a log and fed him his lunch. He's a father now and lives far from here, but if I should meet him I'd want to kiss him all over. One day I came with my bowl of soup and the slice of bread, but the courtyard was empty. Only one little boy came out to urinate. I asked him, 'Where are all the boys?' He said, 'Today is whipping day.' I didn't understand. The door to the cheder was half open and I saw Fivke standing at a bench with a strap in his hand, calling out the boys to be whipped one after another—Berele, Schmerele, Koppele, Hershele. Each boy came over, pulled down his little pants, and was hit once or twice on his naked behind. Then he walked back to the long benches. The older boys laughed as if the whole thing was a game, but the very young ones burst out crying. That my heart did not break on the spot proved I was stronger than iron. I began to search for Chazkele among the children. The cruel teacher was so busy whipping he didn't see me. I had made up my mind that if he called Chazkele I would run over and throw the hot soup into his face and tear out his beard. However, it seemed my Chazkele had already been whipped, because the performance ended quickly.

"I ran to my husband's store like a poisoned rat and told him what my eyes had seen, but all he said was, 'Children should be punished once in a while.' He opened the Bible and showed me the passage in the Book of Proverbs: 'He that spareth his rod hateth his son.' The child did not make any fuss. He was a good soul and said, 'Mama, it did not hurt.' Still, I insisted that my husband take Chazkele away from those malicious hands. When a wife stands up to something, a man listens. Only God knew the tears I shed."

"What wild people live in this world," Reitze Breindels remarked.

"I would have called the police and had him bound in chains and sent to Siberia," Chaya Riva said. "Such a murderer should rot in prison."

"That's easier said than done," answered Aunt Yentl. "Why

didn't you have Michael Scratch Me arrested? To have a tooth knocked out is worse than being whipped."

"Yes, you are right."

"The story is only beginning," Aunt Yentl said in a singsong. "Yes, we took Chazkele out, and after the High Holidays he went to a different cheder. Not more than two or three months had passed before I heard a horrible story. The whole of Lublin was in turmoil. Fivke had his whipping day each month. Once when Dacha, Reb Yissar Mandlebroit's wife, brought lunch for her Yankele, she opened the door and saw her little treasure bent over the whipping bench being lashed by Fivke. The child was crying bitterly. Dacha did what I should have done—threw the hot soup into Fivke's face. Another person would have wiped off his mouth and kept silent. But Fivke had the nature of a Cossack. He let Yankele go, ran over to Dacha, and threw her onto the whipping bench. He had the strength of ten lions. Forgive me, but Fivke lifted her dress, tore down her bloomers, and whipped her with all his might. He used the belt from his pants, not the strap for the children. You can imagine the commotion. Dacha screamed as if he was slaughtering her. It's true that Lublin is a noisy city, but people heard her yelling, and they came to see what was going on. Her wig fell off and her red locks showed. This slut didn't shave her head. Some of the bystanders tried to hold Fivke back, but whoever tried got a kick with his boot. There happened to be only women there, and what female can fight such a brigand? He flogged Dacha thirty-nine times, as the beadles did in ancient days. Then he dragged her outside and threw her into the gutter."

"Father in Heaven, where do you find such an outlaw among Jews?" Reitze Breindels asked.

"There is no lack of filth anywhere," Chaya Riva said.

"Golden words," Aunt Yentl agreed. "If I tried to tell you what went on in Lublin that day, you wouldn't believe your ears. Dacha rushed home more dead than alive. Her howling could be heard all over the street. When Reb Yissar heard what had happened to his beloved wife, he ran to the rabbi immediately. There was talk about excommunication and black candles. Who has ever heard of a teacher thrashing a married woman and bringing her to such disgrace? The rabbi sent his sexton to Fivke and summoned him to a rabbinical trial, but Fivke stood at the door of his house with a cudgel and roared, 'If you want to take me by force, try!' He spoke nasty words about the rabbi, the elders, the whole community. Of course, he soon had to give up the cheder. Who would send a child to such a ruffian? Just talking about it makes me feel ants crawling up my spine."

"Maybe he was possessed by a dybbuk?" Chaya Riva asked.

Aunt Yentl put on her brass-rimmed glasses, took them off, and put them on her lap. She said, "Reb Yissar spoke to his wife: 'Dachele, what can I do? Since Fivke refuses to go to the rabbi, he will be humiliated in another way.' Dacha yelled, 'You are a coward! You're afraid of your own shadow—if you really loved me, you would take revenge on that criminal!' Just the same, she soon realized her husband was too old and weak to fight a savage like Fivke. She grabbed a handful of silver money from her strongbox and went to the place where the toughs and the riffraff met. She called out, 'Whoever wants to earn money, take a stick or a knife and come with me!' She tossed copper coins and showed the silver to the rabble. They rushed to pick up the coins, but only a few were willing to go with her. Even rogues avoid getting mixed up in a brawl. A boy who saw what went on ran to warn Fivke that men were out to get him. Fivke shouted, 'Let them try! I'm ready!' When the men approached, he took up an ax and challenged them. 'Come nearer and you will not walk back—they will have to carry you!' They got frightened. They could see in his eyes he was ready to chop off heads. They ran, and Dacha stood abandoned with her money. Fivke chased her with the ax. There was bedlam. Some women went to the chief of police for help, but he said, 'First let him kill her and then we will imprison him. We are not allowed to punish anyone before he commits the crime.'

"Since Fivke could not be a teacher any more and people ran from him like from a leper, he had nothing to do in Lublin. I guess you all know that there is a village called Piask not far from Lublin. In my time, the thieves of Piask were famous all over Poland. They would get up in the middle of the night, harness their horses, go to some town in their britskas, and rob the stores. A few were assigned to fight off the night watchmen. I'll make it short. Fivke went to Piask and became a teacher there. Bad as they were, the thieves wanted their boys to have some education. It wasn't easy for them to get a teacher, so they were happy when Fivke came. He took into his cheder only the children of the thieves. Sooner or later thieves are caught and put in jail, so there were always more women than men in those narrow streets. The storekeepers sold them merchandise on credit until their husbands were freed. They always paid back what they owed. Someone said that Fivke took the grass widows under his protection. He acted as a kind of healer—cupping them and applying leeches when they felt sick. He went to Lublin and came back with gifts he stole for them. My dear friends, not only did Fivke become a thief but a leader of the thieves—their rabbi. He went with them to fairs, and if there was a clash with the police Fivke was the first to fight back. As a rule, thieves don't carry guns—it's one thing to steal and another thing to shed blood—but Fivke got a pistol and became a horse thief. When peasants caught him stealing, he shot at them or set fire to their stables. In many places the villagers guarded their property all night with knives and rattles. Somehow he managed to escape them. If he was ever put to trial, he always got off. You know that judges and lawyers are on the side of the criminal. It isn't from the victims that they make a living. He was a smooth talker and disentangled himself every time. People began to tell wonders about him. Even if he was put into jail, he broke the bars in the middle of the night and ran away. Sometimes he released the other jailbirds."

"What happened then?" Chaya Riva asked.

"Wait. My throat is dry. I will bring some Sabbath fruit and prune juice."

I came out from the storage room and let Aunt Yentl treat me to a Sabbath cookie and a pear. She asked, "Where were you? Did you study the *Ethics of the Fathers?*"

I said, "I have finished this week's chapter."

"Go back to the study house," Aunt Yentl said. "Stories like these are not for you."

I returned to the storage room and Aunt Yentl continued: "Reb Yissar Mandlebroit grew old and could not longer attend to his business. Dacha, that blabbermouth, took over the whole trade. Her son, Yankele, studied with the rabbi. In the evenings, Dacha would come to our house for a chat. Whenever the talk rolled round to Fivke she would say, 'What do you think about my whipper?' This is how she referred to him. My mother, peace be with her, used to say, 'It's not worth talking about scum like him. There is fine flour and there is chaff.' But Dacha would smile and lick her lips. 'How could I have known that a teacher, a scholar could be so shameless?' She cursed him with all the curses of the book, yet at the same time she seemed to admire his prowess. When she left, my mother would say, 'If she wasn't Reb Yissar's wife I wouldn't let her through my door. She is proud that that monster abused her.' My mother forbade me to have anything to do with her.

"One day Reb Yissar died, and since Yankele was still a minor, Dacha became the guardian of the estate. At once, she dismissed her husband's employees and hired new ones. The former remained without bread, but this didn't bother her.

She bought a plot of ground where the nobles lived and had a house built, with two balconies and a gable. She bedecked herself in so much jewelry she could hardly be seen. She used perfume and all kinds of powders and pastes. Although the matchmakers flooded her with matches, she held off. She insisted on seeing every candidate and talking with him. This one was not a businessman, the next was not handsome, the third was not shrewd. It is written somewhere in the Bible that when a slave becomes a king the earth trembles.

"Now hear something. Not far from Lublin there is a village called Wawolic. This village is known for celebrating Purim two days—the fourteenth and the fifteenth of the month of Adar. People living there had found remnants of a wall supposedly built before the time of Moses. This wall made the village so special that Purim for them was a great holiday. Everyone got drunk. This created a perfect opportunity for the thieves of Piask. As it is on Purim, the moon was full. Late at night when everybody was asleep, they went with their wagons and quick horses to rob the stores. They did not know that the Russian Army was carrying out maneuvers in the area. It was not long after the Polish uprising; the authorities were keeping a lookout for rebels. As the thieves were on their way, a regiment of Cossacks was riding toward them, led by a colonel. When the thieves saw them, their stomachs dropped. The Russians asked where they were going, and Fivke, who knew Russian, said they were a group of merchants going to a fair. But the colonel was no fool—he knew there was no fair in the neighborhood. He gave an order to put the thieves in chains and carry them to jail in Lublin. Fivke dared to resist, but no one can beat Cossacks who have guns and lances. He was bound like a ram and taken to prison. There were fences in Lublin who bought stolen goods, and they were waiting for the thieves to come with their loot. But when the sun rose and the wagons were not there the fences guessed what had happened and dispersed like mice. Soon the bad tidings reached the wives of the thieves in Piask. Never before had so many thieves been arrested at one time, and while there was Purim in Wawolic it was Tishah-b'Ab in Piask. As if this was not enough, one old and sickly thief could not hold up under the beatings and informed against the fences. They, too, were imprisoned. Some of them were quite rich and considered important members of the community. They were all disgraced, along with their families. When the peasants heard that Fivke was in chains, they came in large numbers to bear witness against him, and there was talk of Fivke's being hanged.

"During that time I happened to need lace for a dress and went to Dacha's store. She had stopped coming to us after my mother passed away. However, one could get the best merchandise from her. I went into the store and she was sitting behind the counter, her red hair uncovered, dressed like a countess. She pretended not to know me. I said to her, 'Dacha, you have lived to see your revenge.' With an angry look she answered, 'Revenge is not a Jewish trait,' and turned away. I wanted to ask her when she had become so steeped in Jewishness, but since she played the great lady I let her go. A clerk gave me what I wanted. Outside, I met an acquaintance and told her how high and mighty Dacha had become. She said to me, 'Yentl, have you been asleep or something? Don't you know what's going on?' She told me that Dacha had become a benefactress. She went to Piask and took bread and cheese to the wives of the thieves, and anything else they needed. She left the store for hours and got chummy with the wives of the fences. My dear, she had fallen in love with that Fivke—'my whipper,' as she called him—and was determined to save him. The woman told me she had hired the best lawyer in Lublin. I didn't know whether to laugh or cry. How could this be? Really, I'm afraid it's not right to tell a story like this on the Sabbath."

"Did she save him?" Reitze Breindels asked.

"She married him," Aunt Yentl said.

It was quiet for some time, and then Chaya Riva asked, "How did she get him out?"

Aunt Yentl put two fingers to her lips and thought it over. "The truth is that no one ever knew for sure," she said. "Such things are done stealthily. I heard that she gave a large sum to the governor, and herself in addition. You can believe anything about a bitch like that. Someone saw her enter the governor's palace dressed up to kill. She stayed maybe three hours. They certainly didn't chant psalms. The only thing I know is that the governor freed all the thieves except two, who remained in prison for some time. I was told that Dacha waited for Fivke at the gate of the jail, and when he came out she fell on him, kissed him, and cried. The hoodlums from Lublin who were present called her names and made catcalls at her.

"Yes, they married, but they waited a few months. He had shaved his beard and wore Gentile clothing. He sold his house in Piask and lived with Dacha in her new house. Yankele refused to stay with his mother and stepfather, and he moved to a yeshiva. Those who saw how Fivke became a merchant overnight didn't need to go to the theater. He knew as much about the drygoods business as I know Turkish. If Reb Yissar Mandlebroit could see what happened to his fortune, he would turn over in his grave.

"In the beginning it seemed that everything was fine between the pair. She called him Fivkele and he called her Dachele. They ate from one plate. Because they were rich they became greedy for prestige. He bought himself a pew in the synagogue at the eastern wall, and she at the grate in the women's section. The truth was that they only went to pray on High Holidays. She could not read and he said openly that he was a disbeliever. She wanted to join some charity circle, but the women would not allow it. The couple got nicknames: the Whipper and the Whippress. When it became clear to them that they would not get honors from the Jews, they began to cater to the Gentiles. The Polish squires shunned them just as had the Jews, so they turned to the Russians. When you give Ivan tasty food and plenty of vodka, he melts like wax. Officers and policemen visited the pair constantly. In the evening, they made *vetcherinkas* for the Russians—played cards with them, and got drunk. Dacha became so deeply involved in these lecherous parties that she began to neglect the store. Reb Yissar Mandlebroit's clerks were all honest, but Dacha had chosen swindlers for her assistants.

"As long as there was no competition, the store kept up. Then another drygoods store opened a half block from Dacha's store. The owner was Zelig from Bechow—a little man, a stranger in Lublin. He specialized in buying goods from bankruptcies. He did well from the very first day, and to the degree he succeeded Dacha and Fivke went down. It was like a curse from a holy man. Fivke threatened to burn the new store, but it was so close to his own that a fire would have consumed both. He could have killed Zelig or crippled him, but if Providence says no, it's no. Small and frail as this Zelig was, he was afraid of no one. He didn't walk; he ran like a weasel. He could scream louder than Fivke and Dacha together. He also bribed the *nachalniks*. He hired the clerks Dacha dismissed, and they divulged all her trade secrets to him. Zelig's wife was a quiet dove and seldom came to the store. She stayed home and bore one child after another. People expected Dacha to have children with Fivke, but no child was born. Only Yankele remained to her. He married someone in Lithuania and didn't even invite his mother to the wedding. I forgot to mention that Fivke became exceedingly fat. He got a big belly, and a red nose with the broken veins of a drunkard.

"One morning when Dacha's clerks came to open the store, they found the doors ajar. The thieves of Piask had come in the middle of the night and emptied all the shelves—the same thieves Dacha had saved from prison and whose wives Fivke once played with. When things begin to go bad, there's no limit. Fivke roared that he would murder them all, but he could do nothing. There is a hidden power in every human being and when this is gone the strong become weak and the proud humble. It is written somewhere in a holy book that each animal has its time. When the fox is king, the lion must bow to him."

"What happened then?" Chaya Riva asked.

"It's not for the Sabbath. I don't want to defile my mouth."

"Tell it, Yentl. Don't keep us in suspense."

"She became a whore. The Russians came to her. Fivke was the procurer. When the Poles learned what was going on, they set fire to her house. If there was fire insurance in those times, Dacha didn't have any. They lost their store, their home. They moved to a suburb close to the barracks, and their apartment became a whorehouse. I will tell you about their terrible end another time."

"What happened?"

"Not on the Sabbath."

"Yentl, I won't sleep the whole night." Chaya Riva raised her voice.

Aunt Yentl grimaced and she spat into a handkerchief. "He whipped her, and she died from his whipping."

"Someone saw it?"

"No one. Early one morning he came running to the burial society, crying that his wife had suddenly collapsed and died. The society women went to their house and the corpse was taken to the cleansing hut. When they put her on the cleansing board and saw her naked body, there was a hue and a cry. She was swollen and covered with welts. Women from the burial society are not softhearted; still, one of them fainted dead away."

"Wasn't Fivke arrested?"

"He hanged himself. Both of them were buried in the middle of the night behind the fence."

It became quiet. Aunt Yentl touched the tip of her bonnet. "I told you it was not for the Sabbath."

"What was the sense of it?" Reitze Breindels asked.

"No sense."

I had come out from the storage room, but Aunt Yentl didn't notice me. She began to murmur and look up to the sky. "The sun is setting," she said. "It's time to recite 'God of Abraham.'"

The Safe Deposit

SOME FIVE YEARS BACK, when Professor Uri Zalkind left New York for Miami after his wife Lotte's death, he had decided never to return to this wild city. Lotte's long sickness had broken his spirit. His health, too, it seemed. Not long after he buried her, he fell sick with double pneumonia and an obstruction of the kidneys. He had been living and teaching philosophy in New York for almost thirty years, but he still felt like a stranger in America. The German Jews did not forgive him for having been raised in Poland, the son of some Galician rabbi, and speaking German with an accent. Lotte herself, who was German, called him *Ostjude* when she quarreled with him. To the Russian and Polish Jews he was a German, since, besides being married to a German, for many years he had lived in Germany. He might have made friends with American members of the faculty or with his students, but there was little interest in philosophy at the university, and in Jewish philosophy in particular. He and Lotte had no children. Through the first years they still had relatives in America, but most of the old ones had died and he never kept in touch with the younger generation. Just the same, this winter morning Dr. Uri Zalkind had taken a plane to New York—a man over eighty, small, frail, with a bent back, a little white beard, and bushy eyebrows that retained a trace of having once been red. Behind thick-lensed glasses, his eyes were gray, permanently inflamed. It was a bad day to have come to New York. The pilot had announced that there was a blizzard in the city, with gusting winds. A dark cloud covered the area, and in the last minutes before landing at LaGuardia an ominous silence settled over the passengers. They avoided looking one another in the eye, as if ashamed beforehand of the panic that might soon break out. Whatever happens, I have rightly deserved it, Dr. Zalkind thought. His Miami Beach neighbors in the senior-citizens apartment complex had warned him that flying in such weather was suicide. And for what was he risking his life? For the manuscript of a book no one would read except possibly a few reviewers. He was glad that he carried no other luggage than his briefcase. He raised the fur collar of the long coat he had brought with him from Germany, and clutching his case in his right hand and holding on to his broad-brimmed hat with his left, he went out of the terminal to look for a taxi. From sitting three hours in one position his legs had become numb. Snow fell at an angle, dry as sand. The wind was icy. Although he had made a firm decision that morning to forget nothing, Professor Zalkind now realized that he had left his muffler and rubbers at home. He had planned to put on his woolen sweater in the plane and this he had forgotten, too. By the time a taxi finally stopped for him, he could not tell the driver the address of the bank to which he wanted to go. He remembered only that it was on Fifty-seventh Street between Eighth Avenue and Broadway.

Professor Zalkind had more than one reason for undertaking this journey. First, the editor of the university press that was to publish his book, *Philo Judaeus and the Cabala*, had called to tell him that he would be visiting New York in the next few days. According to the contract, Professor Zalkind was to have delivered the manuscript some two years ago. Because he had added a number of footnotes and made many alterations in the text, he decided he should meet with the editor personally rather than send the manuscript by mail. Second, he wanted to see Hilda, the only living cousin of his late wife. He hadn't seen her for five years, and her daughter had written to him that her mother was seriously ill. Third, Professor Zalkind had read in the Miami *Herald* that last Saturday thieves had broken into a bank in New York and by boring a hole in the steel door leading to the vault they had stolen everything they could. True, this theft had not occurred in the bank where Zalkind rented a safe-deposit box. Still, the news item, headlined "How Safe Is a Safe?," disturbed him to such a degree that he could not sleep the whole night after he read it. In his box were deposited Lotte's jewelry, his will, and a number of important letters, as well as a manuscript of essays on metaphysics he had written when he was young—a work he would never dare publish while he was alive but one he did not want to lose. In addition to the safe-deposit box, he had in the same bank a savings account of some seventeen thousand dollars, which he intended to withdraw and deposit in Miami. It was not that he needed money. He had a pension from his years of teaching at the university. He had been receiving a Social Security check each month since he became seventy-two; regularly, reparation money came from Germany, which he had escaped after Hitler came to power. But why keep his belongings in New York now that he was a resident of Florida?

Another motive—perhaps the most important—brought the old man to New York. For many years he had suffered from prostate trouble, and the doctors he consulted had all advised him to have an operation. Procrastination could be fatal, they told him. He had made up his mind to visit a urologist in New York—a physician from Germany, a refugee like himself.

After crawling in traffic for a long time, the taxi stopped at Eighth Avenue and Fifty-seventh Street. No matter how Professor Zalkind tried, he couldn't read the meter. Lately, the retinas of his eyes had begun to degenerate and he could read only with a large magnifying glass. Assuming that he would get change, he handed the driver a ten-dollar bill, but the driver complained that it was not enough. Zalkind gave him two dollars more. The blizzard was getting worse. The afternoon was as dark as dusk. The moment Zalkind opened the door of the taxi, snow hit his face like hail. He struggled against the wind until he reached Seventh Avenue. There was no sign of his bank. He continued as far east as Fifth. A new building was being constructed. Was it possible that they had torn down the bank without letting him know? In the midst of the storm, motors roared, trucks and cars honked. He wanted to ask the construction workers where the bank had moved, but in the clang and clamor no one would hear his voice. The words in the Book of Job came to his mind: "He shall return no more to his house, neither shall his place know him any more."

Now Zalkind had come to a public telephone, and somehow he got out a dime and dialed Hilda's number. He heard the voice of a stranger, and could not make out what was being said to him. Well, everything is topsy-turvy with me today, he thought. Presently it occurred to him that he had looked only on one side of the street, sure that the bank was there. Perhaps he was mistaken? He tried to cross the street, but his glasses had become opaque and he couldn't be sure of traffic-light colors. He finally made it across, and after a while he saw a bank that resembled his, though it had a different name. He entered. There was not a single customer in the place. Tellers sat idly behind the little windows. A guard in uniform approached him and Zalkind asked him if this was indeed his bank. At first the guard didn't seem to understand his accent. Then he said it was the same bank—it had merged with another one and the name had been changed.

"How did it come that you didn't let me know?"

"Notices went out to all our depositors."

"Thank you, thank you. Really, I began to think I was getting senile," Dr. Zalkind said to the guard and himself. "What about the safe-deposit boxes?"

"They are where they were."

"I have a savings account in this bank, and a lot of interest must have accumulated in the years I've been away. I want to withdraw it."

"As you wish."

Dr. Zalkind approached a counter and began to search for his bankbook. He remembered positively that he had brought it with him in one of the breast pockets of his jacket. He emptied both and found everything except his bankbook—his Social Security card, his airplane ticket, old letters, notebooks, a telephone bill, even a leaflet advertising a dancing school which had been handed to him on the street. "Am I insane?" Dr. Zalkind asked himself. "Are the demons after me? Maybe I put it into my case. But where is my case?" He glanced right and left, on the counter and under it. There was no trace of a briefcase. "I have left it in the telephone booth!" he said with a tremor in his voice. "My manuscript too!" The bank suddenly became dark, and a golden eye lit up on a black background—otherworldly, dreamily radiant, its edges jagged, a blemish in the pupil, like the eye of some cosmic embryo in the process of formation. This vision baffled him, and for some time he forgot his briefcase. He watched the mysterious eye growing both in size and in luminosity. What he saw now was not altogether new to him. As a child, he had seen similar entities—sometimes an eye, other times a fiery flower that opened its petals or a dazzling butterfly or some unearthly snake. Those apparitions always came to him at times of distress, as when he was whipped in cheder, was attacked by some vicious urchin, or was sick with fever. Perhaps those hallucinations were incompatible forms that the soul created without any pattern in the Ideas, Professor Zalkind pondered in Platonic terms. He leaned on the counter in order not to fall. I'm not going to faint, he ordered himself. His belly had become bloated and a mixture of a belch and a hiccup came from his mouth. This is my end!

Dr. Zalkind opened the outside door of the bank with difficulty, determined to find the telephone booth. He looked around, but no telephone booth was in sight. He choked from the blast of the wind. In all his anguish his brain remained playful. Is the North Pole visiting New York? Has the Ice Age returned? Is the sun being extinguished? Dr. Zalkind had often seen blind men crossing the streets of New York without a guide, waving a white stick. He could never understand where they acquired the courage for this. The wind pushed him back, blew up the skirts of his coat, tore at his hat. No, I can't go looking for the phantom of a telephone booth in this hurricane. He dragged himself back to the bank, where he searched again for his briefcase on the counters and floor. He had no copy of the manuscript, just a pile of papers written in longhand—actually, not more than notes. He saw a bench and collapsed onto it. He sat silent, ready for death, which, according to Philo, redeems the soul from the prison of the flesh, from the vagaries of the senses. Although Zalkind had read everything Philo wrote, he could never conclude from his writings whether matter was created by God or always existed—a primeval chaos, the negative principle of the Godhead. Dr. Zalkind found contradictions in Philo's philosophy and puzzles no mind could solve as long as it was chained in the errors of corporality. "Well, I may soon see the truth," he murmured. For a while he dozed and even began to dream. He woke with a start.

The guard was bending over him. "Is something wrong? Can I help?"

"Oh, I had a briefcase with me and I lost it. My bankbook was there."

"Your bankbook? You can get another one. No one can

take out your money without your signature. Where did you lose it? In a taxi?"

"Perhaps."

"All you have to do is notify the bank that you lost the bankbook and after thirty days they will give you another one."

"I would like to go to the safe-deposit boxes."

"I'll take you in the elevator."

The guard helped Dr. Zalkind get up. He half led him, half pushed him to the elevator and pressed the button to the basement. There, in spite of his confusion, Professor Zalkind recognized the clerk who sat in front of the entrance to the safe-deposit boxes. His hair had turned gray, but his face remained young and ruddy. The man also recognized Zalkind. He clapped his hands and called, "Professor Zalkind, whom do I see! We already thought that . . . you were sick or something?"

"Yes, no."

"Let me get the figures on your account," the clerk said. He went into another room. Zalkind heard his name mentioned on the telephone.

"Everything is all right," the clerk said when he returned. "What you owe us is more than covered by the interest in your account." He gave Zalkind a slip to sign. It took some time. His hand shook like that of a person suffering from Parkinson's disease. The clerk stamped the slip and nodded. "You don't live in New York any more?"

"No, in Miami."

"What is your new address?"

Dr. Zalkind wanted to answer, but he had forgotten both the street and the number. The heavy door opened and he gave the slip to another clerk, who led him into the room holding the safe-deposit boxes. Zalkind's box was in the middle row. The clerk motioned with his hand. "Your key."

"My key?"

"Yes, your key, to open the box."

Only now did it occur to Dr. Zalkind that one needed a key to get into a safe-deposit box. He searched through his pockets and took out a chain of keys, but he was sure they were all from Miami. He stood there perplexed. "I'm sorry, I haven't the key to my box."

"You do have it. Give me those keys!" The man grabbed the key chain and showed Professor Zalkind one that was larger than the others. He had been carrying a key to his safe-deposit box with him all those years, not knowing what it was for. The clerk pulled out a metal box and led Zalkind into a long corridor, opened a door to a room without a window, and turned on the light. He put the box on the table and showed Zalkind a switch on the wall to use when he had finished.

After some fumbling, Zalkind managed to open the box. He sat and gaped. Time had turned him sick, defeated, but for these objects in the box it did not exist. They had lain there for years without consciousness, without any need—dead matter, unless the animists were correct in considering all substance alive. To Einstein, mass was condensed energy. Could it perhaps also be condensed spirit? Though Professor Zalkind had packed his magnifying glass in his briefcase, he recognized stacks of Lotte's love letters tied with ribbons, his diary, and his youthful manuscript with the title "Philosophical Fantasies"—a collection of essays, feuilletons, and aphorisms.

After a while he lifted out Lotte's jewelry. He never knew that she possessed so many trinkets. There were bracelets, rings, earrings, brooches, chains, a string of pearls. She had inherited all this from her mother, her grandmothers, perhaps her great-grandmothers. It was probably worth a fortune, but what would he do with money at this stage? He sat there and took stock of his life. Lotte had craved children, but he had refused to increase the misery of the human species and Jewish troubles, he had said. She wanted to travel with him. He deprived her of this, too. "What is there to see?" he would ask her. "In what way is a high mountain more significant than a low hill? How is the ocean a greater wonder than a pond?" Even though Dr. Zalkind had doubts about Philo's philosophy and was sometimes inclined toward Spinoza's pantheism or David Hume's skepticism, he had accepted Philo's disdain for the deceptions of flesh and blood. He had come to New York with the decision to take all these things back with him to Miami. Yet, how could he carry them now that he had no briefcase? And what difference did it make where they were kept?

How strange. On the way to the airport that morning, Zalkind still had some ambitions. He planned to make final corrections on his manuscripts. He toyed with the idea of looking over "Philosophical Fantasies" to see what might be done with it. He had sworn to himself to make an appointment with the urologist the very next day. Now he was overcome by fatigue and had to lean his forehead on the table. He fell asleep and found himself in a temple, with columns, vases, sculptures, marble staircases. Was this Athens? Rome? Alexandria? A tall man with a white beard, dressed in a toga and sandals, emerged. He carried a scroll. He recited a poem or a sermon. Was the language Greek? Latin? No, it was Hebrew, written by a scribe.

"Peace unto you, Philo Judaeus, my father and master," Dr. Zalkind said.

"Peace unto you, my disciple Uri, son of Yedidyah."

"Rabbi, I want to know the truth!"

"Here in the Book of Genesis is the source of all truth: 'In the beginning God created the heaven and the earth. And the earth was without form, and void; and darkness was upon the face of the deep. And the Spirit of God moved upon the face of the waters.' "

Philo intoned the words like a reader in the synagogue. Other old men entered, with white hair and white beards, wearing white robes and holding parchments. They were all there—the Stoics, the Gnostics, Plotinus. Uri had read that Philo was not well versed in the Holy Tongue. What a lie! Each word from his lips revealed secrets of the Torah. He quoted from the Talmud, the Book of Creation, the Zohar, Rabbi Moshe from Córdoba, Rabbi Isaac Luria. How could this be? Had the Messiah come? Had the Resurrection taken place? Had the earth ascended to Heaven? Had Metatron descended to the earth? The figures and statues were not of stone but living women with naked breasts and hair down to their loins. Lotte was among them. She was also Hilda. One female with two bodies? One body with two souls?

"Uri, my beloved, I have longed for you!" she cried out. "Idolators wanted to defile me, but I swore to be faithful."

In the middle of the temple there was a bed covered with rugs and pillows; a ladder was suspended alongside it. Uri was about to climb up when a stream of water burst through the gate of the temple. Had Yahweh broken his covenant and sent a flood upon the earth?

Uri Zalkind woke up with a start. He opened his eyes and saw the bank clerk shaking his shoulder. "Professor Zalkind, your briefcase has been found. A woman brought it. She opened it and on top there was your bankbook."

"I understand."

"Are you sick?" the clerk asked. He pointed to a wet spot on the floor.

It took a long while before Dr. Zalkind answered. "I'm kaput, that's all."

"It's five minutes to three. The bank will be closing."

"I will soon go."

"The woman with the briefcase is upstairs." The clerk went out, leaving the door half open.

For a minute, Dr. Zalkind sat still, numbed by his own indifference. His briefcase was found but he felt no joy. Beside the box, Lotte's jewelry shimmered, reflecting the colors of the rainbow. Suddenly Dr. Zalkind began to fill his coat pockets with the jewels. It was the spontaneous act of a cheder boy. A passage from the Pentateuch came into his mind: "Behold, I am at the point to die: and what profit shall this birthright do to me?" Zalkind even repeated Esau's words with the teacher's intonation.

The clerk came in with a woman who carried a wet mop and a pail. "Should I call an ambulance?" he asked.

"An ambulance? No."

Zalkind followed the clerk, who motioned for the key. It was underneath Lotte's jewelry, and Zalkind had to make an effort to pull it out. The clerk took him up in the elevator, and there was the woman with his briefcase—small, darkish, in a black fur hat and a mangy coat. When she saw Zalkind, her eyes lit up.

"Professor Zalkind! I went to make a telephone call and saw your briefcase. I opened it and there with your papers was your bankbook. Since you use this bank, I thought they would know your address. And here you are." The woman spoke English with a foreign accent.

"Oh, you're an honest person. I thank you with all my heart."

"Why am I so honest? There is no cash here. If I had found a million dollars, the *Yetzer Hora* might have tempted me." She pronounced the Hebrew words as they did in Poland.

"It's terrible outside. Maybe you should take him somewhere," the guard suggested to the woman.

"Where do you live? Where is your hotel?" she asked. "I heard that you just arrived from Miami. What a time to come from Florida in your condition. You may, God forbid, catch the worst kind of cold."

"I thank you. I thank you. I have no hotel. I had planned to stay over with the cousin of my late wife, but it seems her telephone is out of order."

"I will take you to my own place for the time being. I live on 106th and Amsterdam. It is quite far from here, but if we get a taxi it won't be long. My dentist moved to this neighborhood and that is why I'm here."

One of the bank employees came over and asked, "Should I try to get a taxi for you?"

Even though it wasn't clear whom he addressed, Zalkind replied, "Yes—I really don't know how to express my gratitude."

Other clerks came over with offers of help, but Zalkind noticed that they winked at one another. The outside door opened and one of them called, "Your taxi!"

The snow had stopped, but it had got colder. The woman took Zalkind's arm and helped him into the taxi. She got in after him and said, "My name is Esther Sephardi. You can call me Esther."

"Are you a Sephardi?"

"No, a Jewish daughter from Lodz. My husband's surname was Sephardi. He was also from Lodz. He died two years ago."

"Do you have children?"

"One daughter in college. Why did you come in such a weather to New York?"

Dr. Zalkind didn't know where to begin.

"You don't need to answer," the woman said. "You live alone, huh? No wife would allow her husband to go to New York on a day like this. You won't believe me, in frost worse than this I stood in a forest in Kazakhstan and sawed logs. That's where the Russians sent us in 1941. We had to build our own barracks. Those who couldn't make it died, and those who were destined to live lived. I took your briefcase with me to the Automat to get a cup of coffee and I looked into your papers. Is this going to be a book?"

"Perhaps."

"Are you a professor?"

"I was."

"My daughter studies philosophy. Not exactly philosophy but psychology. What does one need so much psychology for? I wanted her to study for a doctor but nowadays children do what they want, not what their mother tells them. For twenty years I was a bookkeeper in a big firm. Then I got sick and had to have a hysterectomy. Dr. Zalkind, I don't like to give you advice, but what you have should not be neglected. An uncle of mine had it and he delayed until it was too late."

"It's too late for me, too."

"How do you know? Did you have tests made?"

The taxi stopped in a half-dark street, with cars buried under piles of snow. Dr. Zalkind managed to get a few bills from his purse and gave them to Esther. "I don't see so well. Be so good—pay him and give him a tip."

The woman took Zalkind's hand and led him up three flights of stairs. Until now, Professor Zalkind had believed that his heart was in order, but something must have happened—after one flight he was short of breath. Esther opened a door and led him into a narrow corridor, and from there into a shabby living room. She said, "We used to be quite wealthy, but first my husband got sick with cancer and then I got sick. I'm working as a cashier during the day in a movie theater. Wait, let me take off your coat." She weighed it in her hands, glanced at the bulging pockets, and asked, "What do you have there—stones?"

After some haggling she took off his shirt and pants as well. He tried to resist, but she said, "When you are sick, you can't be bashful. Where is the shame? We are all made from the same dough."

She filled the bathtub with hot water and brought him clean underwear and a robe that must have been her late husband's. Then she made tea in the kitchen and warmed up soup from a can. Professor Zalkind had forgotten that he had had nothing to eat or drink since breakfast. As she served him, Esther kept on talking about her years in Lodz, in Russia, in New York. Her father had been a rich man, a partner in a textile factory, but the Poles had ruined him with their high taxes. He grew so distraught that he got consumption and died. Her mother lived a few years more and she, too, passed away. In Russia Esther became sick with typhoid fever and anemia. She worked in a factory where the pay was so low that one had to steal or starve. Her husband was taken away by the NKVD, and for years she didn't know if he had been killed in a slave-labor camp. When they finally reunited, they had to wait two years in Germany in a DP camp for visas to America. "What we went through in all those years only God the merciful knows."

For a moment, Professor Zalkind was inclined to tell her that even though God was omniscient, the well of goodness, one could not ascribe any attribute to Him. He did not provide for mankind directly but through Wisdom, called Logos by the Greeks. But there was no use discussing metaphysics with this woman.

After he had eaten, Dr. Zalkind could no longer fight off his weariness. He yawned; his eyes became watery. His head kept dropping to his chest. Esther said, "I will make you a bed on the sofa. It's not comfortable, but when you are tired you can sleep on rocks. Ask me."

"I will never be able to repay you for your kindness."

"We are all human beings."

Dr. Zalkind saw with half-closed eyes how she spread a sheet over the sofa, brought in a pillow, a blanket, pajamas. "I hope I don't wet the bed," he prayed to the powers that have the say over the body and its needs. He went into the bathroom and saw himself in a mirror for the first time that day. In one day his face had become yellow, wrinkled. Even his white beard seemed shrunken. When he returned to the living room, he remembered Hilda and asked Esther to call her. Esther learned from an answering service that Hilda had gone into a hospital the day before. "Well, everything falls to pieces," Zalkind said to himself. He noticed a salt shaker that Esther had neglected to take from the table, and while she lingered in the bathroom he put some of the salt on his palm and swallowed it, since salt retains water in the body. She returned in a house robe and slippers. She's not so young any more, he thought appraisingly, but still an attractive female; in spite of his maladies he had not lost his manhood.

The instant he lay down on the sofa he fell into a deep sleep. This is how he used to pass out as a boy on Passover night after the four goblets of wine. He awoke in the middle of the night with an urgent need to urinate. Thank God, the sheet was dry. The room was completely dark; the window shades were down. He groped like a blind man, bumping into a chest, a chair, an open door. Did it lead to the bathroom? No, he touched a headboard of a bed and could hear someone breathing. He was overcome with fear. His hostess might suspect him of dishonorable intentions. Eventually, he found the bathroom. He wanted light but he could not find the switch. On the way back, in the corridor, he accidentally touched the switch and turned on the light. He saw his briefcase propped against the wall, his coat hanging on a clothes tree. Yes, Lotte's jewelry was still there. He had fallen into honest hands. It had become cold during the night, and he put the coat on his shoulders over his pajamas and took the briefcase with him in order to place the jewelry in it. He had to smile—he looked as if he were going on a journey. I will give it to this goodhearted woman, he resolved. At least a part of it. I have no more need for worldly possessions. If some part of Lotte's mind still exists, she will forgive me. Suddenly his head became compressed with heat and he fell. He could hear his body thud against the floor. Then everything was still.

Professor Zalkind opened his eyes. He was lying on a bed with metal bars on both sides. Above the bed a small lamp glimmered. He stared in the semi-darkness, waiting for his memory to return. An ice bag rested on his forehead. His belly was bandaged and his hand touched a catheter. "Am I still alive?" he asked himself. "Or is it already the hereafter?" He felt like laughing, but he was too sore inside. In an instant everything he had gone through on this trip came back to him. Had it been today? Yesterday? Days before? It did not matter. Although he was aching, he felt a rest he had never known before—the sublime enjoyment of fearing nothing, having no wish, no worry, no resentment. This state of mind was not of this world and he listened to it. It was both astoundingly simple and beyond anything language could convey. He was granted the revelation he yearned for—the freedom to look into the innermost secret of being, to see behind the curtain of phenomena, where all questions are answered, all riddles solved. "If I could only convey the truth to those who suffer and doubt!"

A figure slid through the half-opened door like a shadow— the woman who had found the briefcase. She bent over his bed and asked, "You have wakened, huh?"

He did not answer and she said, "Thank God, the worst is over. You will soon be a new man."

The Betrayer of Israel

WHAT COULD BE BETTER than to stand on a balcony and be able to see all of Krochmalna Street (the part where the Jews lived) from Gnoyna to Ciepla and even farther, to Iron Street, where there were trolley cars! A day never passed, not even an hour, when something did not happen. One moment a thief was caught and then Itcha Meyer, the drunkard—the husband of Esther from the candy store—became wild and danced in the middle of the gutter. Someone got sick and an ambulance was called. A fire broke out in a house and the firemen, wearing brass hats and high rubber boots, came with their galloping horses. I stood on the balcony that summer afternoon in my long gaberdine, a velvet cap over my red hair, with two disheveled sidelocks, waiting for something more to happen. Meanwhile, I observed the stores across the street, their customers, and also the Square, which teamed with pickpockets, loose girls, and vendors running a lottery. You pulled a number from a bag, and if good luck was with you, you could win three colored pencils, or a rooster made of sugar with a comb of chocolate, or a cardboard clown that shook his arms and legs if you pulled a string. Once a Chinaman with a pigtail passed the street. In an instant it became black with people. Another time a dark-skinned man appeared in a red turban with a tassel, wearing a cloak that resembled a prayer shawl, with sandals on his bare feet. I learned later that he was a Jew from Persia, from the town of Shushan—the ancient capital where King Ahasuerus, Queen Esther, and the wicked Haman lived. Since I was the rabbi's boy, everybody on the street knew me. When you stand on a balcony you are afraid of no one. You are like a general. When an enemy of mine passed I could spit on his cap and all he could do was shake a fist and call me names. Even the policeman didn't look so tall and mighty from above. Flies with violet bellies, bees and butterflies landed on the rail of the balcony. I tried to catch them or I just admired them. How did they manage to fly to Krochmalna Street, and where did they get their flamboyant colors? I had tried to read an article about Darwin in the Yiddish newspaper but I hardly understood it.

Suddenly a tumult broke out again. Two policemen were leading a little man, and screaming women ran after him. To my amazement, they all entered our gate. I could barely believe it: the policemen led this little man to our home, into my father's courtroom. He was accompanied by Shmuel Smetena, an unofficial lawyer, a crony of both the thieves and the police. Shmuel knew Russian and often served the Jews of the Street as an interpreter between them and the authorities. I soon discovered what had happened. That little man, Koppel Mitzner, a peddler of old clothes, was the husband of four wives. One lived on Krochmalna Street, one on Smocza Street, one on Praga, and one on Wola. It took quite a while for my father to orient himself to the situation. The senior policeman, with a golden insignia on his cap, explained that Koppel Mitzner had not married the women legally, with a license from the magistrate, but only according to Jewish law. The government could hardly prosecute him since the women had only Jewish marriage contracts, not Russian certificates. Koppel Mitzner contended that they were not his wives but his lovers. On the other hand, the officials could not allow him to break the law without punishment. So the head of the police had ordered the culprit brought to the rabbi. How strange that I, a mere boy, caught on to all these complications more quickly than my father. He was busy with his volumes of the Talmud and commentaries when Koppel, his wives, and the whole crowd of curious men and women burst into our apartment. Some of them laughed, others rebuked Koppel. My father, a small man, frail, wearing a long robe and with a velvet skull cap above his high forehead, his eyes blue, and his beard red, reluctantly put away pen and paper on his lectern. He sat down at the head of the table and asked others to be seated. Some sat on chairs, others on a long bench along the wall, which was lined to the ceiling with books. Between the windows stood the Ark of the holy scrolls with its gilded cornice, on which two lions held the tablets with the Ten Commandments between their curled tongues.

I listened to every word and observed each face. Koppel Mitzner, as small as a cheder boy, skin and bones, had a narrow face, a long nose, and a pointed Adam's apple. On his tiny chin grew a sparse little beard the color of straw. He wore a checked jacket and a shirt which closed at the collar with an ornate brass button. He had no lips, only a crevice of a mouth. He smiled cunningly and tried to outscream the others with his thin voice. He pretended that the whole event was nothing but a joke or a mistake. When my father finally grasped what Koppel had done, he asked, "How did you dare to commit a sin like this? Don't you know that Rabbi Gershom decreed a penalty of excommunication for polygamy?"

Koppel Mitzner signaled with his index finger for everyone to be quiet. Then he said, "Rabbi, first of all, I didn't marry them of my own free will. They caught me in a trap. A hundred times I told them I had a wife, but they attached themselves to me like leeches. The fact that I didn't end up in the insane asylum on Bonifrate Street proves that I'm stronger than iron. Second, I need not to be more pious than our patriarch Jacob. If Jacob could marry four wives, I am allowed to have ten, perhaps even a thousand, like King Solomon. I also happen to know that the ruling of Rabbi Gershom was made for one thousand years, and nine hundred of those thousand have already passed. Only one hundred years are left. I take the punishment upon myself. You, Rabbi, will not roast in my Gehenna."

There was an uproar of laughter. A few of the young men applauded. My father clutched his beard. "What will happen a hundred years from now we cannot know. For the time being the ruling of Rabbi Gershom is valid and the one who breaks it is a betrayer of Israel."

"Rabbi, I did not steal, I did not swindle. Rich Hasidim go bankrupt twice a year and then travel to their rabbi on holidays and sit at his table. When I buy something I pay cash. I don't owe anybody a penny. I provide for four Jewish daughters and nine good children."

His wives tried to interrupt Koppel but the police did not let them. Shmuel Smetena translated Koppel's words into Russian. Even though I did not understand the language it occured to me that he shortened Koppel's arguments—he gesticulated, winked, and it seemed he did not want the Russians to understand all of Koppel's defenses. Shmuel Smetena was tall, fat, with a red neck. He wore a corduroy jacket with gilded buttons and on his vest a watch chain made of silver rubles. The uppers of his boots shone like lacquer. I kept glancing at Koppel's wives. The one from Krochmalna Street was short, broad like a Sabbath stew pot, and she had a potato nose and a huge bosom. She seemed to be the oldest of the lot. Her wig was disheveled and as black as soot. She cried and wiped the tears with her apron. She pointed a thick finger with a broken nail at Koppel, calling him criminal, pig, murderer, lecher. She warned him that she would break his ribs.

One of the women looked as young as a girl. She wore a straw hat with a green band and carried a purse with a brass clasp. Her red cheeks were like those of the streetwalkers who stood at the gates and waited for guests. I heard her say, "He is a liar, the greatest cheat in the whole world. He has promised me the moon and the stars. Such a faker and braggart you cannot find in the whole of Warsaw. If he will not divorce me this very moment he must rot in prison. I have six brothers and each of them can make mincemeat out of him."

As she said these angry words, her eyes smiled and she showed dimples. She seemed lovely to me. She opened her purse, took out a sheet of paper, and shoved it in front of my father's face. "Here is my marriage contract."

The third woman was short, blond, older than the one with the straw hat but much younger than the one from Krochmalna Street. She said she was a cook in the Jewish hospital, where she had met Koppel Mitzner. He introduced himself to her as Morris Kelzer. He came to the hospital because he suffered from severe headaches and Dr. Frankel told him to remain two days for observation. The woman said to my father, "Now I understand why his head ached. If I had cooked up such a kasha as he did, my head would have ruptured and I would have lost my mind ten times a day."

The fourth woman had red hair, a face full of freckles, and eyes as green as gooseberries. I noticed a golden tooth on the side of her mouth. Her mother, who wore a bonnet with beads and ribbons, sat on the bench, screaming each time her daughter's name was mentioned. The latter tried to quiet her by giving her smelling salts, which are used on Yom Kippur for those who are neither strong enough to fast nor willing to break the fast. I heard the daughter say, "Mother, crying and wailing won't help. We have got into a mess and we must get out of it."

"There is a God, there is," the old woman screeched. "He waits long, but He punishes severely. He will see our shame and disgrace and pass judgment. Such an evildoer, such a whoremonger, such a beast!"

Her head fell back as if she was about to faint. The daughter rushed to the kitchen and returned with a wet towel. She rubbed the old woman's temples with it. "Mother, come to yourself. Mother, Mother, Mother!" The old woman woke up with a start, and began to yell again. "People, I'm dying!" "Here, swallow this." The daughter pushed a pill between her empty gums.

After a while the policemen left, ordering Koppel Mitzner to appear at police headquarters the next day, and Shmuel Smetena began to scold Koppel. "How can a man, especially a businessman, do something like this?" My father told Koppel that he must divorce the three other wives without delay and keep the original wife, the one from Krochmalna Street. Father requested that the women approach the table, and he asked them if they agreed to a divorce. But somehow they did not answer clearly. Koppel had six children with the wife from Krochmalna Street, two with the cook from the Jewish Hospital, and one with the redhead. Only with the youngest one did he have no children. By now I had learned the names of the women. The one from Krochmalna Street was called Trina Leah, the cook Gutsha, the redhead Naomi. The youngest one had a Gentile name, Pola. Usually when people came for a Din Torah—a judgment—Father made a compromise. If one litigant sued for twenty rubles and the other denied owing anything, my father's verdict would be to pay ten. But what kind of compromise could be made in this case? Father shook his head and sighed. From time to time he glanced toward his books and manuscripts. He disliked being disturbed in his studies. He nodded to me as if to say, "See where the Evil One can lead those who forsake the Torah."

After much haggling Father sent the women to the kitchen to discuss their grievances and the financial details with my mother. She was more experienced then he in wordly matters.

She had peered into the courtroom once or twice and threw Koppel a look of disdain. The women immediately rushed into the kitchen and I followed. My mother, taller than my father, lean, sickly white, with a sharp nose and large gray eyes, was, as always, reading some Hebrew morality book. She wore a white kerchief over her blond wig. I heard her say to Koppel's wives, "Divorce him. Run away from him like from the fire. I should be forgiven for my words, but what did you see in him? A debaucher!"

Gutsha the cook replied, "Rebbetzin, it's easy to divorce a man, but we have two children. It's true that what he pays for their support is a pittance but it's still better than nothing. Once we divorce, he will be as free as a bird. A child needs shoes, a little skirt, underpants. Well, and what should I tell them when they grow up? He used to come on Saturdays only, still to the girls he was Daddy. He brought them candy, a toy, a cookie. And he pretended to love them."

"Didn't you know that he had a wife?" my mother asked.

Gutsha hesitated for a while. "In the beginning I didn't know, and when I found out it was already too late. He said he didn't live with his wife, and they would be divorced any day. He dazzled me and bewitched me. He's a smooth talker, a sly fox."

"She knew, the whore, she knew!" Trina Leah called out. "When a man visits a woman on the Sabbath only, he's as kosher as pork. She's no better than he is. People like her only want to grab other women's husbands. She's a slut, an outcast." And Trina Leah spat in Gutsha's face.

Gutsha wiped off her face with a handkerchief. "She should spit blood and pus."

"Really, I cannot understand," my mother said to the women and to herself. Then she added, "Perhaps he could be ordered to pay for the children by the law of the Gentiles."

"Rebbetzin," Gutsha said, "if a man has a heart for his children, he doesn't need to be forced. This one came every week with a different excuse. He doled out the few guldens like alms. Today the policemen came to the hospital and took me away as if I were a lawbreaker. My enemies rejoiced at my downfall. I left my children with a nurse who must leave at four o'clock and then they will be alone."

"In that case, go home at once," my mother said. "Something will be done. There is still a remnant of order in the world."

"No order whatsoever. I dug my own grave. I must have been insane. I deserve all the blows I'm getting. I'm ready to die, but who will take care of my darlings? It is not their fault."

"She's as much of a mother as I'm a countess," Trina Leah hollered. "Bitch, leper, hoodlum!"

I had great compassion for Gutsha; nevertheless, I was curious about the men, and I ran back to the room where they were arguing. I heard Shmuel Smetena say, "Listen to me, Koppel. No matter what you say, the children should not be the victims. You will have to provide for them, and if not the Russians will put you into the cage for three years and no one would bat an eyelid. No lawyer would take a case like this. If you fall into a rage and stab someone, the judge may be lenient. But what you did day in and day out was not the act of a human being."

"I will pay, I will pay—don't be so holier-than-thou," Koppel said. "These are my children, and they will not have to go begging. Rabbi, if you permit me, I will swear on the holy scroll." And Koppel pointed to the Ark.

"Swear? God forbid!" Father replied. "First you have to sign a paper that you will obey my judgment and fulfill your obligations to your children. Woe is me!" My father changed his tone. "How long does a man live altogether? Is it worth losing the world to come because of such evil passions? What becomes of the body after death? It's eaten up by the worms. As long as one breathes, one can still repent. In the grave there is no longer free choice."

"Rabbi, I'm ready to fast and to do penances. I have one explanation: I lost my senses. A demon or evil spirit entered me. I got entangled like a fly in a spider's web. I'm afraid people will take revenge on me and no one will enter my store any more."

"Jews have mercy," my father said. "If you repent with all your heart, no one will persecute you."

"Absolutely true," Shmuel Smetena agreed.

I left the men and went back to the kitchen. The old woman, Naomi's mother, was saying, "Rebbetzin, I didn't like him from the very beginning. I took one look at him and I said, 'Naomi, run from him like from the pest. He's not going to divorce his wife. First let him divorce her,' I said, 'then we will see.' My dear lady, we are not just people from the gutter. My late husband, Naomi's father, was a Hasid. Naomi was an honest girl. She became a seamstress to support me. But he has a quick tongue that spouts sweet words. The more he tried to please me with his flattery, the more I recognized what a serpent he was. But my daughter is a fool. If you tell her that there is a horse fair in Heaven, she wants to go up and buy a horse there. She had bad luck in addition. She was married and became a widow after three months. Her husband, a giant of a man, fell down like a tree. Woe what I have lived to see in my old age. I wish I had died a long time ago. Who needs me? I just spoil bread."

"Don't say this. When God tells us to live, we must live," my mother said.

"What for? People sneer at us. When she told me that she was pregnant from that mooncalf I grabbed her hair and . . . People, I'm dying!"

That day, all three women agreed to divorce Koppel Mitzner. The divorce proceedings were to take place in our house. Koppel signed a paper and gave my father an advance of five rubles. Father had already written down the names of the three women. The name Naomi was a good Jewish name. Gutsha was a diminutive of Gutte, which used to be Tovah. But what kind of name was Pola? My father looked the name up in a book with the title *People's Names*, but there was no Pola there. He asked me to bring Isaiah the scribe and they talked it over. Isaiah had much experience in such matters. He told my father that he drew a circle in a notebook each time he wrote a divorce paper and recently his son counted over eight hundred such circles. "According to the law," Isaiah said, "a Gentile name is acceptable in a divorce paper."

Naomi was supposed to be divorced first. The ritual ceremony was to take place on Sunday. But that Sunday neither Koppel nor his wives showed up. The news spread on Krochmalna Street that Koppel Mitzner had vanished together with his youngest wife, Pola. He deserted the three other wives, and they would never be permitted to remarry. Where he and Pola went, no one knew, but it was believed that they had run away to Paris or to New York. "Where else," Mother said, "would charlatans like these run to?"

She gave me an angry look as if suspecting that I envied Koppel his journey, and, who knows, perhaps even his companion. "What are you doing in the kitchen?" she cried. "Go back to your book. Such depravities are not for you!"

Tanhum

TANHUM MAKOVER buttoned his gaberdine and twisted his earlocks into curls. He wiped his feet on the straw mat before the
door, as he had been told to do. His prospective father-in-law,
Reb Bendit Waldman, often reminded him that one could study
the Torah and serve the Almighty and still not behave like an
idle dreamer. Reb Bendit Waldman offered himself as an example. He was everything at once—a scholar, a fervent Hasid
of the Sadgora rabbi as well as a successful lumber merchant,
a chess player, and the proprietor of a water mill. There was
time for everything if one wasn't lazy, Reb Bendit said—even
to teach yourself Russian and Polish and glance into a newspaper. How his prospective father-in-law managed all this was
beyond Tanhum. Reb Bendit never seemed to hurry. He had a
friendly word for everyone, even an errand boy or servant girl.
Women burdened down by a heavy spirit came to him for advice. Nor did he neglect to visit the sick or—God forbid—to
escort a corpse. Tanhum often resolved to be like his prospective father-in-law, but he simply couldn't manage it. He would
grow absorbed in some sacred book and before he knew it
half the day had gone by. He tried to maintain a proper appearance, but a button would loosen and dangle by a thread
until it dropped off and got lost. His boots were always mud-

died, his shirt collars frayed. As often as he knotted the band
of his breeches it always came untied again. He resolved to
commit two pages of the Gemara to memory each day so that
in three and a half years he might finish with the Talmud, but
he couldn't manage even this. He would become preoccupied
with some Talmudic controversy and linger over it for weeks
on end. The questions and doubts wouldn't let him rest. Certainly there was mercy in Heaven, but why did little children
or even dumb animals have to suffer? Why did man have to
end up dying, and a steer under the slaughterer's knife? Why
had the miracles ceased and God's chosen people been forced
to suffer exile for two thousand years? Tanhum probed in the
Hasidic lore, the cabala volumes, the ancient philosophy books.
The questions they raised in his mind plagued him like flies.
There were mornings when Tanhum awoke with a weight in
his limbs, a pain in his temples, and no urge at all to study, pray,
or even perform his ablutions. Today was one of those days.
He opened the Gemara and sat there for two hours without
turning a page. At prayer, he couldn't seem to grasp the meaning of the words. While reciting the eighteen benedictions, he
transposed the blessings. And it just so happened that today he
was invited for lunch at his prospective father-in-law's.

Reb Bendit Waldman's house was constructed in such a way
that one had to pass through the kitchen to get to the dining
room. The kitchen was aswarm with women—Tanhum's prospective mother-in-law, her daughters-in-law, her daughters,
including Tanhum's bride-to-be, Mira Fridl. Even before enter-
ing the house he heard the racket and commotion inside. The
women of the house were all noisy and inclined to laughter,
and often there were neighbors present. The cooking, baking,
knitting, and needlepoint went on with a vengeance, and games
of checkers, knucklebones, hide-and-seek, and wolf-and-goat
were played. On Hanukkah they rendered chicken fat; after
Succoth they made coleslaw and pickled cucumbers; in the
summers they put up jam. A fire was always kept going in the

stove and under a tripod. The kitchen smelled of coffee, braised meat, cinnamon, and saffron. Cakes and cookies were baked for the Sabbath and holidays, to go with the roast geese, chickens, and ducks. One day they prepared for a circumcision and another day for the ceremony of redeeming the firstborn son; now one of the family was becoming engaged, and now they all trouped off to a wedding. Tailors fitted coats, cobblers measured feet for shoes. At Reb Bendit Waldman's there was ample occasion to have a drink of cherry or sweet brandy and to nibble at an almond cookie, a babka, or a honey cake.

Reb Bendit made fun of the women of the house and their exaggerated sense of hospitality, but apparently he, too, enjoyed having his house full of people. Each time he went to Warsaw or Krakow he brought back various trinkets for the women—embroidered headkerchiefs, rings, shawls, and pins— and for the boys, pocketknives, pens, gold embossed skullcaps, and ornate phylactery bags. Apart from the usual wedding gifts—a set of the Talmud, a gold watch, a wine goblet, a spice box, a prayer shawl with silver brocade—Tanhum had already received all kinds of other presents. It wasn't mere talk when Tanhum's former fellow students at the Brisk Yeshiva said that he had fallen into a gravy pot. His bride-to-be, Mira Fridl, was considered a beauty, but Tanhum had not yet had a good look at her. How could he? During the signing of the marriage contract the women's parlor was jammed, and in the kitchen Mira Fridl was always surrounded by her sisters and sisters-in-law.

The moment Tanhum crossed the threshold he lowered his eyes. True, everyone had his destined mate; forty days before he, Tanhum, had been born it had already been decided that Mira Fridl would become his spouse. Still, he fretted that he wasn't a suitable enough son-in-law for Reb Bendit Waldman. All the members of the family were jolly, while he was reticent. He wasn't good at business or quick of tongue, not playful. He knew no games, was unable to perform stunts or do swimming tricks in the river. At twelve he already had to take free board at the homes of strangers in the towns where he was sent to study at the yeshivas. His father died when Tanhum was still a child. His mother had remarried. Tanhum's stepfather was a poor peddler and had six children from a previous marriage. From childhood on, Tanhum went around in rags. He constantly berated himself for not praying fervently enough or devoting himself sufficiently to Jewishness, and he warred eternally with evil thoughts.

This day, the tumult in the kitchen was louder than ever. Someone had apparently just told a joke or performed some antic, for the women laughed and clapped their hands. Usually when Tanhum came in, a respectful path was cleared for him, but now he had to push his way through the throng. Who knows, maybe they were making fun of him? The back of his neck felt hot and damp. He must be late, for Reb Bendit was already seated at the table, with his sons and sons-in-law, waiting for him to appear. Reb Bendit, in a flowered robe, his silver-white beard combed into two points and a silk skullcap high over his forehead, lolled grandly in his armchair at the head of the table. The men had apparently had a drink, for a carafe and glasses stood on the table, along with wafers to crunch. The company was in a joking mood. Reb Bendit's eldest son, Leibush Meir, a big, fleshy fellow with a huge potbelly and a round reddish beard circling his fat face, shook with laughter. Yoshe, a son-in-law—short and round as a barrel and with black eyes and thick lips—giggled into a handkerchief. Another son-in-law, Shlomele, the wag, jokester, and mimic, impudently imitated someone's gestures.

Reb Bendit asked Tanhum amiably, "You have a gold watch. Why aren't you on time?"

"It stopped running."

"You probably didn't wind it."

"He needs an alarm clock," Shlomele jested.

"Well, go wash your hands," and Reb Bendit pointed to the washstand.

While washing his hands Tanhum wet his sleeves. There was a towel hanging on the rack, but he stood helplessly dripping water on the floor. He often tripped, caught his clothing, and bumped into things, and he constantly had to be told where to go and what to do. There was a mirror in the dining room and Tanhum caught a glimpse of himself—a stooped figure with sunken cheeks, dark eyes below disheveled brows, a tiny beard on the tip of the chin, a pale nose, and a pointed Adam's apple. It took him a few seconds to realize that he was looking at his reflection. At the table, Reb Bendit praised the dish of groats and asked the woman who had prepared it what ingredients she had used. Leibush Meir demanded a second helping as usual. Shlomele complained that he had found only one mushroom in his portion. After the soup, the conversation turned serious. Reb Bendit had bought a tract of forest in partnership with a Zamość merchant, Reb Nathan Vengrover. The two partners had fallen out, and Reb Nathan had summoned Reb Bendit to the rabbi's the following Saturday night for a hearing. Reb Bendit complained to the company at lunch that his partner was totally lacking in common sense, a dolt, a ninny, a dunderhead. The sons and sons-in-law agreed that he was a jackass. Tanhum sat in terror. This was evil talk, slander, and who knows what else! According to the Gemara, one lost the world to come for speaking so disrespectfully of another man. Had they forgotten this or did they only pretend to forget? Tanhum wanted to warn them that they were violating the law: Thou shalt not go up and down as a talebearer among thy people. According to the Gemara, he should have stuffed up his ears with the lobes so as not to hear, but he couldn't embarrass his prospective father-in-law this way. He sank even lower in his chair. Two women now brought in the main course—a platter of beef cutlets and a tray of roast chicken floating in sauce. Tanhum grimaced. How could one eat such a repast on a weekday? Didn't they remember the destruction of the Temple?

"Tanhum, are you eating or sleeping?"

It was his intended, Mira Fridl, speaking. Tanhum came to with a start. He saw her now for the first time—of medium build, fair, with golden hair and blue eyes, wearing a red dress. She smiled at him mischievously and even winked.

"Which would you prefer—beef or chicken?"

Tanhum wanted to answer, but the words stuck in his throat. For some time already, he had felt an aversion to meat. No doubt everything here was strictly kosher, but it seemed to him that the meat smelled of blood and that he could hear the bellowing of the cow writhing beneath the slaughterer's knife.

Reb Bendit said, "Give him some of each."

Mira Fridl served a cutlet and then, with her serving spoon poised over the platter of chicken, asked, "Which would you like—the breast or a leg?"

Again Tanhum was unable to answer. Instead, Shlomele the wag said with a leer, "He lusts for both."

As Mira Fridl bent over Tanhum to put a chicken leg on his plate, her bosom touched his shoulder. She added potatoes and carrots, and Tanhum shrank away from her. He heard Shlomele snicker, and he was overcome with shame. I don't belong among them, he thought. They're making a fool of me . . . He had an urge to stand up and flee.

"Eat, Tanhum, don't dillydally," Reb Bendit said. "One must have strength for the Torah."

Tanhum put his fork into the sauce and dug out a sliver of meat, doused it in horseradish, and sprinkled it with salt to blot out the taste. He ate a slice of bread. He was intimidated by Mira Fridl. What would they talk about after the wedding? She was a rich man's daughter, accustomed to a life of luxury. Her mother had told him that a goldsmith from Lublin had fashioned jewelry for Mira Fridl. All sorts of fur coats, jackets, and capes were being sewn for her, and she would be provided with furniture, rugs, and porcelain. How could he, Tanhum, exercise control over such a pampered creature? And why would she want him for a husband? Her father had undoubtedly coerced her into it. He wanted a Talmudist for a son-in-law. Tanhum envisioned himself standing under the wedding canopy with Mira Fridl, eating the golden soup, dancing the wedding dance, and then being led off to the marriage chamber. He felt a sense of panic. None of this seemed fitting for his oppressed spirit. He began to sway and to beg the Almighty to guard him from temptations, impure thoughts, Satan's net. *Father in Heaven, save me!*

Leibush Meir burst into laughter. "What are you swaying for? It's a chicken leg, not Rashi's commentary."

Reb Nathan was expected to bring his arbitrator, Reb Feivel, to the hearing. Reb Bendit Waldman also had his own arbitrator, Reb Fishel, but nevertheless he invited Tanhum to attend the proceedings, too. He said that it would do Tanhum good to learn something about practical matters. If he turned to the rabbinate, he would have to know a little about business. It was entirely feasible that that stubborn villain, Reb Nathan, wouldn't agree to a compromise and would insist on the strict letter of the law, and Reb Bendit asked Tanhum therefore to take down the books and go over the sections that dealt with the codes governing business partnerships. Tanhum agreed reluctantly. The entire Torah was holy, of course, but Tanhum wasn't drawn to those laws dealing with money, manipulation, interests, and swindle. In former years when he studied these subjects in the Gemara, it hadn't occurred to him that there really were Jews who reneged on written agreements, stole, swore falsely, and cheated. The idea of meeting in the flesh a person who would deny a debt, violate a trust, and grow rich from deception was too painful to contemplate. Tanhum wanted to tell Reb Bendit that he had no intention of becoming a rabbi, and that it would be hard for him now to lay aside the treatise in which he was absorbed and turn to matters that were alien to him. But how could he refuse Reb Bendit, who had raised him out of poverty, and given him his daughter for a bride? This would have enraged his future mother-in-law and turned Mira Fridl against him. It would have incited a feud and provoked evil gossip. It would have led to who knows what quarrels.

During the next few days, Tanhum didn't have enough time to get deeply into *The Breastplate of Judgment* and its many commentaries. He quickly scanned the text of Rabbi Caro and the annotations of Rabbi Moshe Isserles. He hummed and bit his lips. Obviously even in the old days there had been no lack of frauds and of rascals. Was it any wonder? Even the generation that received the Torah had its Korah, its Dathan, its Abiram. Still, how could theft be reconciled with faith? How could one whose soul had stood on Mount Sinai defile it with crime?

The Din Torah, the hearing, began on Saturday evening, and it looked as though it would last a whole week. The rabbi, Reb Efraim Engel, a patriarch of seventy and author of a book of legal opinions, told his wife to send all those who came seeking advice about other matters to the assistant rabbi. He bolted the door of his study and ordered his beadle to let only the participants enter. On the table stood the candles that had ushered out the Sabbath. The room smelled of wine, wax, and the spice box. From the way the family had described Reb Nathan Vengrover as a tough man and a speculator, Tanhum expected him to be tall, dark, and with the wild gaze of a gypsy, but in came a thin, stooped little man with a sparse beard the color of pepper, with a milky-white cataract in his left eye, and wearing a faded gaberdine, a sheepskin hat, and coarse boots. Pouches of bluish flesh dangled beneath his eyes and he had warts on his nose. Being the plaintiff, he was the first to speak. He immediately began to shout in a hoarse voice, and he kept on shouting and grunting throughout the proceedings.

Reb Bendit smoked an aromatic blend of tobacco in a pipe with an amber cover; Reb Nathan rolled cigarettes of cheap, stinking tobacco. Reb Bendit spoke deliberately and graced his words with proverbs and quotations from the saints; Reb Nathan slammed the table with his fist, yanked hairs from his beard, and called Reb Bendit a thief. He wouldn't even let his own arbitrator, Reb Feivel—who was the size of a cheder boy, with eyes as mild as a child's and a red beard that fell to his loins—get a word in edgewise. Reb Bendit recalled the details of the agreement from memory, but Reb Nathan consulted whole stackfuls of papers that were filled with row upon row of a clumsy scribble and stained with erasures and blots. He didn't sit in the chair provided for him but paced to and fro, coughed, and spat into a handkerchief. Reb Bendit was sent all kinds of refreshments and drinks from home, but Reb Nathan didn't even go near the tea that the rabbi's wife brought in. From day to day his face grew more drawn, and was gray as dust and wasted as if from consumption. From nervous tension, he chewed his fingernails and tore his own notes into shreds.

For the first two days, Tanhum was completely bewildered by what went on. The rabbi again and again implored Reb Nathan to speak to the point, not to mix up dates or inject matters that had no bearing on the subject. But it all came gushing out of Reb Nathan like water from a pump. Gradually Tanhum came to understand that his prospective father-in-law was being accused of holding back profits and falsifying accounts. Reb Nathan Vengrover maintained that Reb Bendit had bribed Prince Sapieha's steward to chop down more acres of timber than had been stipulated in the contract. Nor would Reb Bendit allow Reb Nathan and his associate near the Squire, or to get in contact with the merchants who purchased the timber, which was tied in rafts and floated down the Vistula to Danzig. Reb Bendit had allegedly announced one price to Reb Nathan, when he had in fact got a higher one from the merchants. Reb Bendit had claimed to have paid the brokers, loggers, and sawyers more than he actually did. He employed every trick and device to oust Reb Nathan from the partnership and to seize all the profits for himself. Reb Nathan pointed out that Reb Bendit had already twice gone bankrupt and subsequently settled for a third of his debts.

Reb Bendit had kept silent most of the time, awaiting his turn to speak, but finally he lost his patience. "Savage!" he shouted. "Hothead! Lunatic!"

"Usurer! Swindler! Robber!" Reb Nathan responded.

On the third day, Reb Bendit calmly began to refute Reb Nathan's charges. He proved that Reb Nathan contradicted himself, exaggerated, and didn't know a pine from an oak. How could he be allowed near the Squire when his Polish was so broken? How could he lay claim to half the income when he, Reb Bendit, had to lay out hush money to the gentry, stave off unfavorable decrees, shower assessors and marshals with gifts out of his own pocket? The more glibly Reb Bendit spoke, the more apparent it became to Tanhum that his prospective father-in-law had broken his agreement and had indeed sought to rob Reb Nathan of the profits and even part of his original investment. But how could this be? Tanhum wondered. How could Reb Bendit, a man in his sixties, a scholar, and a Hasid, commit such iniquities? What was his justification? He knew all the laws. He knew that no repentance could excuse the sin of robbery and theft unless one paid back every penny. The Day of Atonement didn't forgive such transgressions. Could a man who believed in the Creator, in reward and punishment and in immortality of the soul, risk the world to come for the sake of a few thousand gulden? Or was Reb Bendit a secret heretic?

In the closing days, Reb Bendit, his arbitrator, Reb Fishel, and Tanhum didn't go home for dinner—the maid brought them meat and soup. But Tanhum didn't touch the food. There was a gnawing in his stomach. His tongue was dry. He had a bad taste in his mouth, and he felt like vomiting. Although he fasted, his belly was bloated. A lump formed in his throat that he could neither swallow nor disgorge. He didn't weep but his eyes kept tearing over, and he saw everything as if through a mist. Tanhum reminded himself that only that past Succoth, when Reb Bendit had gone to the Sadgora rabbi, he had brought the rabbi an ivory ethrog box that was decorated with silver and embossed in gold. Inside, couched in flax, lay an ethrog from Corfu that was pocked and budding. The Hasidim knew that besides contributing generously to the community, of which he was an elder, Reb Bendit also gave the rabbi a tithe. But what was the sense of robbing one person to give to another? Did he do all this to be praised in the Sadgora study houses and be seated at the rabbi's table? Had the greed for money and honors so blinded him that he didn't know the wrongs he committed? Yes, so it seemed, for during evening prayers Reb Bendit piously washed his fingers in the basin, girdled his loins with a sash, stationed himself to pray at the eastern wall, swayed, bowed, beat his breast, and sighed. From time to time he stretched his hands up to Heaven. Several times during the arbitration he had invoked God's name.

Thursday night, when it came time to pass judgment, Reb Nathan Vengrover demanded a clear-cut decision: "No compromises! If the law says that what my partner did was right, then I don't demand even a groschen."

"According to law, Reb Bendit has to take an oath," Reb Nathan's arbitrator, Reb Feivel, asserted.

"I wouldn't swear even for a sackful of gold," Reb Bendit countered.

"In that case, pay up!"

"Not on your life!"

Both arbitrators, Reb Feivel and Reb Fishel, began to dispute the law. The rabbi drew *The Breastplate of Judgment* down from the bookcase.

Reb Bendit cast a glance at Tanhum. "Tanhum, why don't you speak up?"

Tanhum wanted to say that to appropriate another's possession was as serious an offense as swearing falsely. He also wanted to ask, "Why did you do it?" But he merely mumbled, "Since Father-in-Law signed an agreement, he must honor it."

"So you, too, turn on me, eh?"

"God forbid, but—"

" 'Art thou for us or for our adversaries?' " Reb Bendit quoted from the Book of Joshua, in a dry voice.

"We don't live forever," Tanhum said haltingly.

"You go home!" Reb Bendit ordered.

Tanhum left the rabbi's study and went straight to his room at the inn. He didn't recite the Shema, or undress, but sat on the edge of his cot the whole night. When the light began to break, he packed his Sabbath gaberdine, a few shirts, socks, and books in a straw basket, and walked down Synagogue Street to the bridge that led out of town. Months went by without any news of him. They even dredged the river for his body. Reb Bendit Waldman and Reb Nathan Vengrover reached an agreement. The rabbi and the arbitrators wouldn't permit it to come to oath-taking. Mira Fridl became engaged to a youth from Lublin, the son of a sugar manufacturer. Tanhum had left all his presents behind at the inn, and the bridegroom from Lublin inherited them. One winter day, a shipping agent brought news of Tanhum: he had gone back to the Brisk Yeshiva, from which Reb Bendit originally brought him to his town. Tanhum had become a recluse. He ate no meat, drank no wine, put pebbles inside his shoes, and slept on a bench behind the stove at the study house. When a new match was proposed to him in Brisk, he responded, "My soul yearns for the Torah."

The Manuscript

WE SAT, shaded by a large umbrella, eating a late breakfast at a sidewalk café on Dizengoff Street in Tel Aviv. My guest—a woman in her late forties, with a head of freshly dyed red hair—ordered orange juice, an omelette, and black coffee. She sweetened the coffee with saccharine, which she plucked with her silvery fingernails from a tiny pillbox covered with mother-of-pearl. I had known her for about twenty-five years —first as an actress in the Warsaw Variety Theater, Kundas; then as the wife of my publisher, Morris Rashkas; and still later as the mistress of my late friend, the writer Menashe Linder. Here in Israel she had married Ehud Hadadi, a journalist ten years younger than herself. In Warsaw, her stage name was Shibtah. Shibtah, in Jewish folklore, is a she-demon who entices yeshiva boys to lechery and steals infants from young mothers who go out alone at night without a double apron—one worn front and back. Her maiden name was Kleinmintz.

In Kundas, when Shibtah sang her salacious songs and recited the monologues which Menashe Linder wrote for her, she made the "very boards burn." The reviewers admired her pretty face, her graceful figure, and her provocative movements. But Kundas did not last longer than two seasons. When

Shibtah tried to play dramatic roles, she failed. During the Second World War, I heard that she died somewhere, in the ghetto or a concentration camp. But here she was, sitting across from me, dressed in a white mini-skirt and blouse, wearing large sunglasses and a wide-brimmed straw hat. Her cheeks were rouged, her brows plucked, and she wore bracelets and cameos on both wrists, and many rings on her fingers. From a distance she could have been taken for a young woman, but her neck had become flabby. She called me by a nickname she had given me when we were both young—Loshikl.

She said, "Loshikl, if someone had told me in Kazakhstan that you and I would one day be sitting together in Tel Aviv, I would have thought it a joke. But if one survives, everything is possible. Would you believe that I could stand in the woods sawing logs twelve hours a day? That is what we did, at twenty degrees below zero, hungry, and with our clothes full of lice. By the way, Hadadi would like to interview you for his newspaper."

"With pleasure. Where did he get the name Hadadi?"

"Who knows? They all give themselves names from the Haggadah. His real name is Zeinvel Zylberstein. I myself have already had a dozen names. Between 1942 and 1944, I was Nora Davidovna Stutchkov. Funny, isn't it?"

"Why did you and Menashe part?" I asked.

"Well, I knew that you would ask this question. Loshikl, our story is so strange that I sometimes don't believe it really happened. Since 1939 my life has been one long nightmare. Sometimes I wake up in the middle of the night and I don't remember who I am, what my name is, and who is lying next to me. I reach out for Ehud and he begins to grumble. '*Mah at rotzah?* ('What do you want?') Only when I hear him talk in Hebrew do I recall that I am in the Holy Land."

"Why did you part with Menashe?"

"You really want to hear it?"

"Absolutely."

"No one knows the whole story, Loshikl. But I will tell you everything. To whom else, if not to you? In all my wanderings, not a day passed that I did not think of Menashe. I was never so devoted to anyone as I was to him—and I never will be. I would have gone through fire for him. And this is not just a phrase—I proved it with my deeds. I know that you consider me a frivolous woman. Deep in your heart, you have remained a Hasid. But the most pious woman would not have done a tenth of what I did for Menashe."

"Tell me."

"Oh, well, after you left for America, our few good years began. We knew that a terrible war was approaching and every day was a gift. Menashe read to me everything he wrote. I typed his manuscripts and brought order into his chaos. You know how disorganized he was, he never learned to number his pages. He only had one thing on his mind—women. I had given up the struggle. I said to myself, 'That's how he is and no power can change him.' Just the same, he became more and more attached to me. I had gotten myself a job as a manicurist and was supporting him. You may not believe me, but I cooked for his paramours. The older he became, the more he had to convince himself that he was still the great Don Juan. Actually, there were times when he was completely impotent. One day he was a giant and the next day he was an invalid. Why did he need all those sleazy creatures? He was nothing but a big child. So it went on until the outbreak of the war. Menashe seldom read a newspaper. He rarely turned on the radio. The war was not a complete surprise to anyone—they were digging trenches and piling up barricades on the Warsaw streets already in July. Even rabbis took shovels and dug ditches. Now that Hitler was about to invade them, the Poles forgot their scores with the Jews and we all became, God help us, one nation. Still, when the Nazis began to bombard us, we were shocked. After you left, I bought some new chairs and a sofa. Our home became a regular *bonbonnière*. Loshikl, disaster came in a matter of minutes. There was an alarm, and soon buildings were crumbling and corpses lay strewn in the gutters. We were told to go into the cellars, but the cellars were no safer than the upper stories. There were women who had sense enough to prepare food, but not I. Menashe went to his room, sat down in his chair, and said, 'I want to die.' I don't know what happened in other houses—our telephone stopped functioning immediately. Bombs exploded in front of our windows. Menashe pulled down the shades and was reading a novel by Alexandre Dumas. All his friends and admirers had vanished. There were rumors that journalists were given a special train—or perhaps special cars on a train—to flee from the city. In a time like this, it was crazy to isolate yourself, but Menashe did not stir from the house until it was announced on the radio that all physically able men should cross the Praga bridge. It was senseless to take luggage because trains were not running and how much can you carry when you go on foot? Of course, I refused to remain in Warsaw and I went with him.

"I forgot to tell you the main thing. After years of doing nothing, in 1938, Menashe suddenly developed an urge to write a novel. His muse had awakened and he wrote a book which was, in my opinion, the best thing he had ever written. I copied it for him, and when I did not like certain passages, he always changed them. It was autobiographical, but not entirely. When the newspapers learned that Menashe was writing a novel, they all wanted to start publishing it. But he had made up his mind not to publish a word until it was finished. He polished each sentence. Some chapters he rewrote three or four times. Its tentative title was *Rungs*—not a bad name since every chapter described a different phase of his life. He had finished only the first part. It would have become a trilogy.

"When it came to packing our few belongings, I asked

Menashe, 'Have you packed your manuscripts?' And he said, 'Only *Rungs*. My other works will have to be read by the Nazis.' He carried two small valises and I had thrown some clothes and shoes, as much as I could carry, into a knapsack. We began to walk toward the bridge. In front of us and behind us trudged thousands of men. A woman was seldom seen. It was like a huge funeral procession—and that is what it really was. Most of them died, some from bombs, others at the hands of the Nazis after 1941, and many in Stalin's slave camps. There were optimists who took along heavy trunks. They had to abandon them even before they reached the bridge. Everyone was exhausted from hunger, fear, and lack of sleep. To lighten their loads, people threw away suits, coats, and shoes. Menashe could barely walk, but he carried both valises throughout the night. We were on the way to Bialystok because Stalin and Hitler had divided Poland and Bialystok now belonged to Russia. En route, we met journalists, writers, and those who considered themselves writers. They all carried manuscripts, and even in my despair I felt like laughing. Who needed their writings?

"If I were to tell you how we reached Bialystok, we would have to sit here until tomorrow. Menashe had already discarded one of the valises. Before he did, I opened it to make sure his manuscript wasn't there, God forbid. Menashe had fallen into such a gloom that he stopped talking altogether. He started to sprout a gray beard—he had forgotten his razor. The first thing he did when we finally stopped in a village was to shave. Some towns were already obliterated by the Nazi bombings. Others remained untouched, and life was going on as if was no war. Strange, but a few young men —readers of Yiddish literature—wanted Menashe to lecture to them on some literary topic. This is how people are—a minute before their death, they still have all the desires of the living. One of these characters even fell in love with me and tried to seduce me. I did not know whether to laugh or cry.

"What went on in Bialystok defies description. Since the city belonged to the Soviets and the dangers of the war were over, those who survived behaved as though they had been resurrected. Soviet-Yiddish writers came from Moscow, from Kharkov, from Kiev, to greet their colleagues from Poland in the name of the party, and Communism became a most precious commodity. The few writers who really had been Communists in Poland became so high and mighty you would think they were about to go to the Kremlin to take over Stalin's job. But even those who had been anti-Communists began to pretend they had always been secret sympathizers or ardent fellow travelers. They all boasted of their proletarian origins. Everyone managed to find an uncle who was a shoemaker; a brother-in-law a coachman; or a relative who went to prison for the cause. Some suddenly discovered that their grandparents were peasants.

"Menashe was, in fact, a son of working people, but he was too proud to boast about it. The Soviet writers accepted him with a certain respect. There was talk of publishing a large anthology, and of creating a publishing company for these refugees. The editors-to-be asked Menashe if he had brought some manuscripts with him. I was there and told them about *Rungs*. Although Menashe hated it when I praised him—we had many quarrels because of this—I told them what I thought of this work. They all became intensely interested. There were special funds to subsidize such publications. It was decided that I was to bring them the manuscript the next day. They promised us a big advance and also better living quarters. Menashe did not reproach me for lauding his work this time.

"We came home, I opened the valise, and there lay a thick envelope with the inscription *Rungs*. I took out the manuscript, but I recognized neither the paper nor the typing. My dear, some beginner had given Menashe his first novel to read, and Menashe had put it into the envelope in which he had once kept his own novel. All this time, we had been carry-ing the scribblings of some hack.

"Even now when I speak about it, I shudder. Menashe had lost more than twenty pounds. He looked wan and sickly. I was afraid that he would go mad—but he stood there crest-fallen and said, 'Well, that's that.'

"Besides the fact that he now had no manuscript to sell, there was danger that he might be suspected of having written an anti-Communist work which he was afraid to show. Bialystok teemed with informers. Although the NKVD did not yet have an address in Bialystok, a number of intellectuals had been arrested or banished from the city. Loshikl, I know you are impatient and I will give you the bare facts. I did not sleep the whole night. In the morning, I got up and said, 'Menashe, I am going to Warsaw.'

"When he heard these words, he became as pale as death, and asked, 'Have you lost your mind?' But I said, 'Warsaw is still a city. I cannot allow your work to get lost. It's not only yours, it's mine, too.' Menashe began to scream. He swore that if I went back to Warsaw, he would hang himself or cut his throat. He even struck me. The battle between us raged for two days. On the third day, I was on my way back to Warsaw. I want to tell you that many men who left Warsaw tried to return. They missed their wives, their children, their homes— if they still existed. They had heard what was going on in Stalin's paradise and they decided that they could just as well die with their dear ones. I told myself: To sacrifice one's life for a manuscript, one has to be insane. But I was seized with an obsession. The days had become colder and I took a sweater, warm underwear, and a loaf of bread. I went into a drugstore and asked for poison. The druggist—a Jew—stared at me. I told him that I had left a child in Warsaw and that I did not want to fall alive into the hands of the Nazis. He gave me some cyanide.

"I didn't travel alone. Until we reached the border, I was

in the company of several men. I told them all the same lie—
that I was pining away with longing for my baby—and they
surrounded me with such love and care that I was embarrassed.
They did not permit me to carry my bundle. They hovered
over me as if I were an only daughter. We knew quite well
what to expect from the Germans if we were caught, but in
such situations people become fatalistic. At the same time,
something within me ridiculed my undertaking. The chances
of finding the manuscript in occupied Warsaw, and returning
to Bialystok alive, were one in a million.

"Loshikl, I crossed the border without any incident, reached
Warsaw, and found the house intact. One thing saved me—
the rains and the cold had started. The nights were pitch dark.
Warsaw had no electricity. The Jews had not yet been herded
into a ghetto. Besides, I don't look especially Jewish. I had
covered my hair with a kerchief and could easily have been
taken for a peasant. Also, I avoided people. When I saw someone from a distance, I hid and waited until he was gone. Our
apartment was occupied by a family. They were sleeping in
our beds and wearing our clothes. But they had not touched
Menashe's manuscripts. The man was a reader of the Yiddish
press and Menashe was a god to him. When I knocked on the
door and told them who I was, they became frightened,
thinking that I wanted to reclaim the apartment. Their own
place had been destroyed by a bomb and a child had been
killed. When I told them that I had come back from Bialystok
for Menashe's manuscript, they were speechless.

"I opened Menashe's drawer and there was his novel. I
stayed with these people two days and they shared with me
whatever food they had. The man let me have his bed—I mean
my bed. I was so tired that I slept for fourteen hours. I awoke,
ate something, and fell asleep again. The second evening, I
was on my way back to Bialystok. I had made my way from
Bialystok to Warsaw, and back to Bialystok, without seeing
one Nazi. I did not walk all the time. Here and there a

peasant offered me a ride. When one leaves the city and begins to hike through field, woods, and orchards, there are no Nazis or Communists. The sky is the same, the earth is the same, and the animals and birds are the same. The whole adventure took ten days. I regarded it as a great personal victory. First of all, I had found Menashe's work, which I carried in my blouse. Besides, I had proved to myself that I was not the coward I thought I was. To tell the truth, crossing the border back to Russia was not particularly risky. The Russians did not make difficulties for the refugees.

"I arrived in Bialystok in the evening. A frost had set in. I walked to our lodgings, which consisted of one room, opened the door, and lo and behold, my hero lay in bed with a woman. I knew her quite well: an atrocious poetess, ugly as an ape. A tiny kerosene lamp was burning. They had got some wood or coal because the stove was heated. They were still awake. My dear, I did not scream, I did not cry, I did not faint as they do in the theater. Both gaped at me in silence. I opened the door of the stove, took the manuscript from my blouse, and put it in the fire. I thought that Menashe might attack me, but he did not utter a word. It took a while before the manuscript caught fire. With a poker, I pushed the coals onto the paper. I stood there, watching. The fire was not in a hurry and neither was I. When *Rungs* became ashes, I walked over to the bed with the poker in hand and told the woman, 'Get out or you will soon be a corpse.'

"She did as I told her. She put on her rags and left. If she had uttered a sound, I would have killed her. When you risk your own life, other people's lives, too, are worthless.

"Menashe sat there in silence as I undressed. That night we spoke only a few words. I said, 'I burned your *Rungs*,' and he mumbled, 'Yes, I saw.' We embraced and we both knew that we were doing it for the last time. He was never so tender and strong as on that night. In the morning, I got up, packed my few things, and left. I had no more fear of the cold, the rain, the snow, the lonesomeness. I left Bialystok and that is the reason I am still alive. I came to Vilna and got a job in a soup kitchen. I saw how petty our so-called big personalities can be and how they played politics and maneuvered for a bed to sleep in or a meal to eat. In 1941, I escaped to Russia. "Menashe, too, was there, I was told, but we never met—nor would I have wanted to. He had said in an interview that the Nazis took his book from him and that he was about to rewrite it. As far as I know, he has never rewritten anything. This really saved his life. If he had been writing and publishing, he would have been liquidated with the others. But he died anyhow."

For a long while we sat in silence. Then I said, "Shibtah, I want to ask you something, but you don't have to answer me. I am asking from sheer curiosity."

"What do you want to know?"

"Were you faithful to Menashe? I mean physically?"

She remained silent. Then she said, "I could give you a Warsaw answer: 'It's none of your leprous business.' But since you are Loshikl, I will tell you the truth. No."

"Why did you do it, since you loved Menashe so much?"

"Loshikl, I don't know. Neither do I know why I burned his manuscript. He had betrayed me with scores of women and I never as much as reproached him. I had made up my mind long ago that you can love one person and sleep with someone else; but when I saw this monstrosity in our bed, the actress in me awoke for the last time and I had to do something dramatic. He could have stopped me easily; instead, he just watched me doing it."

We were both silent again. Then she said, "You should never sacrifice yourself for the person you love. Once you risk your life the way I did, then there is nothing more to give."

"In novels the young man always marries the girl he saves," I said.

She tensed but did not answer. She suddenly appeared tired, haggard, wrinkled, as if old age had caught up with her at that very moment. I did not expect her to utter another word about it, when she said, "Together with his manuscript, I burned my power to love."

The Power of Darkness

THE DOCTORS ALL AGREED that Henia Dvosha suffered from nerves, not heart disease, but her mother, Tzeitel, the wife of Selig the tailor, confided to my mother that Henia Dvosha was making herself die because she wanted her husband, Issur Godel, to marry her sister Dunia.

When my mother heard this strange story she exclaimed, "What's going on at your house? Why should a young woman, the mother of two little children, want to die? And why would she want her husband to marry her sister, of all people? One mustn't even think such thoughts!"

As usual when she became excited, my mother's blond wig grew disheveled as if a strong wind had suddenly blown up.

I, a boy of ten, heard what Tzeitel said with astonishment, yet somehow I felt that she spoke the truth, wild as it sounded. I pretended to read a storybook but I cocked my ears to listen to the conversation.

Tzeitel, a dark, wide woman in a wide wig, a wide dress with many folds, and men's shoes, went on, "My dear friend, I'm not talking just to hear myself talk. This is a kind of madness with her. Woe is me, what I've come to in my old age. I ask but one favor of God—that He take me before He takes her."

"But what sense does it make?"

"No sense whatever. She started talking about it two years ago. She convinced herself that her sister was in love with Issur Godel, or he with her. As the saying goes—'A delusion is worse than a sickness.' Rebbetzin, I have to tell someone: Sick as she is, she's sewing a wedding dress for Dunia."

Mother suddenly noticed me listening and cried, "Get out of the kitchen and go in the other room. The kitchen is for women, not for men!"

I started to go down to the courtyard, and as I was passing the open door to Selig the tailor's shop I glanced inside. Selig was our next-door neighbor at No. 10 Krochmalna Street, and his shop was in the same apartment where he lived with his family. Selig sat at a sewing machine stitching the lining of a gaberdine. As wide as his wife was, so narrow was he. He had narrow shoulders, a narrow nose, and a narrow gray beard. His hands were narrow too, and with long fingers. His glasses, with brass rims and half lenses, were pushed up onto his narrow forehead. Across from him, before another sewing machine, sat Issur Godel, Henia Dvosha's husband. He had a tiny yellow beard ending in two points.

Selig was a men's tailor. Issur Godel made clothes for women. At that moment, he was ripping a seam. It was said that he had golden hands, and that if he had his own shop in the fancy streets he would make a fortune, but his wife didn't want to move out of her parents' apartment. When she got pains in the chest and couldn't breathe, her mother was there to take care of her. It was her mother—and occasionally her sister Dunia—who eased her with drops of valerian and rubbed her temples with vinegar when she grew faint. Dunia worked in a dress shop on Mead Street, wore fashionable clothes, and avoided the pious girls of the neighborhood. Tzeitel also watched over Henia Dvosha's two small children—Elkele and Yankele. I often went into Selig the tailor's shop. I liked to watch the machines stitch, and I collected the empty spools from the floor. Selig didn't speak like the people in Warsaw—

he came from somewhere in Russia. He often discussed the Pentateuch and the Talmud with me, and he would speculate about what the saints did in Paradise and how sinners were roasted in Gehenna. Selig had been touched by Enlightenment and often sounded like a heretic. He would say to me, "Were your mother and father up in Heaven, and did they see all those things with their own eyes? Maybe there is no God? Or, if there is, maybe He's a Gentile, not a Jew?"

"God a Gentile? One mustn't say such things."

"How do you know one mustn't? Because it says so in the holy books? *People* wrote those books and people like to make up all kinds of nonsense."

"Who created the world?" I asked.

"Who created God?"

My father was a rabbi and I knew wouldn't want me to listen to such talk. I would cover my ears with my fingers when Selig began to blaspheme, and resolved to never enter his place again, but something drew me to this room where one wall was hung with gaberdines, vests, and trousers and the other with dresses and blouses. There was also a dressmaker's dummy with no head and wooden breasts and hips. This time I felt a strong urge to peek into the alcove where Henia Dvosha lay in bed.

Selig promptly struck up a conversation with me. "You don't go to cheder any more?"

"I've finished cheder. I'm studying the Gemara already."

"All by yourself? And you understand what you read?"

"If I don't, I look it up in Rashi's commentary."

"And Rashi himself understood?"

I laughed. "Rashi knew the whole Torah."

"How do you know? Did you know him personally?"

"Know him? Rashi lived hundreds of years ago."

"So how can you know what went on hundreds of years ago?"

"Everyone knows that Rashi was a great saint and a scholar."

"Who is this 'everybody'? The janitor in the courtyard doesn't know it."

Issur Godel said, "Father-in-Law, leave him alone."

"I asked him a question and I want an answer," Selig said.

Just then a small woman round as a barrel came in to be fitted for a dress. Issur Godel took her into the alcove. I saw Henia Dvosha sitting up in bed sewing a white satin dress that fell to the floor on both sides of the bed. Tzeitel hadn't lied. This was the wedding dress for Dunia.

I raced out of the shop and down the stairs. I had to think the whole matter out. Why would Henia Dvosha sew a dress for her sister to wear when she married Issur Godel after she, Henia Dvosha, died? Was this out of great love for her sister or love for her husband? I thought of the story of how Jacob worked seven years for Rachel and how her father, Laban, cheated Jacob by substituting Leah in the dark. According to Rashi, Rachel gave Leah signs so that she, Leah, wouldn't be shamed. But what kind of signs were they? I was filled with curiosity about men and women and their remarkable secrets. I was in a rush to grow up. I had begun watching girls. They mostly had the same high bosom as Selig's dummy, smaller hands and feet than men's, and hair done up in braids. Some had long, narrow necks. I knew that if I should go home and ask Mother what signs girls had and what Rachel could have given to Leah, she would only yell at me. I had to observe everything for myself and keep silent.

I stared at the passing girls, and thought I saw something like mockery in their eyes. Their glances seemed to say, "A little boy and he wants to know everything . . ."

Although the doctors assured Tzeitel that her daughter would live a long time and prescribed medicines for her nerves, Henia Dvosha grew worse from day to day. We could hear her moans in our apartment. Freitag the barber-surgeon gave her injections. Dr. Knaister ordered her taken to the hospital on

Czysta Street, but Henia Dvosha protested that the sick were poisoned there and dissected after they died.

Dr. Knaister arranged a consultation of three—himself and two specialists. Two carriages pulled up before the gates of our building, each driven by a coachman in a top hat and a cloak with silver buttons. The horses had short manes and arched necks. While they waited they kept starting forward impatiently, and the coachmen had to yank on the reins to make them stand still. The consultation lasted a long time. The specialists couldn't agree, and they bickered in Polish. After they had received their twenty-five rubles, they climbed into their carriages and drove back to the rich neighborhoods where they lived and practiced.

A few days later Selig the tailor came to us in his shirtsleeves, a needle in his lapel and a thimble over the index finger of his left hand, and said to my father, "Rabbi, my daughter wants you to recite the confession with her."

My father gripped his red beard and said, "What's the hurry? With the Almighty's help, she'll live a hundred and twenty years yet."

"Not even a hundred and twenty hours," Selig replied.

Mother looked at Selig with reproof. Although he was a Jew, he spoke like a Gentile; those who came from Russia lacked the sensitivity of the Polish Jew. She began to wipe away her tears. Father rummaged in his cabinet and took out *The Ford of the Jabbok*, a book that dealt with death and mourning. He turned the pages and shook his head. Then he got up and went with Selig. This was the first time Father had been to Selig's apartment. He never visited anyone except when called to officiate in a religious service.

He stayed there a long time, and when he came back he said, "Oh, what kind of people are these? May the Almighty guard and protect us!"

"Did you recite the confession with her?" Mother asked.

"Yes."

"Did she say anything?"

"She asked if you could marry right after shivah, the seven days of mourning, or if you had to wait until after sheloshim, the full thirty."

Mother made a face as if to spit. "She's not in her right mind."

"No."

"You'll see, she'll live years yet," Mother said.

But this prediction didn't come true. A few days later a lament was heard in the corridor. Henia Dvosha had just passed away. The front room soon filled with women. Tzeitel had already managed to cover the sewing machines and drape the mirror with a black cloth. The windows had been opened, according to Law. Issur Godel appeared among the throng of women. He was dressed in a vented gaberdine cut to the knee, a paper dickey, a stiff collar, a black tie, and a small cap. He soon was on his way to the community office to arrange for the funeral. Then Dunia walked into the courtyard wearing a straw hat decorated with flowers and a red dress and carrying a bag in ladylike fashion. Dunia and Issur Godel met on the stairs. For a moment they stood there without speaking, then they mumbled something and parted—he going down and she up. Dunia wasn't crying. Her face was pale, and her eyes expressed something like rage.

During the period of mourning, men came twice a day to pray at Selig the tailor's. Selig and Tzeitel sat on little benches in their stocking feet. Selig glanced into the Book of Job printed in Hebrew and Yiddish that he had borrowed from my father. His lapel was torn as a sign of mourning. He chatted with the men about ordinary matters. The cost of everything was rising. Thread, lisle, and lining material were all higher. "Do people work nowadays?" Selig complained. "They play. In my time an apprentice came to work with the break of day. In the winter you started working while it was still dark. Every worker had to furnish a tallow candle at his own expense. Today the machine does everything and the worker knows only one thing—a new raise every other month. How can you have a world of such loafers?"

"Everyone runs to America!" Shmul the carpenter said.

"In America there's a panic. People are dying of hunger."

I went to pray each day at Selig the tailor's, but I never saw Issur Godel or Dunia there. Was Dunia hiding in the alcove or had she gone to work instead of observing shivah? As soon as this period of mourning was over, Issur Godel trimmed his beard, and exchanged his traditional cap for a fedora and the gaberdine for a short jacket. Dunia informed her mother that she wouldn't wear a wig after she was married.

The night before the wedding, I awoke just as the clock on the wall struck three. The window of our bedroom was covered with a blanket, but the moonlight shone in from each side. My parents were speaking softly, and their voices issued from one bed. God in Heaven, my father was lying in bed with my mother!

I held my breath and heard Mother say, "It's all their fault. They carried on in front of her. They kissed, and who knows what else. Tzeitel told me this herself. Such wickedness can cause a heart to burst."

"She should have got a divorce," Father said.

"When you love, you can't divorce."

"She spoke of her sister with such devotion," Father said.

"There are those that kiss the Angel of Death's sword," Mother replied.

I closed my eyes and pretended to be asleep. The whole world was apparently one big fraud. If my father, a rabbi who preached the Torah and piety all day, could get into bed with a female, what could you expect from an Issur Godel or a Dunia?

When I awoke the next day, Father was reciting the morning prayers. For the thousandth time he repeated the story of how the Almighty had ordered Abraham to sacrifice his son Isaac on an altar and the angel shouted down from Heaven, "Lay not thy hand upon the lad." My father wore a mask—a saint by day, a debaucher at night. I vowed to stop praying and to become a heretic.

Tzeitel mentioned to my mother that the wedding would be a quiet one. After all, the groom was a widower with two children, the family was in mourning—why make a fuss? But for some reason all the tenants of the courtyard conspired to make the wedding noisy. Presents came pouring in to the couple from all over. Someone had hired a band. I saw a barrel of beer with brass hoops being carried up the stairs, and baskets of wine. Since we were Selig's next-door neighbors, and my father would officiate at the ceremony besides, we were considered part of the family. Mother put on her holiday dress and had her wig freshly set at a hairdresser's. Tzeitel treated me to a slice of honeycake and a glass of wine. There was such a crush at Selig's apartment that there was no room for the wedding canopy, and it had to be set up in my father's study. Dunia wore the white satin wedding gown her sister had sewn for her. The other brides who had been married in our building smiled, responded to the wishes offered them in a gracious way, laughed and cried. Dunia barely said a word to anyone, and held her head high with wordly arrogance.

It was whispered about that Tzeitel had had to plead with her to get her to immerse herself in the ritual bath. Dunia had invited her own guests—girls with low-cut dresses and clean-shaven youths with thick mops of hair and broad-brimmed fedoras. Instead of shirts they wore black blouses bound with sashes. They smoked cigarettes, winked, and spoke Russian to each other. The people in our courtyard said that they were all socialists, the same as those who rebelled against the czar in 1905 and demanded a constitution. Dunia was one of them.

My mother refused to taste anything at the affair: some of the guests had brought along all kinds of food and drinks, and one could no longer be sure if everything was strictly kosher. The musicians played theater melodies, and men danced with women. Around eleven o'clock my eyes closed from weariness and Mother told me to go to bed. In the night I awoke and heard the stamping, the singing, the pagan music—polkas, mazurkas, tunes that aroused urges in me that I felt were evil even though I didn't understand what they were.

Later I woke again and heard my father quoting Ecclesiastes: "I said of laughter, It is mad, and of mirth, What doeth it?"

"They're dancing on graves," Mother whispered.

Soon after the wedding, scandals erupted at Selig's house. The newlyweds didn't want to stay in the alcove, and Issur Godel rented a ground-floor apartment on Ciepla Street. Tzeitel came weeping to my mother because her daughter had trimmed Yankele's earlocks and had removed him from cheder and enrolled him in a secular school. Nor did she maintain a kosher kitchen but bought meat at a Gentile butcher's. Issur Godel no longer called himself Issur Godel but Albert. Elkele and Yankele had been given Gentile names too—Edka and Janek.

I heard Tzeitel mention the number of the house where the newlyweds were living, and I went to see what was going on there. To the right of the gate hung a sign in Polish: ALBERT LANDAU, WOMEN'S TAILOR. Through the open window I could see Issur Godel. I hardly recognized him. He had dispensed with his beard altogether and now wore a turned-up mustache; he was bareheaded and looked young and Christian. While I was standing there, the children came home from school—Yankele in shorts and a cap with an insignia and with a knapsack on his shoulders, Elkele in a short dress and knee-high socks. I called to them, "Yankele . . . Elkele . . ." but they walked past and didn't even look at me.

Tzeitel came each day to cry anew to my mother: Henia Dvosha had come to her in a dream and shrieked that she couldn't rest in her grave. Her Yankele didn't say Kaddish for her, and she wasn't being admitted into Paradise.

Tzeitel hired a beadle to say Kaddish and study the Mishnah in her daughter's memory, but, even so, Henia Dvosha came to her mother and lamented that her shrouds had fallen off and she lay there naked; water had gathered in her grave; a wanton female had been buried beside her, a madam of a brothel, who cavorted with demons.

Father called three men to ameliorate the dream, and they stood in front of Tzeitel and intoned, "Thou hast seen a *goodly* vision! A goodly vision hast thou seen! Goodly is the vision thou hast seen!"

Afterward, Father told Tzeitel that one dared not mourn the dead too long, or place too much importance in dreams. As the Gemara said, just as there could be no grain without straw, there couldn't be dreams without idle words. But Tzeitel could not contain herself. She ran to the community leaders and to the Burial Society demanding that the body be exhumed and buried elsewhere. She stopped taking care of her house, and went each day to Henia Dvosha's grave at the cemetery.

Selig's beard grew entirely white, and his face developed a network of wrinkles. His hands shook, and the people in the courtyard complained that he kept a gaberdine or a pair of trousers for weeks, and when he finally did bring them back they were either too short or too narrow or the material was ruined from pressing. Knowing that Tzeitel no longer cooked for her husband and that he lived on dry food only, Mother frequently sent things over to him. He had lost all his teeth, and when I appeared with a plate of groats, or some chicken soup or stuffed noodles, he smiled at me with his bare gums and said, "So you're bringing presents, are you? What for? It's not Purim."

"One has to eat the year round."

"Why? To fatten up for the worms?"

"A man has a soul, too," I said.

"The soul doesn't need potatoes. Besides, did you ever see a soul? There is no such thing. Stuff and nonsense."

"Then how does one live?"

"It's Breathing. Electricity."

"Your wife—"

Selig interrupted me. "She's crazy!"

One evening Tzeitel confided to my mother that Henia Dvosha had taken up residence in her left ear. She sang Sabbath and holiday hymns, recited lamentations for the Destruction of the Temple, and even bewailed the sinking of the *Titanic*. "If you don't believe me, Rebbetzin, hear for yourself."

She moved her wig aside and placed her ear against Mother's.

"Do you hear?" Tzeitel asked.

"Yes. No. What's that?" Mother asked in alarm.

"It's the third week already. I kept quiet, figuring it would pass, but it grows worse from day to day."

I was so overcome by fear that I dashed from the kitchen. The word soon spread through Krochmalna Street and the surrounding streets that a dybbuk had settled in Tzeitel's ear, and that it chanted the Torah, sermonized, and crowed like a rooster. Women came to place their ears against Tzeitel's and swore that they heard the singing of Kol Nidre. Tzeitel asked my father to put his ear next to hers, but Father wouldn't consent to touch a married woman's flesh. A Warsaw nerve specialist became interested in the case—Dr. Flatau, who was famous not only in Poland but in all Europe and maybe in America, too. And an article about the case appeared in a Yiddish newspaper. The author borrowed its title from Tolstoy's play *The Power of Darkness*.

At just about that time, we moved to another courtyard in Krochmalna Street. A few weeks later, in Sarajevo, a terrorist assassinated the Austrian Archduke Ferdinand and his wife.

From this one act of violence came the war, the shortages of food, the exodus of refugees from the small towns to Warsaw, and the reports in the newspapers of thousands of casualties.

People had other things to talk about than Selig the tailor and his family. After Succoth, Selig died suddenly, and a few months later Tzeitel followed him to the grave.

One day that winter, when the Germans and Russians fought at the Bzura River, and the windowpanes in our house rattled from the cannon fire and the oven stayed unheated because we could no longer afford coal, a former neighbor from No. 10, Esther Malka, paid a call on my mother. Issur Godel and Dunia, she said, were getting a divorce.

Mother asked, "Why on earth? They were supposed to be in love."

And Esther Malka replied, "Rebbetzin, they *can't* be together. They say Henia Dvosha comes each night and gets into bed between them."

"Jealous even in the grave?"

"So it seems."

Mother turned white and said words I've never forgotten: "The living die so that the dead may live."

Translated by Joseph Singer

The Bus

WHY I UNDERTOOK that particular tour in 1956 is something I haven't figured out to this day—dragging around in a bus through Spain for twelve days with a group of tourists. We left from Geneva. I got on the bus around three in the afternoon and found the seats nearly all taken. The driver collected my ticket and pointed out a place next to a woman who was wearing a conspicuous black cross on her breast. Her hair was dyed red, her face was thickly rouged, the lids of her brown eyes were smeared with blue eyeshadow, and from beneath all this dye and paint emerged deep wrinkles. She had a hooked nose, lips red as a cinder, and yellowish teeth.

She began speaking to me in French, but I told her I didn't understand the language and she switched over to German. It struck me that her German wasn't that of a real German or even a Swiss. Her accent was similar to mine and she made the same mistakes. From time to time she interjected a word that sounded Yiddish. I soon found out that she was a refugee from the concentration camps. In 1946, she arrived at a DP camp near Landsberg and there by chance she struck up a friendship with a Swiss bank director from Zurich. He fell in love with her and proposed marriage but under the condition that she accept Protestantism. Her name at home had been Celina Pultusker. She was now Celina Weyerhofer.

Suddenly she began speaking to me in Polish, then went over into Yiddish. She said, "Since I don't believe in God anyway, what's the difference if it's Moses or Jesus? He wanted me to convert, so I converted a bit."

"So why do you wear a cross?"

"Not out of anything to do with religion. It was given to me by someone dying whom I'll never forget till I close my eyes."

"A man, eh?"

"What else—a woman?"

"Your husband has nothing against this?"

"I don't ask him. There he is."

Mrs. Weyerhofer pointed out a man sitting across the way. He looked younger than she, with a fair, smooth face, blue eyes, and a straight nose. To me he appeared the typical banker—sober, amiable, his trousers neatly pressed and pulled up to preserve the crease, shoes freshly polished. He was wearing a panama hat. His manner expressed order, discipline. Across his knee lay the *Neue Zürcher Zeitung*, and I noticed it was open to the financial section. From his breast pocket he took a piece of cloth with which he polished his glasses. That done, he glanced at his gold wristwatch.

I asked Mrs. Weyerhofer why they weren't sitting together.

"Because he hates me," she said in Polish.

Her answer surprised me, but not overly so. The man glanced at me sidelong, then averted his face. He began to converse with a lady sitting in the window seat beside him. He removed his hat, revealing a shining bald pate surrounded by a ruff of pale-blond hair. "What could it have been that this Swiss saw in the person next to me?" I asked myself, but such things one could not really question.

Mrs. Weyerhofer said, "So far as I can tell, you are the only Jew on the bus. My husband doesn't like Jews. He doesn't like

Gentiles, either. He has a million prejudices. Whatever I say displeases him. If he had the power, he'd kill off most of mankind and leave only his dogs and the few bankers with whom he's chummy. I'm ready to give him a divorce but he's too stingy to pay alimony. As it is, he barely gives me enough to keep alive. Yet he's highly intelligent, one of the best-read people I've ever met. He speaks six languages perfectly, but, thank God, Polish isn't one of them."

She turned toward the window and I lost any urge to talk to her further. I had slept poorly the night before, and when I leaned back I dozed off, though my mind went on thinking wakeful thoughts. I had broken up with a woman I loved—or at least desired. I had just spent three weeks alone in a hotel in Zakopane.

I was awakened by the driver. We had come to the hotel where we would eat dinner and sleep. I couldn't orient myself to the point of deciding whether we were still in Switzerland or had reached France. I didn't catch the name of the ciy the driver had announced. I got the key to my room. Someone had already left my suitcase there. A bit later, I went down to the dining room. All the tables were full, and I didn't want to sit with strangers.

As I stood, a boy who appeared to be fourteen or fifteen came up to me. He reminded me of prewar Poland in his short pants and high woolen stockings, his jacket with the shirt collar outside. He was a handsome youth—black hair worn in a crewcut, bright dark eyes, and unusually pale skin. He clicked his heels in military fashion and asked, "Sir, you speak English?"

"Yes."

"You are an American?"

"An American citizen."

"Perhaps you'd like to join us? I speak English. My mother speaks a little, too."

"Would your mother agree?"

"Yes. We noticed you in the bus. You were reading an

American newspaper. After I graduate from what you call high school, I want to study at an American university. You aren't by chance a professor?"

"No, but I have lectured at a university a couple of times."

"Oh, I took one look at you and I knew immediately. Please, here is our table."

He led me to where his mother was sitting. She appeared to be in her mid-thirties, plump, but with a pretty face. Her black hair was combed into two buns, one at each side of her face. She was expensively dressed and wore lots of jewelry. I said hello and she smiled and replied in French.

The son addressed her in English: "Mother, the gentleman is from the United States. A professor, just as I said he would be."

"I am no professor. I was invited by a college to serve as writer-in-residence."

"Please. Sit down."

I explained to the woman that I knew no French, and she began to speak to me in a mixture of English and German. She introduced herself as Annette Metalon. The boy's name was Mark. The waiters hadn't yet managed to serve all the tables, and while we waited I told the mother and son that I was a Jew, that I wrote in Yiddish, and that I came from Poland. I always do this as soon as possible to avoid misunderstandings later. If the person I am talking to is a snob, he knows that I'm not trying to represent myself as something I'm not.

"Sir, I am also a Jew. On my father's side. My mother is Christian."

"Yes, my late husband was a Sephardi," Mrs. Metalon said. Was Yiddish a language or a dialect? she asked me. How did it differ from Hebrew? Was it written in Latin letters or in Hebrew? Who spoke the language and did it have a future? I responded to everything briefly. After some hesitation, Mrs. Metalon told me that she was an Armenian and that she lived in Ankara but that Mark was attending school in London. Her husband came from Saloniki. He was an importer and exporter

of Oriental rugs and had had some other businesses as well. I
noticed a ring with a huge diamond on her finger, and mag-
nificent pearls around her neck. Finally, the waiter came over
and she ordered wine and a steak. When the waiter heard I was
a vegetarian he grimaced and informed me that the kitchen
wasn't set up for vegetarian meals. I told him I would eat whatever I could get—potatoes, vegetables, bread, cheese. Anything
he could bring me.

As soon as he had gone, the questions started about my veg-
etarianism: Was it on account of my health? Out of principle?
Did it have anything to do with being kosher? I was accustomed to justifying myself, not only to strangers but even to
people who had known me for years. When I told Mrs. Metalon
that I didn't belong to any synagogue, she asked the question
for which I could never find the answer—what did my Jewishness consist of?

According to the way the waiter had reacted, I assumed that
I'd leave the table hungry, but he brought me a plateful of
cooked vegetables and a mushroom omelette as well as fruit
and cheese. Mother and son both tasted my dishes, and Mark
said, "Mother, I want to become a vegetarian."

"Not as long as you're living with me," Mrs. Metalon replied.

"I don't want to remain in England, and certainly not in
Turkey. I've decided to become an American," Mark said. "I
like American literature, American sincerity, democracy, and
the American business sense. In England there are no opportunities for anyone who wasn't born there. I want to marry an
American girl. Sir, what kind of documents are needed to get
a visa to the United States? I have a Turkish passport, not an
English one. Would you, sir, send me an affidavit?"

"Yes, with pleasure."

"Mark, what's wrong with you? You meet a gentleman for
the first time and at once you make demands of him."

"What do I demand? An affidavit is only a piece of paper
and a signature. I want to study at Harvard University or at

the University of Princeton. Sir, which of these two universities has the better business school?"

"I really wouldn't know."

"Oh, he has already decided everything for himself," Mrs.
Metalon said. "A child of fourteen but with an old head. In
that sense, he takes after his father. He always planned down
to the last detail and years in advance. My husband was forty
years older than I, but we had a happy life together." She took
out a lace-edged handkerchief and dabbed at an invisible tear.

The bus routine required that each day passengers exchanged
seats. It gave everyone a chance to sit up front. Most couples
stayed together, but individuals kept changing their partners.
On the third day, the driver placed me next to the banker from
Zurich, who was apparently determined not to sit with his
wife.

He introduced himself to me: Dr. Rudolf Weyerhofer. The
bus had left Bordeaux, where we had spent the night, and was
approaching the Spanish border. At first neither of us spoke;
then Dr. Weyerhofer began to talk of Spain, France, the situation in Europe. He questioned me about America, and when I
told him that I was a staff member of a Yiddish newspaper his
talk turned to Jews and Judaism. Wasn't it odd that a people
should have retained its identity through two thousand years of
wandering across the countries of the world and after all that
time returned to the land and language of its ancestors? The
only such instance in the history of mankind. Dr. Weyerhofer
told me he had read Graetz's *History of the Jews* and even
something of Dubnow's. He knew the works of Martin Buber
and Klausner's *Jesus of Nazareth*. But for all that, the essence
of the Jew was far from clear to him. He asked about the Talmud, the Zohar, the Hasidim, and I answered as best I could.
I felt certain that shortly he would begin talking about his
wife.

Mrs. Weyerhofer had already managed to irritate the other

passengers. Both in Lyons and in Bordeaux the bus had been forced to wait for her—for a half hour in Lyons and for over an hour in Bordeaux. The delays played havoc with the travel schedule. She had gone off shopping and had returned loaded down with bundles. From the way she had described her husband to me as a miser who begrudged her a crust of bread, I couldn't understand where she got the money to buy so many things. Both times she apologized and said that her watch had stopped, but the Swiss women claimed that she had purposely turned back the hands of her gold wristwatch. By her behavior Celina Weyerhofer humiliated not only her husband, who accused her in public of lying, but also me, for it was obvious to everyone on the bus that she, like me, was a Jew from Poland.

I no longer recall how it came about but Dr. Weyerhofer began to unburden himself to me. He said, "My wife accuses me of anti-Semitism, but what kind of anti-Semite am I if I married a Jewish woman just out of concentration camp? I want you to know that this marriage has caused me enormous difficulties. At that time many people in financial circles were infected with the Nazi poison, and I lost important connections. I was seriously considering emigrating to your America or even to South Africa, since I had practically been excommunicated from the Christian business community. How is this called by your people . . . cherem? My blessed parents were still living then and they were both devout Christians. You could write a thick book about what I went through.

"Though my wife converted, she did it in such a way that the whole thing became a farce. This woman makes enemies wherever she goes, but her worst enemy is her own mouth. She has a talent for antagonizing everyone she meets. She tried to establish a connection with the Jewish community in Zurich, but she said such shocking things and carried on so that the members would have nothing to do with her. She'd go to a rabbi and represent herself as an atheist; she'd launch a debate with him about religion and call him a hypocrite. While she accuses everyone of anti-Semitism, she herself says things about Jews you'd expect from a Goebbels. She plays the role of a rabid feminist and joins protests against the Swiss government for refusing to give women the vote, yet at the same time she castigates women in the most violent fashion.

"I noticed her talking to you when you were sitting together and I know she told you how mean I am with money. But the woman has a buying mania. She buys things that will never be used. I have a large apartment she's crowded with so much furniture, so many knickknacks and idiotic pictures that you can barely turn around. No maid will work for us. We eat in restaurants even though I hate not eating at home. I must have been mad to agree to go on this trip with her. But it looks as if we won't last out the twelve days. While I sit talking here with you, my mind is on forfeiting my money and leaving the bus before we even get to Spain. I know I shouldn't be confiding my personal problems like this, but since you are a writer maybe they can be of use to you. I tell myself that the camps and wanderings totally destroyed her nerves, but I've met other women who survived the whole Hitler hell, and they are calm, civilized, pleasant people."

"How is it that you didn't see this before?" I asked.

"Eh? A good question. I ask myself the same thing. The very fact that I'm telling you all this is a mystery to me, since we Swiss are reticent. Apparently ten years of living with this woman have altered my character. She is the one who allegedly converted, but I seem to have turned into almost a Polish Jew. I read all the Jewish news, particularly any dealing with the Jewish state. I often criticize the Jewish leaders, but not as a stranger—rather as an insider."

The bus stopped. We had come to the Spanish frontier. The driver went with our passports to the border station and lingered there a long time.

Dr. Weyerhofer began talking quietly, in almost a mumble,

"I want to be truthful. One good trait she did have—she could attract a man. Sexually, she was amazingly strong. I don't believe myself that I am speaking of these things—in my circles, talk of sex is taboo. But why? Man thinks of it from cradle to grave. She has a powerful imagination, a perverse fantasy. I've had experience with women and I know. She has said things to me that drove me to frenzy. She has more stories in her than Scheherazade. Our days were cursed, but the nights were wild. She wore me out until I could no longer do my work. Is this characteristic of Jewish women in Eastern Europe? The Swiss Jewish women aren't much more interesting than the Christian."

"You know, Doctor, it is impossible to generalize."

"I have the feeling that many Jewish women in Poland are of this type. I see it in their eyes. I made a business trip to the Jewish state and even met Ben-Gurion, along with other Israeli leaders. We did business with the Bank Leumi. I have a theory that the Jewish woman of today wants to make up for all the centuries in the ghetto. Besides, the Jews are a people of imagination, even though in modern literature they haven't yet created any great works. I've read Jakob Wassermann, Stefan Zweig, Peter Altenberg, and Arthur Schnitzler, but they disappointed me. I expected something better from Jews. Are there interesting writers in Yiddish or Hebrew?"

"Interesting writers are rare among all peoples."

"Here is our driver with the passports."

We crossed the border, and an hour later the bus stopped and we went to have lunch at a Spanish restaurant.

In the entrance, Mrs. Weyerhofer came up to me and said, "You sat with my husband this morning and I know that the whole time he talked about me. I can read lips like a deaf-mute. You should know that he's a pathological liar. Not one word of truth leaves his lips."

"It so happens he praised you."

Celina Weyerhofer tensed. "What did he say?"

"That you are unusually interesting as a woman."

"Is that what he said? It can't be. He has been impotent several years, and being next to him has made me frigid. Physically and spiritually he has made me sick."

"He praised your imagination."

"Nothing is left me except my imagination. He drained my blood like a vampire. He isn't sexually normal. He is a latent homosexual—not so latent—although when I tell him this he denies it vehemently. He only wants to be with men, and when we still shared a bedroom he spent whole nights questioning me about my relationships with other men. I had to invent affairs to satisfy him. Later, he threw these imaginary sins up to me and called me filthy names. He forced me to confess that I had relations with a Nazi, even though God knows I would sooner have let them skin me alive. Maybe we can find a table together?"

"I promised to eat with some woman and her son."

"The one I saw you with yesterday in the dining room? Her son is a beauty, but she is too fat and when she gets older she'll go to pieces. Did you notice how many diamonds she wears? A jewelry store—tasteless, disgusting. In Lyons and Bordeaux none of us had a bathroom, but she got one. Since she is so rich, why does she ride in a bus? They don't give her a plain room but a suite. Is she Jewish?"

"Her late husband was a Jew."

"A widow, eh? She's probably looking for a match. The diamonds are more than likely imitations. What is she, French?"

"Armenian."

"Foolish men kill themselves and leave such bitches huge estates. Where does she live?"

"In Turkey."

"Be careful. One glance was enough to tell me this is a spider. But men are blind."

I couldn't believe it, but I began to see that Mark was trying to arrange a match between his mother and myself. Strangely, the mother played as passive a role in the situation as some old-time maiden for whom the parents were trying to find a husband. I told myself that it was all my imagination. What would a rich widow, an Armenian living in Turkey, want with a Yiddish writer? What kind of future could she see in this? True, I was an American citizen, but it wouldn't have been difficult for Mrs. Metalon to obtain a visa to America without me. I concluded that her fourteen-year-old son had hypnotized his mother—that he dominated her as his father had probably done before him. I also toyed with the notion that her husband's soul had entered into Mark and that he, the dead Sephardi, wanted his wife to marry a fellow Jew. I tried to avoid eating with the pair, but each time Mark found me and said, "Sir, my mother is waiting for you."

His words implied a command. When it was my turn to order my vegetarian dishes, Mark took over and told the waiter or waitress exactly what to bring me. He knew Spanish because his father had had a partner with whom he had conversed in Ladino. I wasn't accustomed to drinking wine with my meals, but Mark ordered it without consulting me. When we came to a city, he always managed that his mother and I were left alone to shop for bargains and souvenirs. On these occasions he warned me sternly not to spend any money on his mother, and if I had already done so he demanded to know how much and told his mother to pay me back. When I objected, he arched his brows. "Sir, we don't need gifts. A Yiddish writer can't be rich." He opened his mother's pocketbook and counted out whatever the amount had been.

Mrs. Metalon smiled sheepishly at this and added, half in jest, half in earnest, that Mark treated her as if she were his daughter. But she had obviously accepted the relationship.

Is she so weak? I wondered. Or is there some scheme behind this?

The situation struck me as particularly strange because the mother and son were together only during vacations. The rest of the year she remained in Ankara while he studied in Lon-

don. As far as I could determine, Mark was dependent on his
mother; when he needed something he had to ask for money.

At first, the two of them sat in the bus together, but one day
after lunch Mark told me that I was to sit with his mother. He
himself sat down next to Celina Weyerhofer. He had arranged
all this without the driver's permission, and I doubted if he had
discussed it with his mother.

I had been sitting next to a woman from Holland, and this
changing of seats provoked whispering among the passengers.
From that day on, I became Mrs. Metalon's partner not only
in the dining room but in the bus as well. People began to wink,
make remarks, leer. Much of the time I looked out of the window. We drove through regions that reminded me of the
desert and the land of Israel. Peasants rode on asses. We passed
an area where gypsies lived in caves. Girls balanced water jugs
on their heads. Grandmothers toted bundles of wood and herbs
wrapped in linen sheets over their shoulders. We passed ancient
olive trees and trees that resembled umbrellas. Sheep browsed
among cracked clods of earth on the half-burned plain. A horse
circled a well. The sky, pale blue, radiated a fiery heat. Something Biblical hovered over the landscape. Passages of the Pentateuch flashed across my memory. It seemed to me that I was
somewhere in the plains of Mamre, where presently would
materialize Abraham's tent, and the angel would bring Sarah
tidings that she would be blessed with a male child at the age
of ninety. My head whirled with stories of Sodom, of the sacrifice of Isaac, of Ishmael and Hagar. The stacks of grain in the
harvested fields brought Joseph's dreams to mind. One morning
we passed a horse fair. The horses and the men stood still, congealed in silence like phantoms of a fair from a vanished time.
It was hard to believe that in this very land, some fifteen years
before, a civil war had raged and Stalinists had shot Trotskyites.

Barely a week had passed since our departure, but I felt that
I had been wandering for months. From sitting so long in one
position I was overcome with a lust that wasn't love or even

sexual passion but something purely animalistic. It seemed that my partner shared the same feelings, for a special heat emanated from her. When she accidentally touched my hand, she burned me.

We sat for hours without a single word, but then we became gabby and said whatever came to our lips. We confided intimate things to one another. We yawned and went on talking half asleep. I asked her how it happened that she had married a man forty years older than herself.

She said, "I was an orphan. The Turks murdered my father, and my mother died soon after. We were rich but they stripped us of everything. I met him as an employee in his office. He had wild eyes. He took one look at me and I knew that he wanted me and was ready to marry me. He had an iron will. He also had the strength of a giant. If he hadn't smoked cigars from early morning till late at night, he would have lived to be a hundred. He could drink fifteen cups of bitter coffee a day. He exhausted me until I developed an aversion to love. When he died, I had the solace that I would be left in peace for a change. Now everything has begun to waken within me again."

"Were you a virgin when you married?" I asked in a half dream.

"Yes, a virgin."

"Did you have lovers after his death?"

"Many men wanted me, but I was raised in such a way I couldn't live with a man without marriage. In my circle in Turkey a woman can't afford to be loose. Everyone there knows what everyone else is doing. A woman has to maintain her reputation."

"What do you need with Turkey?"

"Oh, I have a house there, servants, a business."

"Here in Spain you can do what you want," I said, and regretted my words instantly.

"But I have a chaperon here," she said. "Mark watches over me. I'll tell you something that will seem crazy to you. He guards me even when he is in London and I'm in Ankara. I often feel that he sees everything I do. I sense it isn't he but his father."

"You believe this?"

"It's a fact."

I glanced backward and saw Mark gazing at me sharply as if he were trying to hypnotize me.

When we stopped for the night at a hotel, we first had to line up for the toilets, then wait a long time for our dinner. In the rooms assigned to us, the ceilings were high, the walls thick, and there were old-fashioned washstands with basins and pitchers of water.

That night, we stopped late, which meant that dinner was not served until after ten. Once again, Mark ordered a bottle of wine. For some reason I let myself be persuaded to drink several glasses. Mark asked me if I had had a chance to bathe during the trip, and I told him that I washed every morning out of the washbasin with cold water just like the other passengers.

He glanced at his mother half questioningly, half imperatively.

After some hesitation, Mrs. Metalon said, "Come to our room. We have a bathroom."

"When?"

"Tonight. We leave at five in the morning."

"Sir, do it," Mark said. "A hot bath is healthy. In America everyone has a bathroom, be he porter or janitor. The Japanese bathe in wooden tubs, the whole family together. Come a half hour after dinner. It's not good to bathe immediately following the evening meal."

"I'll disturb both of you. You're obviously tired."

"No, sir. I never go to sleep until between one and two o'clock. I'm planning to take a walk through the city. I have to stretch my legs. From sitting all day in the bus they've become cramped and stiff. My mother goes to bed late, too."

"You're not afraid to walk alone at night in a strange city?" I asked.

"I'm not afraid of anybody. I took a course in wrestling and karate. I also take shooting lessons. It's not allowed boys my age, but I have a private teacher."

"Oh, he takes more courses than I have hairs on my head," Mrs. Metalon said. "He wants to know everything."

"In America, I'll study Yiddish," Mark announced. "I read somewhere that a million and a half people speak this language in America. I want to read you in the original. It's also good for business. America is a true democracy. There you must speak to the customer in his own language. I want my mother to come to America with me. In Turkey, no person of Armenian descent is sure of his life."

"My friends are all Turks," Mrs. Metalon protested.

"Once the pogroms start they'll stop being your friends. My mother tries to hide it from me but I know very well what they did to the Armenians in Turkey and to the Jews in Russia. I want to visit Israel. The Jews there don't bow their heads like those in Russia and Poland. They offer resistance. I want to learn Hebrew and to study at Jerusalem University."

We said goodbye and Mark wrote the number of their room on a small sheet he tore from a notebook. I went to my room for a nap. My legs wobbled as I climbed the stairs. I lay down on the bed in my clothes with the notion of resting a half hour. I closed my eyes and sank into a deep slumber. Someone woke me—it was Mark. To this day I don't know how he got into my room. Maybe I had forgotten to lock it or he had tipped the maid to let him in.

He said, "Sir, excuse me but you've slept a whole hour. You've apparently forgotten that you are coming to our room for your bath."

I assured Mark that I'd be at his door in ten minutes, and after some hesitation he left. Getting undressed and unpacking a bathrobe and slippers from my valise wasn't easy for me. I cursed the day I had decided to take this tour, but I hadn't the courage to tell Mark I wouldn't come. For all his delicacy and politeness Mark projected a kind of childish brutality.

I threw my spring coat over my bathrobe and on unsteady legs began climbing the two floors to their room. I was still half asleep, and for a moment I had the illusion that I was on board ship. When I got to the Metalons' floor, I could not find the slip of paper with the room number. I was sure that it was No. 43, but the tiny lamp on the high ceiling was concealed behind a dull shade and emitted barely any light. In the dimness I couldn't see this number. It took a long time of groping before I found it and knocked on the door.

The door opened, and to my amazement I saw Celina Weyerhofer in a nightgown, her face thickly smeared with cream. Her hair looked wet and freshly dyed. I grew so confused that I could not speak. Finally I asked, "Is this 43?"

"Yes, this is 43. To whom were you going? Oh, I understand. It seems to me that your lady with the diamonds is somewhere on this floor. I saw her son. You've made a mistake."

"Madam, I don't wish to detain you. I just want to tell you they invited me to take a bath there, that's all."

"A bath, eh? So let it be a bath. I haven't had a bath for over a week myself. What kind of tour is this that some passengers get privileges and others are discriminated against? The advertisement didn't mention anything about two classes of passengers. My dear Mr.—what is your name?—I warned you that that person would trap you, and I see this has happened sooner than I figured. Wait a minute—your bath won't run out. Since when do they call it a bath? We call it by a different name. Don't run. Because you've forgotten the number, you'll have to knock on strangers' doors and wake people. Everyone is dead tired. On this tour, before you can even lie down you have to get up again. My husband is a good sleeper. He lies down, opens some book, and two minutes later he's snoring like a lord.

He carries his own alarm clock. I've stopped sleeping altogether. Literally. That's my sickness. I haven't slept for years. I told a doctor in Bern about this—he's actually a professor of medicine—and he called me a liar. The Swiss can be very coarse when they choose to be. He had studied something in a medical book or he had a theory, and because the facts didn't jibe with his theory this made me a liar. I've been watching you sitting with that woman. It looks as if you're telling her jokes from the way she keeps on laughing. My husband sat next to her one time before she monopolized you, and she told him things no decent woman would tell a stranger. I suspect she is a madam of a whorehouse in Turkey. Or something like that. No respectable woman wears so much jewelry. You can smell her perfume a mile away. I'm not even sure that this boy is her son. There seems to be some kind of unnatural relationship between them."

"Madam Weyerhofer, what are you saying?"

"I'm not just pulling things out of the air. God has cursed me with eyes that see. I say 'cursed' because this is for me a curse rather than a blessing. If you absolutely must take a bath, as you call it, do it and satisfy yourself, but be careful—such a person can easily infect you with God knows what."

Just at that moment the door across the hall opened and I saw Mrs. Metalon in a splendid nightgown and gold-colored slippers. Her hair was loose; it fell to her shoulders. She was made up, too. The women glared at each other furiously; then Mrs. Metalon said, "Where did you go? I'm in 48, not 43."

"Oh, I made a mistake. Truly, I'm completely mixed up. I'm terribly sorry—"

"Go take your bath!" Mrs. Weyerhofer said and gave me a light push. She muttered words in French I didn't understand but knew to be insulting. She slammed her own door shut.

I turned to Mrs. Metalon, who asked, "Why did you go to her, of all people? I waited and waited for you. There is no more hot water anyhow. And where has Mark vanished to? He went for a walk and hasn't come back. This night is a total loss to me. That woman—what's her name? Weyerhofer—is a troublemaker, and crazy besides. Her own husband admitted that she's emotionally disturbed."

"Madam, I've made a terrible mistake. Mark wrote down your room number for me, but while changing my clothes I lost the slip. It's all because I'm so tired—"

"Oh, will that red-haired bitch malign me before everyone on the bus now! She is a snake whose every word is venom."

"I truly don't know how to excuse myself. But—"

"Well, it's not your fault. It was Mark who cooked up this stew. The driver told me to keep it secret that we're getting a bathroom. He doesn't want to create jealousy among the passengers. Now he'll be mad at me and he'll be right. I can't continue this trip any longer. I'll get off with Mark in Madrid and take a train or plane back to the border or maybe even to Paris. Come in for a moment. I'm already compromised."

I went inside, and she took me to the bathroom to show me that the hot water was no longer running. The bathtub was made of tin. It was unusually high and long. On its outside hung a kind of pole with which to hold in and let out the water. The taps were copper. I excused myself again and Mrs. Metalon said, "You're an innocent victim. Mark is a genius, but like all geniuses he has his moods. He was a prodigy. At five he could do logarithms. He read the Bible in French and remembered all the names. He loves me and he is determined to have me meet someone. The truth is, he's seeking a father. Each time I join him during vacations he starts looking for a husband for me. He creates embarrassing complications. I don't want to marry—certainly not anyone Mark would pick out for me. But he is compulsive. He gets hysterical. I shouldn't tell you this, but I have a good reason to say it—when I do something that displeases him, he abuses me. Later he regrets it and beats his head against the wall. What can I do? I love him more than life itself. I worry about him day and night.

I don't know exactly why you made such an impression on him. Maybe it's because you're a Jew, a writer, and from America. But I was born in Ankara and that's where my home is. What would I do in America? I've read a number of articles about America, and that's not the country for me. With us, servants are cheap and I have friends who advise me on financial matters. If I left Turkey, I would have to sell everything for a song. I tell you this only to point out there can never be anything between us. You would not want to live in Turkey any more than I want to live in New York. But I don't want to upset Mark and I therefore hope that for the duration of the trip you can act friendly toward me—sit with us at the table and all the rest. When the tour ends and you return home, let this be nothing more for you than an episode. He's due back soon. Tell him that you took the bath. You'll be able to have one in Madrid. We'll be spending almost two days there, and I'm told the hotel is modern. I'm sure you have someone in New York you love. Sit down awhile."

"I've just broken up with a woman."

"Broken up? Why? You didn't love her?"

"We loved each other but we couldn't stay together. This past year we argued constantly."

"Why? Why can't people live in peace? There was a great love between my husband and me, though I must admit I had to give in to him on everything. He bullied me so that I can't even say no to my own child. Oh, I'm worried. He never stayed away this long. He probably wants you to declare your love for me so that when he comes back everything will be settled between us. He is a child, a wild child. My greatest fear is that he might attempt suicide. He has threatened to." She uttered these last words in one breath.

"Why? Why?"

"For no reason. Because I dared disagree with him over some trifle. God Almighty, why am I telling you all this? Only because my heart is heavy. Say nothing about it, God forbid!"

The door opened and Mark came in. When he saw me sitting on the sofa, he asked, "Sir, did you take your bath?"

"Yes."

"It was nice, wasn't it? You look refreshed. What are you talking about with my mother?"

"Oh, this and that. I told her she's one of the prettiest women I've ever met," I said, astonished at my words.

"Yes, she is pretty, but she mustn't remain in Turkey. In the Orient, women age quickly. I once read that an actress of sixty played an eighteen-year-old girl on Broadway. Send us an affidavit and we'll come to you."

"Yes, I'll do that."

"You may kiss my mother good night."

I stood up and we kissed. My face grew moist and hot. Mark began to kiss me, too. I said good night and started down the stairs. Again it seemed to me that I was on board ship. The steps were running counter to my feet. I suddenly found myself in the lobby. In my confusion I had gone down an extra floor. It was almost dark here; the desk clerk dozed behind the desk. In a leather chair sat Mrs. Weyerhofer in a robe, legs crossed, veiled in shadow. She was smoking a cigarette.

When she saw me, she said, "Since I don't sleep anyway, I'd rather spend the night here. A bed is to sleep in or make love in, but when you can't sleep and have no one to love, a bed becomes a prison. What are you doing here? Can't you sleep, either?"

She drew the smoke in deeply and the glow of the cigarette temporarily lit up her eyes. They reflected both curiosity and malaise.

She said, "After that kind of bath, a man should be able to sleep soundly instead of wandering around like a lost soul."

Mark began telling everyone on the bus that his mother and I were engaged. He planned that when the bus came back to Geneva I should ask the American consul for visas for himself and his mother so that all three of us could fly to America to-gether. Mrs. Metalon told him several times that this would be impossible—she had a business appointment in Ankara. I made up the lie that I had to go to Italy on literary business. But Mark argued that his mother and I could postpone our business affairs temporarily. He spoke to me as if I were already his stepfather. He enumerated his mother's financial assets. His father had arranged a trust fund for him, and he had left the remainder of his estate to his wife. According to Mark's calcu-lations she was worth no less than two million dollars—maybe more. Mark wanted his mother to liquidate all her holdings in Turkey and transfer her money to America. He would go to America to study even before he graduated from high school. The interest on his mother's capital would allow us to live in luxury.

Mark had decided that we would settle in Washington. It was childish and silly, but this boy cast a fear over me. I knew that it would be hard to free myself from him. His mother had hinted that another disappointment could drive him to actually attempt suicide. She suggested, "Maybe you'd spend some time with me in Turkey? Turkey is an interesting country. You'd have material to write about for your newspaper. You could spend two or three weeks, then go back to America. Mark wouldn't want to come along. He will gradually realize that we're not meant for each other."

"What would I do in Turkey? No, that's impossible."

"If it's a matter of money, I'll be glad to cover the expenses. You can even stay with me."

"No, Mrs. Metalon, it's out of the question."

"Well, something is bound to happen. What shall I do with that boy? He's driving me crazy."

We had two days in Madrid, a day in Córdoba, and we were on our way to Seville, where we were scheduled to stop for two days. The tour program promised a visit to a nightclub there. Our route was supposed to take us through Málaga, Granada, and Valencia to Barcelona, and from there to Avignon, then back to Geneva.

In Córdoba, Mrs. Weyerhofer delayed the bus for nearly two hours. She vanished from the hotel before our departure and all searching failed to turn her up. On account of her, the passengers had already missed a bullfight. Dr. Weyerhofer pleaded with the driver to go on and leave his lunatic wife alone in Spain as she deserved, but the driver couldn't bring himself to abandon a woman in a strange country. When she finally showed up loaded down with bundles and packages, Dr. Weyerhofer slapped her twice. Her packages fell to the floor and a vase shattered. "Nazi!" she shrieked. "Homosexual! Sadist!" Dr. Weyerhofer said aloud so that everyone could hear, "Well, thank God, this is the end of my martyrdom." And he raised his hand to the sky like a pious Jew swearing a vow.

The uproar caused an additional three-quarters of an hour delay. When Mrs. Weyerhofer finally got into the bus, no one would sit next to her, and the driver, who had seen us speaking together a few times, asked me if I would, since there were no single seats. Mark tried to seat me next to his mother and take my place, but Mrs. Metalon shouted at him to stay with her, and he gave in.

For a long while Mrs. Weyerhofer stared out the window and ignored me as if I were the one responsible for her disgrace. Then she turned to me and said, "Give me your address. I want you to be my witness in court."

"What kind of witness? If it should come to it, the court would find for him, and—if you'll excuse me—rightly so."

"Eh? Oh, I understand. Now that you're preparing to marry the Armenian heiress, you're already lining up on the side of the anti-Semites."

"Madam, your own conduct does more harm to Jews than all the anti-Semites."

"They're my enemies, mortal enemies. Your madam from Constantinople was glowing with joy when those devils humiliated me. I am again where I was—in a concentration camp. You're about to convert, I know, but I will turn back to the Jewish God. I am no longer his wife and he is no longer my husband. I'll leave him everything and flee with my life, as I did in 1945."

"Why do you keep the bus waiting in every city? This has nothing to do with Jewishness."

"It's a plot, I tell you. He organized the whole thing down to the last detail. I don't sleep the whole night, but comes morning, just as I'm catching a nap he turns back the clock. Your knocking on my door the other night—what was the name of the city?—when you were on your way to take a bath at that Turkish whore's, was also one of his tricks. It was a conspiracy to let him catch me with a lover. It's obvious. He wants to drive me out without a shirt on my back, and he has achieved his goal, the sly fox. I won't be allowed to remain in Switzerland, but who will accept me? Unless I can manage to make my way to Israel. Now I understand everything. You'll be the witness for *him*, not for me."

"I'll be a witness for no one. Don't talk nonsense."

"You obviously think I'm mad. That's his goal—to commit me to an asylum. For years he's been talking of this. He's already tried it. He keeps sending me to psychiatrists. He wanted to poison me, too. Three times he put poison in my food and three times my instinct—or maybe it was God—gave me a warning. By the way, I want you to know that this boy, Mark, who wants so desperately for you to sit next to that Turkish concubine, is not her son."

"Then who is he?"

"He is her lover, not her son. She sleeps with him."

"Were you there and saw it?"

"A chambermaid in Madrid told me. She made a mistake and opened the door to their room in the morning and found them in bed together. There are such sick women. One wants a lap-dog, and another a young boy. Really, you're crawling into slime."

"I'm not crawling anywhere."

"You're taking her to America?"

"I'm not taking anyone."

"Well, I'd better keep my mouth shut." Mrs. Weyerhofer turned away from me.

I leaned my head back against the seat and closed my eyes. I knew well that the woman was paranoid; just the same, her last words had given me a jolt. Who knows? What she told me might have been the truth. Sexual perversion is the answer to many mysteries. I was almost overcome with nausea. Yes, I thought, she is right. I'm crawling into a quagmire.

I had but one wish now—to get off this bus as quickly as possible. It occurred to me that for all my intimacy with Mrs. Metalon and Mark, so far I hadn't given them my address.

I dozed, and when I opened my eyes Mark informed me that we were in Seville. I had slept over three hours.

Despite our late start, we still had time for a fast meal. I had sat as usual with Mrs. Metalon and Mark. Mark had ordered a bottle of Malaga and I had drunk a good half of it. Vapors of intoxication flowed from my stomach to my brain.

The topic of conversation at the tables was Dr. and Mrs. Weyerhofer. All the women concluded that Dr. Weyerhofer was a saint to put up with such a horror.

Mrs. Metalon said, "I'd like to think that this is her end. Even a saint's patience has to burst sometime. He is a banker and a handsome man. He won't be alone for long."

"I wouldn't want him for a father," Mark said.

Mrs. Metalon smiled and winked at me. "Why not, my son?"

"Because I want to live and study in America, not in Switzerland. Switzerland is only good for mountain climbing and skiing."

"Don't worry, there's no danger of it."

As she spoke, Mrs. Metalon did something she had never done before—she pressed her knee against mine.

Coaches waited in front of the hotel to take us to a cabaret. Candles flickered in their head lanterns, casting mysterious designs of light and shadow. I hadn't ridden in a horse-drawn carriage since leaving Warsaw. The whole evening was like a magic spell—the ride from the hotel to the cabaret with Mrs. Metalon and Mark, and later the performance. Inside the carriage, driving through the poorly lit Seville streets Mrs. Metalon held my hand. Mark sat facing us and his eyes gleamed like some night bird's. The air was balmy, dense with the scents of wine, olive oil, and gardenias. Mrs. Metalon kept on exclaiming, "What a splendid night! Look at the sky, so full of stars!"

I touched her breast, and she trembled and squeezed my knee. We were both drunk, not so much from wine as from fatigue. Again I felt the heat of her body.

When we got out of the coach Mark walked a few paces in front and Mrs. Metalon whispered, "I'd like to have another child."

"By whom?" I asked.

"Try to guess," she said.

I cannot know whether the actors and actresses and the music and the dancing were as masterly as I thought, but everything I saw and heard that evening enraptured me—the semi-Arabic music, the almost Hasidic way the dancers stamped their feet, their meaningful clicking of the castanets, their bizarre costumes. Melodies supposed to be erotic reminded me of liturgies sung on the night of Kol Nidre. Mark found an unoccupied seat close to the stage and left us alone. We began to kiss with the ardor of long-parted lovers. Between one kiss and the next, Mrs. Metalon (she had told me to call her Annette) insisted that I accompany her to Ankara. She was even ready to visit America. I had scored one of those victories I could never explain except by the fact that in the duel of love the victim is sometimes as eager to surrender as the attacker is to conquer. This woman had lived alone for a number of years. She was accustomed to the embraces of an elderly man. As I thought these things, I warned myself that Mark would not allow our relationship to remain an affair.

From time to time he glanced back at us searchingly. I didn't believe Mrs. Weyerhofer's slanderous tale of mother and son, but it was obvious that Mark was capable of killing anyone he considered to be dishonoring her. The woman's words about wanting another child portended danger. However strong my urge for her body, I knew that I had no spiritual ties with her, that after a while misunderstandings, boredom, and regrets would take over. Besides, I had always been afraid of Turks. As a child, I had heard in detail of Abdul-Hamid's savageries. Later, I read about the pogroms against the Armenians. There in faraway Ankara they could easily fabricate an accusation against me, take away my American passport, and throw me in prison, from which I would not emerge alive. How strange, but when I was a boy in cheder I dreamed of lying in a Turkish prison bound with heavy ropes, and for some reason I had never forgotten this dream.

On the way back from the nightclub, both mother and son asked if I had a bathtub in my room. I told them no, and at once they invited me to bathe in their suite. Mark added that he was going to take a stroll through town. The fact that we were scheduled to stay in Seville through the following night meant that we did not have to get up early the next morning.

Mrs. Metalon and Mark had been assigned a suite of three rooms. I promised to come by and Mrs. Metalon said, "Don't be too late. The hot water may cool soon." Her words seemed to carry a symbolic meaning, as if they were out of a parable.

I went to my room, which was just under the roof. It exuded a scorching heat. The sun had lain on it all day and I switched on the ceiling lamp and stood for a long time, stupefied from the heat and the day's experiences. I had a feeling that soon flames would come shooting from all sides and the room would flare up like a paper lantern. On a brass bed lay a huge pillow and a red blanket full of stains. I needed to stretch out, but the sheet seemed dirty. I imagined I could smell the sperm that who knows how many tourists had spilled here. My bathrobe and pajamas were packed away in my valise, and I hadn't the strength to open it. Well, and what good would it do to bathe if soon afterward I had to lie down in this dirty bed?

In the coach and in the cabaret everything within me had seethed with passion. Now that I had a chance to be alone with the woman, the passion evaporated. Instead, I grew angry against this rich Turkish widow and her pampered son. I made sure that Mark wouldn't wake me. I locked the door with the heavy key and bolted it besides. I put out the light and lay down in my clothes on the sprung mattress, determined to resist all temptation.

The hotel was situated in a noisy neighborhood. Young men shouted and girls laughed wantonly. From time to time, I detected a man's cry followed by a sigh. Was it outside? In another room? Had someone been murdered here? Tortured? Who knows, remnants of the Inquisition might still linger here. I felt bites and I scratched. Sweat oozed from me but I made no effort to wipe it away. "This trip was sheer insanity," I told myself. "The whole situation is filled with menace."

I fell asleep and this time Mark did not come to wake me. By dawn it turned cold and I covered myself with the same blanket that a few hours earlier had filled me with such disgust. When I awoke, the sun was already burning. I washed myself in lukewarm water from the pitcher on the stand and wiped myself with a rusty towel. I seemed to have resolved everything in my sleep. Riding in the carriage through the city the night before, I had noticed branches of Cook's Tours and American Express. I had a return ticket to America, an American passport, and traveler's checks.

When I went down with my valise to the lobby, they told

me that I had missed breakfast. The passengers had all gone off to visit churches, a Moorish palace, a museum. Thank God, I had avoided running into Mrs. Metalon and her son and having to justify myself to them. I left a tip for the bus driver with the hotel cashier and went straight to Cook's. I was afraid of complications, but they cashed my checks and sold me a train ticket to Geneva. I would lose some two hundred dollars to the bus company, but that was my fault, not theirs.

Everything went smoothly. A train was leaving soon for Biarritz. I had booked a bedroom in a Pullman car. I got on and began correcting a manuscript as if nothing had happened.

Toward evening, I felt hungry and the conductor showed me the way to the diner. All the second-class cars were empty. I glanced into the diner. There, at a table near the door, sat Celina Weyerhofer struggling with a pullet.

We stared at each other in silence for a long while; then Mrs. Weyerhofer said, "If this is possible, then even the Messiah can come. On the other hand, I knew that we'd meet again."

"What happened?" I asked.

"My good husband simply drove me away. God knows I've had it up to here with this trip." She pointed to her throat.

She proposed that I join her, and she served as my interpreter to order a vegetarian meal. She seemed more sane and subdued than I had seen her before. She even appeared younger in her black dress. She said, "You ran away, eh? You did right. You would have been caught in a trap you would never have freed yourself from. She suited you as much as Dr. Weyerhofer suited me."

"Why did you keep the bus waiting in every city?" I asked.

She pondered. "I don't know," she said at last. "I don't know myself. Demons were after me. They misled me with their tricks."

The waiter brought my vegetables. I chewed and looked out the window as night fell over the harvested fields. The sun set, small and glowing. It rolled down quickly, like a coal from some heavenly conflagration. A nocturnal gloom hovered above the landscape, an eternity that was weary of being eternal. Good God, my father and my grandfather were right to avoid looking at women! Every encounter between a man and a woman leads to sin, disappointment, humiliation. A dread fell upon me that Mark would try to find me and exact revenge.

As if Celina had read my mind, she said, "Don't worry. She'll soon comfort herself. What was the reason for your taking this trip? Just to see Spain?"

"I wanted to forget someone who wouldn't let herself be forgotten."

"Where is she? In Europe?"

"In America."

"You can't forget anything."

We sat until late, and Mrs. Weyerhofer unfolded to me her fatalistic theory: everything was determined or fixed—every deed, every word, every thought. She herself would die shortly and no doctor or conjurer could help her. She said, "Before you came in here I fantasized that I was arranging a suicide pact with someone. After a night of pleasure, he stuck a knife in my breast."

"Why a knife, of all things?" I asked. "That's not a Jewish fantasy. I couldn't do this even to Hitler."

"If the woman wants it, it can be an act of love."

The waiter came back and mumbled something.

Mrs. Weyerhofer explained, "We're the only ones in the dining car. They want to close up."

"I'm finished," I said. "Gastronomically and otherwise."

"Don't rush," she said. "Unlike the driver of our ill-starred bus, the forces that drive us mad have all the time in the world."

Translated by Joseph Singer